IN THE PANTHER'S WAKE

Maté Jarai

THE BOOKSMITH

The Booksmith
70 Derby Square
Douglas
Isle of Man
IM1 3LR
British Isles

ISBN: 978-1-909588-38-7

A CPI Catalogue for this title is available from the British Library

www.pantherswake.com

1

A thorn will lie buried beneath ash and rust, life hidden below decay. I am that thorn. Awake I sit, eyes open wide. But I'm not alone – my brother Markus is beside me. Two thorns in the pale light, not ready to die yet.

A group of soldiers walk by and we watch from our hiding place under a rusty car wreck. When they pass I emerge, sliding out and pushing myself to my feet.

Markus grabs my ankle, whispers, "Not yet, Bandi. Wait."

I hug the ground, press my fingers onto the tarmac.

"Count to ten," Markus says.

I begin counting in my head, look up at the muddy sky. It's almost dark but we have just enough time. Ten seconds pass and Markus slips out from under the car. He nods, and side by side we creep over to the carcass in the middle of the road, squat down beside it. I avoid looking into the dead horse's eyes. Its chestnut tail is matted with dark red. Markus sets down his back-pack as we both pull small knives from our belts. There is a large saddle bag beside it and we search that first. There are a couple of flares and some matches, a knife and a bag of cornmeal but not much else, not worth taking anyway. We pack the few useful items away and turn our attention to the horse. The carcass has been carved bare but we take what we can, slicing off strips of bloody horsemeat and wrapping them in cloth, before placing them into the back-pack. Flies buzz, they won't leave us alone and I feel itchy, sticky.

We cut quickly so we can move on as soon as possible, shredding the flesh, our hands and wrists wet. Footsteps sound out just ahead and we freeze, lay low to the ground. A soldier appears from around the corner and spots us. He watches us from the roadside ahead for a few minutes, standing there holding his rifle down at his side. There's a large blade on his back and he's smoking, his gas mask pushed up onto his forehead. The cherry glows in the fading light. After a few minutes he moves on and I sigh. Markus has finished stripping the carcass and stands up, putting his bag on his shoulders. It's still not full enough, still light.

"We need to keep looking," he says.

"But it's almost dark."

"I know. But it's been days since we found anything good."

I glance around, I know he's right.

"We came all this way. We need to make it worthwhile."

"Ok."

"Down this road here. Use the cars for cover. Come on."

Markus starts walking quickly in the direction we'd seen the soldier. I run to catch up and carry on past him, quietly hopping onto the hood of a car and climbing onto its roof. I squint and search the road ahead with my eyes. There's smoke rising in the distance but there always is. The sky is brooding, as if ready for a storm but I know it won't rain. It hasn't in almost a year.

Everything is dry and hot, everything is dying. Most of the buildings are ruins; walls missing, windows shattered, bullet holes strewn over the concrete. It's quiet other than the sound of the wind that comes charging down from the desert hills just outside the city. It roars between the buildings, whistling ominously. Markus moves forwards, down the road into my view and I watch him walk carefully, his wavy hair blowing this way and that. There are dark shapes straight ahead, small mounds lying limp in the road.

I hiss, two sharp bursts. Markus looks up at me as I point towards the shapes. He nods and readies himself to approach, while I leap down off the car. I run forwards to catch up with him once more. Then together we run, keeping low and quiet. As we near what I had thought were animal carcasses we both stop dead. What I'd seen as a couple of dogs or cats is a human, a soldier, lying unmasked, torn in two, his body half devoured. I have to look away, hold a hand to my mouth until the ill feeling fades. Markus stands beside me, puts his hand on my back.

"Bandi, you alright?"

I've turned away but can still see the soldier's eyes, open, piercing blue but completely dead, pale. My stomach turns uneasy again and my heart beats faster and faster.

"Come on," says Markus, "let's go back."

I nod and he puts his arm around my shoulder. "Wait here," he says, "I want to see if he has anything useful on him first."

Markus goes over to the soldier's body. I walk in the opposite direction, back the way we came, sit down on the kerb and pull out my sling shot, search the sky for any pigeons. I've never been great around blood and guts. It's the one thing I've not been able to get used to. So I hunt instead but the air is empty, still. I sit staring down a long wide road that leads all the way to the edge of the city in a straight line. Barren sands open out beyond, where the ground rises into hills and I wonder what's beyond that. We've never left the city—as far back as I can remember.

The soldier's dead blue eyes stare at me wherever I look, sealed inside my skull. I feel weak, anxious for Markus to hurry.

My gaze drifts to the hills in the east and that's when I see it, far away, barely visible. It stays low to the ground, stalking forwards at the roads end. I stand up and run forwards a few steps, stare hard in its direction, can't believe my eyes.

It's a black panther, I'm sure it is. The skulking form moves like a cat but it's much bigger. It stops, turns its head towards me. I can feel it looking right at me. Its fur shimmers, and a burning rises inside me; a hot flame that charges, as the soldier's dead blue eyes seem to melt away. They're replaced by bright green, eyes that blaze like copper and fire, and I can feel them flooding all the way inside.

I take a step back, overwhelmed, and I look to see where Markus is. He's still bent low over the body and I want to shout out to him, but I resist, don't want to alert anyone. I look back towards the panther, a huge smile on my face, but it quickly fades. The panther is gone.

Only a few seconds have passed but there's no sign of it. The flames inside me sink away. It's as if I'd imagined it, and for a second I think that maybe I have. But I shake it off—the thought. Those fiery eyes, they were too far away to see yet I saw them clearly, inside my head. I felt them. How could I have felt something that wasn't really there?

A hand grabs me from behind and I jump away. Turning, I draw my knife. But it's only Markus, holding out a hand.

"What is it?" he asks.

His blue eyes are greyer than mine, wet from the wind. I'm about to tell him, but something stops me. I decide to keep it to myself, at least for now.

"Nothing... just waiting for you."

"Well, I'm ready."

"Did you find anything?"

"No. Let's go, it'll be long past dark by the time we make it back."

I look into my big brother's eyes and I know he's lying. I know he's found something. But I let it go. He would tell me if he wanted to, and right now I don't care. I've seen a black panther. It was like magic, the feeling. I want it to mean something. I'm certain it does. It has to. After all it's a black panther, and I'd thought there were none left.

Soon it's completely dark so we stick together. I don't run ahead like I usually do. We keep quiet, not talking at all, and before long we find a sewer opening. I climb down first; then Markus follows. It doesn't matter where we emerge from below, the nearest drain or sewer is always our way back down. It's safest this way. Once in the sewers we make our way back to the metro station through the tunnels. We used to get lost but we know our way around very well now. We've marked arrows on the walls that point the way home, using chalk. It's a very good system and we almost always make it back faster than the others. Our parents are always very proud, especially when we return with horse or even dog and cat meat. They try to hide the disappointment if we return with rats or pigeons.

We youngsters go out because the soldiers don't bother us. They don't see us as a threat. But they would kill our parents. They kill the adults for territory and even for meat sometimes. The soldiers are dangerous, and although they normally leave us alone, we still have to be extremely careful. They're killers and they're ruthless, heartless. We can't let them see us go below ground because we can't ever let them find our home at the metro station. That would surely be the end of everything, so it's up to us to keep low, keep hidden—not ever be followed.

Our job is to search for useful items and carcasses, animals to feed our families. Most carcasses we bring home are grim, the meat tough and barely edible. If we're lucky we find a horse which feeds almost everyone for a couple of days. This doesn't happen often though, and usually we have to settle for less. There used to be hundreds of horses, all over the city, left behind from the wars. Soldiers used them when fuel became scarce. At least that's what my father says. There are few left now, so for the last few weeks we've had only pigeons, rats when things got really tough. My mother tries her best to disguise the meat but the smell is strong, it reeks sour, and I can always tell.

We salvage in groups of two or three. More than three would is too big a group, might bother the soldiers. Being alone is too dangerous so we always stick with at least one other. I always go with Markus. He's older than me and has been going above ground for over five years now, since well before the drought had begun. I only started going with him around three years ago, when I turned eleven, and I even had to beg my mother to let me go then. My father persuaded her, telling her that I would be safe; my big brother would take care of me. Of course

I know that I'm the brave one, and even though he's been going above ground longer, it's me that takes care of him. Unless it involves dead things. I've always struggled with that. But I try and deal with it because I have to. When it comes to real danger, that's when I'm the one that gets us through it.

Markus is the smart one, the one who would have done well in the old world. I'm made for this world. I'm small for my age which helps when it comes to sneaking and being stealthy. I can spot salvage materials and carcasses miles away. That's why I always run ahead, trying to keep a high vantage, usually using the cars or fallen debris from the ruined buildings. We have a good system. My brother and I are a great team. I'm proud of how well we salvage. Plus we have our family call, the hissing sound - two sharp bursts. If we whistled or shouted all the soldiers would hear but a hiss goes un-noticed. It blends with the wind. When we're above ground only Markus knows what to listen for, and if you know what to listen for a hiss can cut through the air and travel a long way.

Sometimes I wonder what I would've done in the old world. Salvaging, hunting for supplies, it's all I know, all I can imagine doing. Maybe I would have been a soldier. They weren't all bad men once. Maybe I could have been a good soldier. Maybe I could have stopped everything. If only everything had happened later, when I was older. But I guess none of that matters now.

I don't remember anything of the old world. I was only two when it all ended and that was more than twelve years ago. The only things I know are the things I'm told or things that have been left behind. My brother was four when things changed and he remembers some stuff. He says he remembers going swimming in the sea, playing in the waves. I know we were all there, as a family. My mother still carries a photo of the four of us standing by a small fishing boat, crinkled water rolling out behind us. We're all smiling. It seems pointless to hold onto it, I don't think those things matter anymore. But my mother says it's important to hold on to the past, even if it is things we'll never see again. Markus always talks about returning to the sea, once we can live above ground for good, when the soldiers are gone. But my father says the sea isn't there anymore. He says it's nothing but dust and flame. Markus is determined to go there because his name means 'of the sea'; he thinks it's his destiny to return to it. Maybe he's just being dramatic. My parents always think he is. He reads too much, they tell him. Real life isn't like stories. He just tells them it's impossible to read too much. But he says a lot of things. He also says he can remember the taste of ice cream. I'm pretty sure he's lying. The taste of things doesn't last long in the memory; except the rat meat. That taste will haunt me forever and I know I'll have to eat it again.

My name, Bandi, means 'man, warrior'. But the war is over and I'm only fourteen. But maybe one day Markus will finally find the sea, and maybe I'll be a warrior, somehow. It's all one giant war we fight in here, every time we rise up from beneath the ground and hit the devastated streets. So I guess in a sense we're all warriors, every one of us. But something bigger is coming. Everything transforms eventually. The dead soldier we found is an indication of that. And the panther. I don't know what that means. It's the kind of thing Markus would go crazy about—get all dramatic. 'It must be an omen', he'd say, 'we need to act on this'. But it's me who saw it. The panther appeared for me, not him. So maybe it's time for me to believe in something that seems more like a story than real life.

2

The sewers are very dark and we can barely see where we're going. We want to move quickly but we keep stopping to search for the chalk arrows. They can be hard to find in the dark. Eventually we have to spark a flare. There's only a very limited supply so we don't feel great about it but we have to. We stayed out too long and night is over us. We move forward by flare-light, the orange glow allows us to see the ground and we pick up our pace as the white arrows take us home. We move straight for a very long time, heading south. There are a couple of left turns and then a right. I immediately recognise where we are, familiar territory. The sewers are dry, our feet patter along, our worn boots kicking up dirt. Soon we reach an opening onto the main metro line that leads to the city's oldest station beneath the zoo. That's where we live.

We toss the flare; it's the home straight. I look at Markus and he's smiling. I smile back at him, but notice the blood dripping from his back-pack. He shrugs. As we stand still to rest I can hear the droplets landing on the stone. Beneath the stone we can hear the dripping of the water channels. Markus glances at me with a smile and then starts to run towards home. I follow him, catching up fast. The glow of the station is just ahead, a little further along the tracks.

We climb up onto the platform and I spot my mother immediately. I run to her and hug her.

"We were so worried!" she says, "Thank God you made it back. What happened?"

I hold her close, close my eyes and let her squeeze me, "We went farther this time, we wanted to come back with something good."

Her face turns sad for an instant, but she covers it with a smile, shaking her head, "You have to be careful. Don't worry about what you bring back. We don't care as long as you're safe."

She worries too much, and I can't contain my smile any more.

"What?" she asks.

I lean close and whisper to her, "We found horse meat."

Markus jumps in and joins the hug. Then I feel my father's strong hand on my back.

"Thank God you're both back. Most of the others returned hours ago. They couldn't find anything."

Markus looks at him proudly, "I've got a back-pack full of horse for you."

My father smiles at us both, "You know we don't care what you return with, as long as you return."

"We know," I reply, but I can see the joy inside my father. Rats and pigeons have been killing us all. He looks thin and hungry. Everyone does. He just doesn't want us to feel responsible for what we bring back. But we are responsible. Without us everyone would starve.

The station's ceiling is high above the ground. It's painted with bright colours, pictures of people and buildings and blue skies and trees and plants that twist over and under each other. A large fire burns in the centre of the platform. It burns there the whole time. It stays very cool down here even in the summer—even during the day. It's May now and on the surface it's getting hot, but down here the air still bites as if it were December. We follow our parents back to our little shack in the west corner of the station. It's built from wood and sheet metal. My father built it when we first came down here, back when the skies first turned black from the smoke and fire of *The End*. We've lived here ever since. There are three rooms in our shack; one for Markus and me, another for my parents, and a third with a table and chairs where we eat. We're surrounded by other shacks, all very similar. They line all the walls of the station, all four platforms.

There are almost two hundred people living in the metro station in around forty separate shacks. There are others hiding out elsewhere. I've seen others I don't recognise on the surface, doing the same thing we're doing. That's how I can be sure. We haven't actually made contact with them though. We keep to our task like we're told. We have our settlement in the metro station and we get by, keeping to ourselves. I'm sure the others do the same. Markus wants all the groups to join up and build an army to fight the soldiers above. My father says it would be too hard, not worth the risk. Most of the people here have families, and that's most important, family.

When we reach our shack Markus and my father begin unpacking the strips of horse meat. There's a bunch of younger children playing by the fire in a big group. I watch them, remembering a time when things were simpler. There are a few other kids around mine and Markus' age but we don't speak to them much. We're a team and get on fine just the two of us. The others aren't as good as us at salvaging. They complain, they're afraid. Markus and I just do it. It's our purpose here. Markus started salvaging with two other twin boys in the beginning. One of them is quiet and the other is loud but both of them are useless. Markus hated it, that's why he was so glad when I could finally join him on the surface. That and the fact that I can watch out for him; even if he is my big brother.

Markus sits outside our hut with a book. He's always reading. Only I notice he's not really looking down at the pages. He's looking across to the other platform. There's a girl there, washing something in a bucket. Her name is Szilvia. I've never spoken to her and I don't think Markus has either. He's been watching her a lot recently but he never says anything, just pretends to read. It makes no sense to me. It's a waste of time.

I'm tired and decide to lie down for a while. We sleep under big blankets, blankets Markus and I found in an old hotel a couple of years back. We were smaller then, and could barely get them home they're so big. We use our old blankets as mattresses and my mother made pillows out of old clothes, using shirts to stuff them as well. I lie on my stomach and open my shoebox. It's full of cool things I've collected. There are all kinds of things; my sling-shot, a few pencils I can draw with, chalk and coal. I still have some of the toys I used to play with when I was little. My favourite was always a small, rubber black panther. I pick it up, twirling it in my hands.

Markus and I have explored the zoo above our home many times and seeing all the animals that used to live there blows my mind. They had everything you could think of, even rhinos and gorillas and a tiger, one of the last ones alive. The animals are long gone now; most of them either escaped or were killed for food in the war. But the signs holding information on all the animals, some of those are still there. Markus and I used to spend hours reading about all the animals. We've read all the information countless times. The zoo is where we used to play when we got bored down here. We still go there sometimes, just to be out in the free air, away from everyone. It's safe, soldier free, and lots of the animal habitats are still intact. The monkey cages have some of the best climbing ropes and trees, it's a good place to practice. Although I know soon we'll have to use the wood for the fire.

They had a black panther at the zoo too. I've spent a lot of time by its old cage. I used to think a black panther was a separate species, most people think that's the case. But a black panther is normally either a black leopard or a black jaguar. If it's from South America it's a Jaguar, if it's from China or India or anywhere in the East then it's a Leopard. The one they had in the zoo was a Jaguar. They call them 'melanistic colour variants' of a species. It works in the same way as eye colour in people; my father explained it to me. It's all genetics, and I can't remember how it works exactly but either way, I'm glad it does. It makes black panthers more special, even rarer. It makes my sighting this morning even more magical. Maybe it was the panther from the zoo, the same one whose cage I've spent hour beside.

I lie back, spinning the small black animal in my hands. I stare at its eyes and remember the emerald flames that burned inside me as it stared from a distance. I try to think what it could have meant. When I saw the panther I was afraid. It was almost like it had appeared to make me feel stronger when I was weak. Maybe it came for a reason. Maybe it wanted to help.

Outside there's commotion, a man shouting. I rise up from my bed, pack my shoe box away and walk out onto the platform. There's a group of men near the centre and my father is among them. One of the men is shouting, the others are trying to calm him down. Markus is watching them too.

"What's going on?" I ask him.

"That same guy is causing issues again," he says.

"What's he saying now?" I ask.

"He's complaining, about the food. I'd like to see him try and find something. He'd be shot and torn apart within five minutes of sticking his head above ground. We should take him up there, tie him up."

"Markus, stop being so dramatic," my mother calls over, "We all find it a little difficult at times living this way."

"I'm not being dramatic," he says, "It's what he deserves."

I walk towards the men. The angry one is flailing his arms, pacing left and right. He's a very large man and his skin sags and hangs off his face in huge, floppy folds. He's dressed in a tattered suit that is much too big for him. He'd arrived recently, alone, wandered into the city one day and followed one of the other salvaging groups down here. He always has something to complain about. His face is red and flustered, the wrinkles jiggling and flapping.

"I just can't believe you entrust these stupid youngsters with getting food for all of us! You call yourselves men?"

"You know how it works, the soldiers don't bother them. You'd be welcome to try, but I guarantee you wouldn't last long," one of the other men says.

"I know it's not ideal but it's the best solution right now," says another.

The wrinkled man starts to laugh, "Ridiculous! And I haven't even mentioned the water situation. What's the plan for that?"

"We're working on it," my father says.

"Working on it? Well that's great. Soon not only will we starve, but we'll all die of thirst down here."

We had an entire channel reserved for water. When we first came down here my father had the idea. They sealed off a section of old water pipe and dug a channel up to the surface. This was before the drought, years ago, when it rained non-stop, after the sky had completely blacked out. My father knew the rain wouldn't last and he wanted to ensure we had drinking water long after it had stopped. But the drought is lasting too long. The adults haven't told us, they don't want us to worry, but we all know we're running low.

Markus says that lots of cities have underground rivers, some of them man-made. If we had one of those, or an underground lake, then we'd have nothing to worry about. But my father says there aren't any here. The only body of water was the big river on the surface that splits the city in two. But it's far away, in the part of the city that was completely flattened in the war. They bombed all the bridges, and all the important buildings that line the river bank. And besides, if the sea isn't there anymore, the river can't be either.

The wrinkled man finally sits down, exhausted from all the complaining.

"It's going to be fine," my father tells him, "my boys brought back horse. There's enough for everyone to have some."

"A bite or two of horse? Oh fantastic! Do you know the kind of life I once lived? Fillet steak, lobster, caviar. And now..." He trails off, shakes his head and storms back to his shack.

My father speak quietly with the others. Then he turns and begins walking back towards me.

"Come on son, let's cook some horse. You and your brother deserve it. Don't worry about him. He has no idea what he's talking about."

He puts his hand on my shoulder and leads me back to the shack. Later we eat the horse. My Dad sneaks an extra strip for Markus and me.

"For the hunters," he says.

My mother flavours it with salt and paprika, spices Markus and I salvaged ourselves. It tastes pretty good.

Later on I'm lying in my bed, staring at the crumpled, metal ceiling. Markus is reading in his bed beside me, this time actually looking at the pages and not other things. But still, I find it boring when he reads. I roll onto my stomach and prop myself up on my elbows.

"What's this one about?" I ask.

"It's about a man who goes to the desert with an Indian chief."

What's it called?"

"The Lessons of Chief Bear."

"What's it about?"

"It's awesome. They eat all kinds of crazy desert plants and see all kinds of crazy things."

"Like what?"

"Markus hesitates, "Like visions of power and stuff, hallucinations, only it's more than that."

I shrug, "What do you mean, *more than that*?"

Markus hesitates, looks up at the ceiling for answers, "I'm not really sure. But they aren't random. They mean stuff." He flicks back a few pages, "The part I just read is all about Death. It says here that Death waits over your left shoulder all the time."

I glance over my left shoulder, there's nothing there.

"You can't always see it. But sometimes, if you look quickly, you might catch a glimpse of it."

I try again, twisting my neck fast, but I still don't see anything. Markus laughs at me.

"It's only a story, it might not be true. But if it is, don't worry. It says here that everyone's death follows them all the time. When it's time, Death will tap you on the shoulder. But you mustn't be afraid. Think of Death as an advisor. Whenever you're scared, whenever you think you're about to die, just turn to your death and ask him. He'll tell you not to worry, it's not time for him to tap you yet. Nothing matters unless you feel his touch, and that's good to know."

I roll onto my back, "I guess so."

"Don't think on it too hard, it's just a story."

I turn to face the wall, close my eyes and I think about Death, right there beside me, snoring in black robes. I don't understand Markus' book. I'm just more afraid because I think Death could tap me at any second, whether I'm in danger or not. Markus blows out the lantern between our beds and I listen to him settle down in his. I try not to think about Death, watching me sleep. Instead I think of the black panther. I think of him as I fall asleep because I want him to be in my dreams, the flames in his eyes warming me. This calms me as I remember the power I felt, and Death is no longer watching me sleep, the panther's warm gaze is guarding me now. It's been a long day. I go out like a light.

3

Anxious voices wake me up—panic on the platform. Markus is already out of his bed and I jump up quickly, pulling on my jeans and hoody. People are rushing everywhere. I spot a woman crying, and another, their husbands try to console them. Markus isn't far off, near the big fire. I run towards him.

"What's happening?" I ask.

"Some of the others never made it back last night."

"Which ones?"

"I don't know. I guess they just got lost or something."

I spot the large, wrinkled man running from his shack—the one who was complaining last night. His face is red with rage again, his wrinkles flapping up and down on his cheeks.

"My watch! Someone stole my watch!"

A few of the others try to calm him down, but he's furious.

"That watch is worth more than your pathetic lives!" I hear him shout at one of the men trying to calm him.

"He deserves it," Markus says.

I look at my brother. He's sitting calmly on one of the chairs he's dragged out from the shack. I can see my father go over to the wrinkled man and put a hand on his shoulder, trying to calm him. The man pushes my father away and someone else tries to grab him, so he swings his fist. He catches a woman in the face. She screams and hits the ground hard. The woman's husband charges at the wrinkled man and knocks him down in one punch. The other men hold the husband back as he crawls away and then staggers to his feet.

"Savages! All of you! I've had enough!" He storms off.

"Where do you think he's going?" I ask Markus.

"Hopefully he's leaving," he smiles at me.

I look back towards the crowd of adults that has grown, and my father's walking towards us. My mother comes out of the shack with some food—a tin of peaches.

I take the tin and start to eat whilst I wait for my father. He smiles at me, telling me not to worry.

"Three youngsters never came back last night," he says.

"Are they dead?" I pass him the tin.

"It doesn't look good. It was some of the older boys, the twins and another, who aren't likely to get lost."

"What does this mean?" my mother asks.

"It could mean the soldiers aren't ignoring the young ones anymore. Things are growing desperate up there. From what I hear from the boys there's hardly any food left to find."

My mother looks worried. "Don't jump to conclusions," she says.

Markus puts his arm around her waist and she leans her head against his.

"I don't understand," I say.

"He means the soldiers probably killed and ate the twins."

"Markus!" My mother is angry at him for even thinking it.

"Easy, Markus, no need to say it like that," my father shakes his head.

"But it's true."

My father tries to give Markus a stern look, but his eyes are overcome with sadness.

"Needless to say you boys can't go out today. We need to wait and hope the lost ones show up, at least for now. Then we'll decide on what comes next."

"But we need food! We barely have any tins left, and the horse we had yesterday was nothing! We're better than the others—smarter too. We'll be fine!"

"Markus, if soldiers are killing youngsters as well now, then you cannot go above ground. That was the whole deal. We sent you up there because they left you alone. Things may have changed. Please, promise me you won't."

Markus is raging, anyone can see that. I know he wants to head up, and so do I. We can't just sit around and wait.

"I promise," Markus says, but he doesn't look up. I can see the fingers on one of his hands are crossed behind his back.

A crowd begins to gather towards the centre of the station. The wrinkled man is there, a bag on his shoulder and a walking stick in his hand. The adults are all trying to stop him.

"Get out of my way, I'm finished with all of you," he shouts.

He pushes past the last few men trying to block him off and, in the end, they let him pass. He doesn't say another word and slumps off like a big, old, useless dog.

"He doesn't stand a chance," Markus says.

"It's a miracle he survived this long. We don't need people like that down here. It's not good for morale. It's hard as it is," my father is shaking his head.

"We can't let him go up there and die," my mother says.

"He's a grown man, we can't control his actions. We can only advise, and that we tried."

"All because of a stupid watch?" I ask.

"This is about more than just a watch," my mother says. "It's about who he was before, in the old world, and who he is now. It's a status thing."

"I don't understand," I say.

"That's because you don't remember the old world. Things like the value of the watch on your wrist mattered a great deal to lots of people. The car you drove and the wine you drank. That watch was probably his last memento of who he once *was*."

"That all sounds ridiculous," I say. "Why do any of those things matter?"

My father nodded, "You're right, Bandi. It was stupid. And some people still can't let go."

I sit by the hut for the rest of the morning, there's so much going on. My father heads off to a meeting with some of the other adults and my mother joins him a bit later. I know they're going to discuss the water and the missing children. I'm nervous. What if soldiers are killing us now—*eating* us? I shudder at the thought.

All of sudden I feel a tap on my left shoulder and I jump up quickly.

"It's not Death, only me," Markus says with a big smile on his face.

He has his back-pack on, his knife in his belt.

"Come on, little brother, let's find some meat."

"Now?"

"They're all too busy worrying about what to do. Fast and silent, like ninjas."

I smile back at him, *ninjas*, a game we always used to play. It seems fitting now. I grab my small knife and slide it into my belt. I join Markus out on the platform and we dart off together, sneaking quietly down the tracks. Nobody sees us leave. What a feast we will bring them, I know it. Markus and I will be heroes tonight.

4

We head towards the surface as soon as we can. We know if the adults notice we're gone they'll try looking for us, on the tracks and in the tunnels, so we climb for the surface the first chance we get. I lead the way and Markus is right on my heels. We scale the ladder, hanging off the metal rungs. I push the drain cover up and slide it along. It's very heavy but I'm used to it.

Outside, everything looks the same. We emerge on a street corner; it's deserted—like everywhere— and silent. Only the dust blows and swirls over the rubble, over the debris and down the streets, as if looking for life to blow upon, finding none but us. Two thorns in the dust.

I look up at the sky and it's stormy and hot, but the air is dry as ever.

Markus stands beside me. "You ready?" he asks.

"Of course," I say, before charging off at speed.

Markus runs after me as quickly as he can, but I'm faster. I look back and I can see him struggling to keep up. He's smiling but his face is red and I notice I'm also starting to sweat in the morning heat. I forget all about everything for a few minutes, the lack of food and water, the missing salvaging group, the wrinkled man, even the dead soldier and the black panther. For a few minutes I run and the breeze blows through my hair and I close my eyes. I feel like I could take off. When we were younger we'd spread our arms out at our sides. We'd pretend to fly, swooping low and flapping our arms like wings and squawking like the seagulls that lived by the sea. Markus showed me the sound they make. He remembers it from before.

He catches up now and I glance at my brother who worries so much, and the smile on his face only pulls mine wider. But Markus stops. Momentum carries me on but he grabs my shoulder and yanks me back, holds me still.

"Shhh," he puts his finger to his lips, "didn't you hear that?"

He looks worried—afraid even. I shake my head and try to listen.

A rumbling scream rattles the air and we both drop to the ground. We lie on our stomachs and crawl to the side of the road where we hide under an old bus. Another scream rises, filled with pain, a man's scream. I look at Markus. His eyes are a little wet, neither of us can move. There's no movement in the distance, no one and nothing. I'm too low to the ground.

Without saying a word I start to slide myself out from under the bus. Markus grabs at my leg.

I turn to look at him, "I'm climbing this bus. Maybe I can see from up there," I whisper.

He looks more afraid than I've ever seen him. Maybe the stories of the soldiers' new ways have really gotten to him.

"Wait here," I say. "I'll be right back."

There's an old car on its side just behind the bus, so I use the parts underneath as a climbing wall. The metal is hot so I move quickly and pull myself up and perch on the door, careful of the broken glass. I crawl slowly forward and a fallen streetlight bridges the gap onto the bus' roof. It's steep and narrow but seems quite sturdy; the bus, the car and the street lamp have almost welded into one over the years. I grip the metal pole tightly, wrapping my legs and arms around it. My jeans slide nicely along the metal and the rubber soles of my shoes grip well, allowing me to push myself along with my feet. I hoist myself up onto the bus' roof and stop for a second to catch my breath. The metal moans as I rise up, but it feels strong enough.

Shielding my eyes, I stare into the distance and I can see the old square up ahead, just down the road we're on. There's a large group of soldiers in a circle, a dark shape on the ground in the middle. It's a man laying in a heap—a large man. I can hear him crying and wailing, the wind carrying the pained sounds towards me.

I quickly climb down and Markus is right where I left him, completely still. I tell him what I've seen. "We should take a closer look, see what's going on."

I can see on my brother's face that he wishes I hadn't said that, but I also know that he has to come with me. He's older. There's nothing he lets me do without him. That's just how it is.

He nods reluctantly and starts to slide himself out from under the bus. I stare down the street towards the square, unable to see it from ground level, but the piercing screams haven't stopped.

"What did you see?" Markus is now beside me, staring with me.

"Soldiers; standing around someone in the middle."

"It sounds like they're torturing him."

I look at Markus and nod. "I think they are."

Keeping low and to the side of the road, I jog towards the square. Markus follows, telling me to slow down. The screams grow louder and louder and soon I can see the shapes, the soldiers in their masks, some of them on lookout, others with their backs to us and facing the screaming man. We stop and lie down on the concrete. I feel terrified all of a sudden, remember the dead soldier, torn in half, and the missing children. Markus' hands are shaking and I look at him. He looks focused but I can see he's trying really hard to be brave.

"We shouldn't stay on this road, they'll see us if we get any closer. We need to go up somehow," he says.

He pushes himself into a squat and starts to look around. I do the same. We're almost at the corner, where the road meets the square, just a hundred metres back from the soldiers. I spot a building to our right with its glass door kicked in. Markus spots it too. We nod at each other and duck behind some wreckage and start to creep towards it.

It's an old apartment building and there's a large stone stairwell right in front of us. There's a carpet that's red and grand; a fallen chandelier lies cracked and broken in the middle of the entrance hall. I can tell this was once a very fancy building for rich people, but it's a ruin like everything else now. We run up the stairs, one flight at a time as we check windows. We want to stay out of sight, but we want to be close enough to see them clearly, maybe even hear what the soldiers are saying.

I stop on the fourth floor. "This should be high enough."

Markus nods and we move to the side of the building that faces the square, where an open window should give us a good view. All the doors are either open or smashed to the floor. We enter one of the apartments and creep through. The living room has been emptied of almost everything and the wooden floor creaks as we step towards the window. It waits for us, its glass long gone, probably lying shattered on the street below. We peer through it side by side, down at the square. The statues of former great leaders lie in heaps of metal, the ones still on their stone podiums limbless and headless. We can see the circle of soldiers has broken up now, the majority of them are heading down the road where Markus and I had just been. I look at my brother and he shakes his head as if to say, 'That was too close.'

Four soldiers remain in the square, all of them armed with pistols and knives strapped to their backs. Their gas-masks make them look like robots, or monsters—only half human. They don't look up at all and I stare hard at the large man who lies in a heap. He's covered in blood and weeping.

"Shut up!" One of the soldiers shouts, then he kicks the large man in the stomach.

"Please, just let me go, I told you everything! I promise I'm not lying!" The man weeps and his voice is distorted, but there's something very familiar about it.

Another soldier walks over and kicks him again. "We'll see, very soon now. If what you're saying is true the others should be there in a few minutes. If we find enough supplies and food, then we won't have to barbeque you."

I start to shake and look at Markus; his eyes are pulled wide and I can see he's struggling to swallow.

"You really are pathetic. Giving up an entire settlement to save your own skin. We should kill you anyway, just for being such a coward."

"They stole my watch, made me look like a fool. They're barbarians, the lot...."

We don't hear anymore. We're already out of the apartment and charging down the stairs. I'm running faster than I ever have before. When we reach the street we can see the other group of soldiers already by the bus where we first emerged. Markus grabs me by the arm and drags me after him, down an alleyway on the left.

"We need to go around," he tells me, "we have to warn everyone!"

We emerge at the other end of the alley and charge down the parallel street. We run so hard I can feel my feet start to bleed. We have to go the long way round to avoid the soldiers, but we know the way, we can make it. I start to feel tired but I can't stop. As the wind blasts into our faces, tears start to stream down, stinging my eyes and cheeks.

I think of the black panther and I feel stronger, run even faster. We reach the drain and slide it open. But then the explosion rings out, rocking my bones. Smoke rises from the old station's entrance a few streets away.

Markus screams desperately, "Come on!"

I feel like I've turned to stone, too heavy to move. Markus is already halfway down the ladder when I start to climb. I can hear gunshots rattling off the concrete walls and metal pipes. Screams come hurtling down the sewer tunnels. We're too late. The soldiers are already there.

Neither of us move for a few minutes. We stand in the dark, side by side, hoping it's all just a twisted nightmare, hoping the tunnel will swallow us whole so we can wake up and forget all of this. I take my brothers hand and he's shaking furiously. We both drop to our knees in the black and weep for our parents, weep in fear—weep for each other.

5

A few minutes go on forever. So many things bolt through my mind, memories flying out of the black tunnels like bullets. I see my mother's face, my father's eyes, the smell of his t-shirt and her hair. I see the station as it was— its painted ceiling, safe and comforting, and its fire warm and strong. I imagine it now, my parents screaming as guns crack and smoke charges, while people fall in heaps to the platform. I see the soldiers' masked faces, their eyes hidden but piercing blue, cold and hollow. Markus sobs beside me and he's squeezing my hand. We collapse into each other as I try to hold back my own tears.

"Quickly, we have to go help them!" Hope surges in me for a moment and I try to rise to my feet, pulling Markus with me, but he's heavy and I can't stand. My legs buckle and give way. I fall to my knees again.

"We can't, you know we can't," Markus says.

I crumble and start to cry again. I know he's right.

"But what if someone's alive?" I say.

"They leave no one alive. You know that. We'll only die too."

"Then we'll die!" I say, my voice choked, my throat sore. "We have to do something!"

I look into my brother's eyes and they're wet like the sea, brimming with wave upon wave of heartache. It seems impossible, surviving now. Everything was fine as it was, we had a home, we had each other—now we have nothing. I gaze at Markus and I know I have to be brave. He's trying so hard but he can't do this alone, he needs me to be strong for both of us.

I listen for a minute and the chaos has subsided. There's still the occasional gunshot or banging, crashing, but the noises are scarce now, the attack likely over.

"We need to get out of here," I say.

Markus looks at me and nods, picks himself up and stands.

"They might come searching the tunnels for survivors," he rubs his eyes with his dirty hands.

"It sounds like it's over. I think they're just shooting any..." my voice trails off.

Markus puts his hand on my shoulder, like he always does. I'm glad he's with me. I know I can't do this alone, and neither can he. At least we're together—together alone.

We run quietly, on the pads of our feet, fast but almost silent. We don't take the same sewer drain to the surface; we use one further down the tunnel. Outside it's later than I'd thought, a few hours past noon at least, the sunlight barely grazing over the taller buildings. I'm out into the daylight first but Markus is just behind me. We stay crouched when we reach the streets, and run low to the safety of an upside down taxi, leaning against the side of an old building. The front wall of the building is half gone, the inside a mess of debris, nothing to tell us what it once was.

"Where now?" I ask.

"I don't know. Where else could be safe?"

I scout our surroundings; we're still close to the station. Smoke is spewing up a few streets away. It's thick and black, and I think of the bodies again; Mother, Father. But I shake my head, toss the thoughts out. I need to focus on staying alive.

"The zoo," Markus says, "it's always been safe before."

"Isn't it too close? Won't they search the area?"

"If we wait, I think we'll be Ok. They probably found all the food they need down there."

His voice crackles and I can feel myself about to break down again. A sickness rises inside me. I vomit on the concrete and collapse onto my hands and knees. I feel Markus' hand on my back. He rubs in circles like my mother always does—did. My body rattles, my hands unable to grasp, too weak. We sit there, shielded from view by the taxi, waiting for the night.

When the darkness comes, we gather ourselves and start off towards the zoo. We creep away quietly and hug the row of buildings heading south. Ten minutes later, we arrive at the gates. There is no sign of anyone; no soldiers and no survivors. We jog around to the side of the main entrance, passing the white stone elephants. The fence is low here, half caved. We jump it and stand still, our backs against the metal. For a few minutes we don't move, listening to the night. There isn't a sound, only the wind whistling through the gaps of the steel fence.

"I think it's safe," Markus says.

I nod and relax, slumping to the ground. He crumples beside me and we sit there for an hour, not saying a word, not feeling safe at all.

"We should find somewhere to sleep," Markus says, as he rises to his feet.

He puts out his hand and I take it. He pulls me up.

"Where to?" he asks.

"The panther enclosure," I say.

"Ok, let's be careful."

I lead the way and Markus follows. We're by the old seal habitat and the big cats aren't far, on the east side of the zoo. We run along the path and stay as low as possible, choosing concealment over speed. All the while I don't hear anything, other than our feet tapping along the concrete, but I still can't feel safe.

The plants are long dead, only some dry stalks and foliage remain in the dust. The trees lining the path are like skeletons, bare bones of their former selves. I can't imagine what they looked like. The closest thing I've seen is the paintings on the platform roofs. Markus remembers, he's wanted to show me a photo for a long time, but hasn't found the right book.

We take a left through the ape house, and the stone floor is covered in shards of glass that were once windows. We walk in between the gorilla and chimpanzee enclosures on tiptoes because of the glass crunching under our heels. As I pass by, I stare into them and they look emptier than ever. I think about how they serve no purpose anymore, but they were once the homes for whole families of apes. I think of the metro station, below us right now, sitting there empty—a hall of ghosts and nothing more. It's pointless now, when for years it was my home, Markus' home, our family's home. It was the only home I ever knew. I try not to think about it and continue to tiptoe on, till we're out in the moonlight again.

We run now, passing the tiger cages, the lions', and beside the leopards' the panther cage sits. We climb through the large hole in the front, which we always use. It's the same as it was when we were last here. It's been a few months at least.

We jump the ditch and land side by side in the dust. There's a large tree in the centre, that's where we always sit, and up it we climb, first me, then Markus once he places his bag safely at the bottom. Through the cage's roof I can see the moon. It's thin, like a clawed finger curling at the stars. But I'm in the black panther's home now and I feel protected, I feel safe—finally.

I sit on my branch and lean against the trunk, letting my legs dangle. Markus sits on his branch beside me and does the same, his legs swinging a little.

"Why did he do it?" I whisper.

Markus looks at me, his eyes shimmering. "Who?"

"Why did he give us up?"

Markus looks away and shakes his head. "Anything to save himself."

"And all because of what? A watch?"

Markus doesn't answer for a moment. I watch as he chews his lip and keeps his face in shadow so that I can't see his tears. It's all too much for him. I shouldn't have said anything.

Then he turns to me, opening his bleary eyes. "It's like Mother said, he didn't like who he was in this world. He was holding on to it all from before, everything he was. But that's all long gone, and now, everything *we* had here is gone with it."

"Why couldn't he just get on with it, like everyone else?"

Markus stares at me blankly, emotionless—zonked. "Once you live life at the top, it's hard to come back down."

"It's not fair."

"All of them, just like that. No hesitation. Mother and Father, Szilvia." I look up at him, his eyes are far away, "She was nice. She didn't deserve this."

"Nobody did," I say.

He shrugs, "I was going to talk to her, you know, soon. I was just waiting for the right moment."

He looks up, returning from the distance, from memory. I try and force a smile but it's pointless. There are no reasons to smile anymore. The moon rises higher and higher and soon it's directly above us. One man's selfishness cost us everything, his pride was too strong. I think about the black panther, how it was once here but now it's out there, somewhere in the wild. And I want to see it again, now more than ever—need it now more than ever. But at least I'm here, in its old home. That's something for sure.

We're alone, surrounded by Death. It's coming for us, I'm sure of that. I close my eyes and wait for that tap on the shoulder. Only it doesn't come. The night drifts along.

6

A cough sounds in the night, a heavy chesty cough. It's close too, and Markus immediately hops off the tree. I jump down after him and he holds his finger to his lips.

We listen.

Glass smashes, along with some muttered swearing. The sounds are coming from the path outside the cages. I creep to the front of the enclosure and hop over the ditch again. I get low and peer out through the gaps in the black metal. It's a soldier, stumbling forward towards us, no mask on his head, just a knife in his belt and not even a pack on his back.

I look back at the tree where Markus is waiting. He looks worried but his brows are pulled low in an attempt to feel fierce.

I creep back across the dirt and whisper, "It's a soldier—just one—and I think he's drunk."

"Drunk?"

"Yeah, he's falling all over the place. Come see."

I crawl forwards and wait for Markus. He's fiddling with something on his belt, his knife probably. Soon he's beside me and we both jump the ditch and squat low, peering out through the hole this time. The soldier carries on stumbling in our direction, his big boots stomping this way and that, as he sways in the moon light. We pull our heads lower as he moves closer. We turn away, ducking completely out of sight and wait. I can hear his hoarse breathing, his scratchy throat. He spits and I hear the saliva hit the stone right beside us, just the other side of the cage. He grunts and then there's a huge crash as his whole body falls to the ground. He moans and I glance at Markus, his fierce expression has returned. Peering out of the hole again I can see the soldier, flat out on his back, still.

"Let's run, now!" I say.

I hop through the hole and onto the path, taking a second to look at the soldier, whose black uniform is dusty and blood stained. He's on his back facing the sky and grimaces in pain.

I start running to the left, past the panther cages, towards the east walls of the zoo. Markus isn't beside me and I stop, spin around to see what's happened. He's just standing there, staring at the drunk soldier, who lies almost motionless. Then Markus pulls a handgun from his belt.

It looks strange in his hands, the charcoal metal gleaming in the skinny moon's light. I can't believe what I'm seeing; has he lost his mind? Where did he get a gun?

"Markus," I shout, "come on!"

He turns to look at me but doesn't take his aim off the soldier. The soldier lies in the centre of the path, Markus between us. There are tears in his eyes.

"What if he's the one who..." his voice trails off.

"Let's just go, he'll die anyway," I say.

"No he won't. He'll wake up with a headache, ready to kill more people, good people, like the ones he killed today!"

"Easy'dere," the soldier's voice stuns us both, sends shivers down my back. He's s sitting up, his hands out in surrender, his upper body swaying – words slurred and dry.

Markus quickly turns and holds the gun out with both hands around the grip, his finger on the trigger.

"Don't move!" he shouts.

"Markus wait," I come running over, stand beside him, "let's just go."

"You should listen to your little friend, I'm not here't hurt you's."

The soldier keeps his hands up and stares at us, his eyes look black in the dark.

Markus keeps the gun held out straight, tears form in his eyes again, "You killed our parents! You destroyed our home!"

"I don't know anything about that s-son," he hiccups, "I only just got in th-the city this evening, from the east."

"I don't believe you, you're drunk. I can tell you're lying," rage builds behind my brother's eyes.

"Ha!" the soldier laughs then coughs hard, raspy, "I can promise you's both, I don't know what... you're talking, about. But you're right… I'm definitely drunk."

He's struggling to speak. I don't know what to think. But I don't care who he is, or where he came from, I just want to leave. Markus' hands are shaking, the gun bouncing up and down, left and right in his grip.

"Please Markus, let's just go."

"We have to kill him, he killed them!"

The gun wavers in his hands. He can no longer hold it straight.

"The only thing I killed was'ome mangy dogs this m-morning. And that's because I woke up with them gnawing at my gammy wound, look at it."

The soldier pulls up his trouser leg. The wound underneath is grim; red, brown and rotting. It's dark but I'm sure I can see things crawling in it; insects, maggots.

"I'm just drinking for the pain," he pulls his trouser leg down, "I'll be dead pretty soon with this...one." He belches loudly and falls back again, onto his back, facing the stars. "Hurt it in a fall in the hills, and those dogs made sure this would be the end of m-me. Infection... nothing that c-can be done."

Markus lowers the gun finally, he's breathing hard.

I put my palm on his back, "Let's go."

Markus rubs his eyes with his hand, then tucks the gun into his belt with the other. "I'm sorry," he says.

"It's Ok," I try to smile.

"It's just, they took it all away, soldiers like him, maybe him. They took it all..." his voice trails off.

I stare at the soldier, still on his back, grunting occasionally, coughing at the moon. I hate him furiously, with everything in me, but maybe he's telling the truth. He doesn't seem like a bad man, and I think maybe he's one of the good soldiers, there have to be some after all.

He starts to snore and I know he's passed out. I look at my brother who's watching him intensely, as if trying to figure something out.

"We should get out of here," I say.

"But where do we even go?"

I don't know the answer to Markus' question. I don't know anything. I look up at the sky and think of the black panther, somewhere out there, and I want nothing more than for it to come to me now, show me where to go.

"We can't stay here," I say after a while.

"Maybe we need to leave the city. We have no reason to stay anymore. I don't think we'd last long. Soldiers are everywhere now, even here."

His words are heavy on my mind, my heart. I know he's right. We don't stand a chance if we stay.

"So then where?" I ask.

"Maybe we should ask him," Markus nods towards the soldier, "he claims he came from the east, then surely he should know."

I look at the soldier too, snoring, his leg slowly killing him. I nod at Markus and he pulls the gun from his belt again, cocks it back skilfully.

He looks at me, see's my puzzlement, "Been playing with it a lot," he shrugs.

"Where did you even get it?"

"The dead soldier, the one we found."

Blue piercing eyes flash in my head. I knew he'd found something but I didn't expect it to be a gun.

"Just be careful," I say.

"I will."

Markus moves over towards the sleeping soldier.

"Wait," I say, "we should search him first."

Markus nods and I hurry to join him. We stand over the soldier's body and foul rot fuses in the air. I can even feel its sting in my eyes. A boozy smell wafts towards us whenever he breathes out, his chest still hoarse, his throat dry.

"I'll keep the gun aimed at his head while you search."

I nod in agreement and wait for him to circle the soldier, stand above his head, the gun aimed directly between his eyes. When he's in position I kneel down and search carefully, first his jacket pockets, then his trousers. I find a small rusty revolver, empty of bullets. I place it on the ground beside me and continue to scour his pockets. There's nothing in his jacket at all.

"He probably had a back-pack and left it somewhere," I say.

"Search his back pockets. He must have some matches or something useful."

I reach under the soldier's back and manage to slip my hands into the back pocket of his trousers. I pull out a photo, but nothing else, hold it up to Markus. It's a picture of the soldier, looking much younger with a woman by his side. His brown hair is much thicker, longer, wavy like mine. She has long dark hair, a smile that calms me for a moment, her eyes remind me of my mother. White mountains rise in the background.

I turn the photo over and there's writing on the back, the words running and flowing into one another.

'Remember day's like this... Always,

With Love'

"Who do you think she is?" I ask.

"Maybe his wife, from before, I don't know."

"He looks so happy," I say.

"A lot of people were happy before, at least compared to now."

I rise to my feet holding the picture and step back, "Now what?"

"Now we wake him up," Markus says.

"How? He's completely passed out"

"Kick him, hard, in the ribs maybe."

I shrug, hesitate.

"Just do it," Markus says, "I've got the gun, remember."

I kick him a little first and he grunts, but no more. I swallow and take a deep breath, then heave my right foot forward into his side.

"Aghh!" he grunts, begins moaning again, "What the?"

He opens his eyes, looks up at me blearily, confused. I step back, Markus grips the guns with both hands.

"Thought you two were a bloody dream. Where the hell am I?"

He rubs his thinning hair, his clammy forehead. He tries to sit up but can't.

"We just want to ask some questions," Markus says, a tremble in his throat.

"Just let me die, there's nothing to tell," he closes his eyes again, his breathing grows heavy once more.

"What's to the east, where you came from?" I ask.

He squints at me, then groans, begins to push himself up into a sitting position.

Markus moves round to stand beside me, holding the gun out all the while, aimed at his chest now.

"Nothing; just hills, then mountains, hills and mountains of dust, deserts, all of it burnt to hell, flattened by bombs and wars fought years ago for years on end. There's nothing left," and he just stares at us, waiting.

"What about beyond that?" I ask.

He sighs, "I don't know, the sea I suppose."

I can feel Markus surge a little beside me at the mention of the sea, "The sea isn't there anymore," he says.

"Course it is," replies the soldier.

"I heard it was all gone, dried up, just dust, fire, like everything else," Markus says.

The soldier shakes his head, "Think about it, it rained for six years. This drought has been long but not that long, do you know how big the sea is? It can never dry up. The sea was here before all of us, and it will be here long after."

We stand in silence, Markus and I, not sure what to think. The soldier searches his pockets for a while, then gives up, finding nothing, looking up at us again, "Don't suppose one of you's has a smoke?"

We shake our heads.

"Will that be all?" he asks, "It's time I die in peace."

He lies back again, this time tucking his arms behind his head, closing his eyes.

"Have you seen it, the sea?" Markus asks.

The soldier opens his eyes, "Not for a long time, but I know it's there. Trust me on that one."

Markus finally lowers the gun. "Let's go," he says.

We start to walk off, away from the soldier, to the east wall of the zoo. I remember I'm still holding his photograph. I turn back, quietly stepping towards him. He opens his eyes again and looks at me as I approach. I'm sure he's not a bad soldier, or at least wasn't always. I hold out the photo and he looks at it.

"How'd you get that?" he asks.

"Sorry," I say, "forgot I'd taken it."

He takes the photo from my hand and holds it out, between the stars and his face. He sighs and lets it drop to the dust.

"Who is she?" I ask.

"Doesn't matter, not in this place."

"Who was she?"

The soldier looks at me, "She was my world, but that world is long gone."

"What happened to her?" I ask.

"Same thing that happened to everything else that was good and true."

He speaks with indifference, and I know he's lost all hope, it's over for him.

"I used to think I'd find her, searched for years after the wars. Eventually I realised there's nothing to find. No love, no good, nothing."

"She might still be out there," I say.

The soldier shakes his head, "Nothing good left out there, and she was good as they come."

I don't say anything else, turn away and walk towards Markus who's waiting a few metres on. He puts his hand on my shoulder and we move forward together, side by side. I turn back to look at the soldier, who lies motionless, just a dark mound in front of the black panther's cage.

"You ready?"Markus asks.

"Ready for what?"

"To leave this city behind."

He unloads the gun, releases the bullet from the chamber, then puts it back together, tucks it in his bag.

"Good thing I didn't have to shoot him," he says, "There's only one bullet."

7

Before moving on we decide to get some sleep. We arrive by the east wall, or where it once was. The entire structure has been destroyed now, blown apart and smashed to pieces. Only a low row of crumbling stone remains, but it's high enough to keep us hidden if we lie down. From here, during the day, we can see far off into the distance, over a large barren plain that was once a huge park, and beyond. The buildings no longer rise high, most of them are smaller houses, the outskirts of the city. Beyond that lies the long desert, stretching out in the heat for several miles, before the ground begins to rise into the mountains. Beyond that, I don't know. And beyond that…we can only hope the drunken soldier is right.

Markus and I lie parallel to the wall, hugging it closely, head to head, the back-pack our pillow. The air is fairly warm, the nights growing hotter as the summer sets in. I struggle to fall asleep even though I'm completely exhausted, drained of everything. There's just too much going on in my head; memories, thoughts of the what lies ahead, screams and screams, tears and pain, death, loss, my mother, my father, up there in the stars now, waiting for me. I think of the dead soldier, who had scared me so much, not two days ago. Now all that seems insignificant, his cold blue eyes make me feel nothing compared to what's happened since. Finding that soldier was the beginning of the end. I should have known. I lie and think about the drunken soldier, his lack of care, his complete loss of hope and faith in anything good left in this world. I know I'm good, I know Markus is good, but if everything else is truly gone, maybe we don't have a chance either. Maybe we should give up too, let dogs devour us, soldiers shoot us or the heat drain us until we can move no more, think no more.

Markus is sleeping beside me, muttering and cursing to himself quietly, fighting his dreams. But at least he's asleep. I give up trying, sit up on the stump of the wall and stare off into the distance, to the east. The moon—the clawed finger—is frightening now and it seems weak; the power of the night—the power of the dark—defeating it. That's when I see it again. The black panther.

This time it's closer, on the other side of the old park just in front of me. My heartbeat starts to flurry as I watch it stalk in a circle, facing me the entire time. Suddenly the night doesn't seem so dark, as if the light within it has been awakened. The moon suddenly seems more powerful, the clawed finger burning brightly in the sky. I stand up on the wall and watch silently. This time I can make out the black panther's emerald eyes, staring unblinkingly at me. I feel its brightness, the warmth ignites my hope once more. I feel its strength again, surging through my veins and erupting through my pores. The panther lies down and curls itself up, just like a cat, and we sit there, in silence, staring at each other for a very long time.

I'm aware of so much so suddenly; things no longer look so bleak. The sea is out there, beyond where the panther sits, I feel sure of that now, though I can't explain why. I feel a purpose again, and above all I feel hope. I know we can make it. I can't explain any of this, it all just happens in my head, suddenly, while I stare at the panther, staring back at me.

I wake up covered in sweat and the sky is grey, brimmed with a golden blue, the sun ready to chase the last of the night away. I'm lying on the other side of the wall, outside the zoo. I'm confused but then I remember the panther, look up and find no sign of it. It may have been a dream. Only it can't have been, because I'm the other side of the wall. That and I'm feeling brave again, ready to carry on. I stand on the rubble and breathe the morning air in slowly. It's surprisingly fresh and cool. The black panther appeared to the east, twice now, always watching me, always from the *east*.

I don't wake Markus, I wait for him to rise on his own. It isn't long before he does, the sun still a small golden curve on the horizon. He's gloomy when he wakes. He doesn't say a lot and lethargically shuffles over to sit beside me. When I ask how he slept he shrugs, seems hollow. I can tell he's starting not to care, and I think of the drunk soldier, his hope depleted, and I know I need to help my big brother. He needs to feel the same strength I feel.

"Markus," I say, "I need to tell you something."

He rubs his eyes, gazes around, "Sure."

"I first saw it two days ago when we were out scavenging. You were searching the dead soldier. I was looking out, and that's when I saw it."

"Saw what?"

"A black panther to the east. It just stood there, and I could feel him looking at me. I could see his eyes, even though he was too far away."

Markus looks at me for a few seconds, "It was probably a cat, or a dog. It probably just seemed further away, so you thought it was something bigger."

I shake my head in frustration, "I know what I saw. I know what happened, what I felt. And last night I saw it again."

Markus looks up at me suddenly, "Where?"

I stand, point out across the park, "Right there. Last night while you were sleeping."

Markus clambers to his feet and looks out to where I'm pointing, "Well, why didn't you wake me?"

"Because you were asleep, and I couldn't sleep, and all kinds of thoughts were going on in my head, and then it was there, to the east again, to the east both times."

Markus stands there, doesn't say anything.

"The east Markus," I say, "The same way the soldier told us to go, to the sea."

Markus still doesn't respond, starts looking around again.

"I think it's trying to help us," I say. "He comes when I need him, like I did last night. It sounds strange, but he makes me feel strong."

Markus stares at me, sees how serious I am, but he shakes his head, "I get it. We've been through a lot. You're finding ways to make sense of it, and that's a good thing."

"I'm not 'finding ways to make sense of it', I know what I saw!" I almost scream in frustration.

"Calm down," he says. "Are you crazy? You'll wake the whole city."

"You're the one always getting all dramatic about things, creating stories, talking about omens and stuff, not me. I wouldn't make this up."

He steps closer and looks at me hard, "Ok. I believe you. Next time you see it, let me know."

I'm angry because I know he doesn't believe me, know he doesn't care. He packs his bag and starts off across the park without saying a word. Then he calls back to me, "Come on, little brother, we have a long way to go."

He turns towards me and smiles, only he's forcing it. I want him to believe me because I know what I saw, and because right now I can see that he's broken.

I catch up with him and we walk on, staying low. We're out in the open so we hurry, start to jog. It's not the safest route but we're sure this part of the city is empty. It's the fastest way out and we need to leave quickly. We try to stay low and I speed up, running fast because I'm suddenly very aware of how easy to spot we must be. Then I hear a blast, a gunshot, and the dust just ahead blows up in a cloud where the bullet hits. We don't say a word to each other, continue to run. Another shot is fired, hits something to my left as I duck. We keep going, almost across the empty plain now. No more gunshots crack the quiet.

The shooter is too far, ammunition is hard to come by. My chest is heavy so I slow down, reaching the street on the other side of the park. I kneel and hug the side of an old tram car.

Markus squats beside me. "You alright?"

I nod vigorously. "We need to keep going. They know where we are."

We stand at the same time. I lead us across the road, staying low, sprinting between cars. We enter a building on the other side, an old apartment block. The building has been blown right through and the stone staircase is a pile of rubble, impossible to climb.

We come out the other side and we're in a dark alley. It leads north, while walls line all other directions. We follow the alley between bullet-strewn buildings and come out just opposite Hero's Square. Tall stone pedestals once reached up into the sky, gleaming white, statues of our country's heroes atop them. A few remain almost fully intact. Others lie crumbled on the ground. All of the statues are gone, but I don't know where to. They probably just crumbled, turned to dust like everything else.

The street heads east and along it we go, keeping low, staying close to walls or debris where we can, cutting quickly across small sections of road that are open, always one at a time. The sun is rising higher and sweat pours from both of us and our chests heave as we power on. I tell Markus to wait, catch his breath. I decide to climb something, scout ahead. The front of an old pharmacy leans down onto the road, a large sign. The back of the sign is made of wire mesh and I climb it, up onto a balcony above the shop front. From there I stare out but can't see much, other than more of the same; cars, stone, broken glass glistening in the sunlight. Maybe it's delirium, but for a second I forget what I'm looking at, in awe of its beauty, how even the ruins of a world can be made beautiful by sunshine. Then I see the bodies up ahead, dark shapes on the side of the road. I shield my eyes from the sun, hoping that maybe it's just some carcasses we can use. But my heart drops; there are blood soaked clothes, maybe a backpack beside them. I quickly climb down from the balcony, over the railings, dropping down onto the street. Markus is waiting, an anxious look on his face.

"It looks clear, but I see bodies, less than a hundred metres down."

Markus looks away, closing his eyes for a moment, sighing. He doesn't want to see them and nor do I.

"We should keep moving," I say, "soldiers might come back for them."

Markus nods and we move on up the road, past more rusting cars and shattered stone. I know the bodies are beside the overturned four-by-four that lies just ahead, the cover we head for next. I dart across the tarmac and wait in the vehicle's shadow. Markus sprints after me and we both squat with our backs against the metal.

"They're on the other side. Should we check them out?"

Markus breathes out slowly, closes his eyes.

"We should just look, as we go past. I'm sure if they were killed by soldiers they would have already been stripped clean."

Markus glances at me, "Ok. Lead the way."

I lean forwards and crawl on my hands and knees. Rounding the corner of the vehicle I see the bodies again, up close this time. The headrush almost knocks me out and I slow my breathing to counteract it.

"Bandi?" Markus grabs my arm, concerned.

"I know who they are," I say, "It's the three who never made it back."

My heart is pounding. I recognise their faces, the twins and András. We didn't care about them, hated them even, but now they're dead, their bodies lying right in front of us. The arms and legs have been stripped, the flesh hacked off with a knife. The bodies are a mess, almost unrecognisable. I have to turn away, my head spinning, and I vomit onto the ground.

Markus is right beside me now, the bodies not ten metres away. His breathing is rapid, mine is too, no longer under control.

"We need to get out of here," he says, almost in a whisper.

Our eyes meet. I grab their discarded backpack and we run.

Staying low is forgotten and I stride at full stretch with Markus on my heels. Only speed matters. We jump over heaps of bricks and stone that lie trickling into the road amongst the cars. We run along the tramlines, the pylons that once carried its power reduced to a web of metal to hop and skip over. Markus is right beside me, ducking and dodging along his own path. The end of the road is up ahead. From there we need to head north for a while, to avoid the factory district to the east, an area where we were told never to go. It's where the soldiers often camp. I don't know what we'll find in the northern edge of the city, but I know that's the way we must go in order to escape. From there we can head east again.

I tear open the twins' backpack. The whole thing is bloody and it sticks to my clothes, my hands. There's nothing inside it and I toss it to the ground. Markus glances hopefully but I shake my head. The bodies of András and the twins are images that flicker in my head as we run onwards. Soldiers have always left us alone. We're young, weak in their eyes. But maybe my father was right—things have changed.

8

By nightfall we are further from the station, further from the zoo than anyone we know of has ever been. All we know is that there isn't much in the northern part of the city, but we can't be sure it's safe. The road we're on is straight and long, although in the dark we can't see too far, only that it seems to carry on for a while. Houses line the roadside, some of them small and others large. Taller buildings become even scarcer, whilst the number of skeletal trees and shrubs has grown. It's dark but our eyes have adjusted, and I thank the stars for helping us conserve flares, knowing on most nights clouds of dust and debris floating up high would choke us into total blackness. We're walking and I can barely keep my eyes open. My feet are sore and blistered, pulsing inside my shoes. Even my calves feel weak and powerless, my toes numb.

"We need to stop soon," I say.

"I know, just a little further. We'll stop and stay in one of these houses. We just have to be very careful; anyone, anything could be out here," he says.

We trudge on warily, my mouth pasty and dry. Our water is running low already and we both know it, but haven't found a solution. The only thing I can think would be to go back to the metro station. But we've come so far already, and going back could be suicide.

As if reading my thoughts Markus passes me a bottle from his bag. I drink, but just a sip. It's half empty, half a litre left. I pass the bottle back to Markus and he puts it away.

"Aren't you having any?" I ask him.

"I'm fine for now," he keeps looking ahead, but I can see his lips are cracked, and I know he must be thirsty.

"Is that all we have left?"

"Yeah, but we'll find something soon."

It's obviouse he's not convinced, and neither am I. It hasn't rained in six years. There might not be water anywhere out here.

The creature seems to appear from thin air, dissolving out of the dark, almost knocking us both to the ground in shock. Markus holds me up as we both stagger backwards. It's a large brown dog, right in front of us, its head lowered, eyes black in the dim starlight. It barks twice, then takes a few steps towards us. It starts growling and I slowly lower myself, pick a stone off the ground, one the size of my fist. I slowly stand again and pull my arm back, before hurling the stone in the dog's direction. It bounces off the tarmac and pings up into the dog's side. It yelps and runs away. Markus pats me on the back.

"What kind of dog was that?" I ask.

"I don't know. But it was big, and I'm glad it's gone."

I smile at Markus, "We should have killed it. We're low on food too."

"Actually, we don't have any food."

I take my knife from my belt, "When it comes back, we'll get it."

We walk on and occasionally I hear a bark fire up from the darkness somewhere nearby. What worries me is that sometimes the bark comes from behind us, sometimes ahead. Sometimes it's to the left of us and sometimes to the right. And it doesn't sound like one dog, it sounds like many.

After a few minutes the brown dog returns, scampering out of the darkness. I raise my knife slowly as it stares at me, hunched forwards, its tail stiff. I can hear Markus pulling out the gun, rattling around as he loads our only bullet, cocks it back.

"Don't", I tell him, "We should save it. I can get him. Just get your knife out and help me if I need it."

"Be careful," he says.

I step towards the dog and it stands staring at me. I hear a bark to my left and spin quickly, turning to face it. A small white dog appears. Then there's a bark behind me and Markus and I both swivel to face that. Two Vizslas are standing right there, brown hunting dogs, slobber dripping slowly to the ground. I turn to face the first dog and beside it two others have appeared, one of them a big black Rottweiler. They all start barking viciously, loudly, all of them frothing, their tongues dangling out of their mouths, hanging over snapping teeth. Markus and I are back to back, holding our knives out as they close in on us. More dogs appear out of the darkness and we're almost totally surrounded.

"What do we do?" Markus says.

"Get the gun. You can shoot one, and maybe the noise will scare them."

He reaches into his belt and pulls out the pistol again. I can hear him fiddling with the metal over my shoulder. The small white dog runs at me and tries to nip at my leg. I kick it away and it scampers back, joins the others in barking again.

"What's happening? Shoot one!" I scream.

Out of the corner of my eye I see Markus' arm go up, the gun in his right hand. He aims at one of the Vizslas. I close my eyes, wait for the blast. It never comes. Instead, a low growl resonates up out the dark. I feel it ripple through me, and I know it's the growl of something big. The dogs all look to the left, where they seem to think the sound came from, they all go silent, some of them cower. We take our chance and charge in the other direction, towards the nearest house.

Markus is in front this time, still holding the gun as he runs. The barking resumes as some of the dogs start to chase us. I can feel them at my heels, biting. I look over my left shoulder, waiting for Death's tap-tap. Instead I see the Rottweiler charging.

"Inside!" I shout.

Markus is at the door and goes straight through it. I don't look back again, run as hard as my aching feet will allow me. I slide across the stone front step and in through the door. Markus slams the door shut and there's a double thud; the second one followed by barking, clawing and growling.

We slump down onto the ground and clamber backwards on our hands and feet, away from the door towards the stairs. We pant as our chests grind and throats rasp. Markus passes me the bottle and we sip, sitting still, till we're sure the dogs have gone.

"That was too close," Markus says. "Whatever that was, growling in the dark, it scared them."

I turn towards my brother, smile widely. "It was the panther! I'm telling you! He's looking out for us!"

Markus looks at me, sees my excitement, and a real smile appears on his face for the first time in a while, "Let's just hope it is your panther, Bandi. I'd hate to think what else could be out there."

I know it's the black panther here for us again. I don't care that we have almost no water, no food, because I know we're going to make it. The panther will make sure of that.

I stand up and Markus is already exploring the downstairs. There isn't much, an old sofa and some dusty books. Markus starts looking through them and I wander around the back to where I suspect the kitchen will be. I open a door at the end of the living room and step through. I can hardly believe my eyes. I'm staring at the stars through a huge hole in the roof. And I'm not in the kitchen, I'm in another sitting room. The house we're in is huge. In the middle of the room is a large metal tube. Markus comes through the door and stands beside me.

"Is it..."

"It's the cockpit of a plane!" Markus almost shouts with joy.

We both seem to forget everything for a moment. It's a piece of a real airplane, and it came from the sky, through the roof, probably shot down in the wars. Markus says we've flown before, like the time we went to the sea, the photo my mother kept. He says he remembers looking down at pink clouds from up there, something I can't even imagine. Any planes that still exist are like this one; in pieces. There's no fuel, barely any tools or machines left to build them. People might never fly again. But once they did and this is a piece of that history.

We rush around to the other side of the room where the rest of the plane must have broken away from the cockpit. There are some boxes and other things inside but we don't investigate just yet. We go straight for the pilot seats in the front, sitting side by side in them. We flick all the buttons and switches but nothing works, obviously. The seats are comfortable, made of real leather. Before I know it I'm yawning. I catch Markus with his mouth open wide doing the same.

"Not a bad place to spend the night," he says.

I smile but my eyes are already closed, leaning back in the pilot's seat.

"Good night, little brother."

"Good night."

Dreams take me away but I sleep too deeply to remember them.

9

Markus isn't next to me when I wake up. He's not in the cockpit but I can hear him rummaging around in the room. I stare through the open wind-shield towards the door and I can see the room we entered through on the other side. The barking seems to have stopped. I climb around towards the back of the cockpit. It's been stripped bare by Markus who's outisde of the cockpit testing a torch. He flicks it on, smiling at me.

"Not bad, right? Working batteries; insane. And I found some rope too."

His seems realtively happy, refreshed.

"What else was there?" I ask him.

"Junk mostly. Apart from a parachute, this," he holds up a screwdriver, "but there is one other thing."

Markus is smiling at me and the intrigue is too much, "What? Come on, tell me!"

He lifts up a small bottle, full to the brim of water.

"Where did you get that?"

I don't wait for an answer, take it, drink a glug full. It's warm but I don't care. The liquid washes the pasty feeling from my mouth, moistens my dry throat.

"Follow me," Markus says.

He leads me to the back of the room where a boarded up window leads to a garden. He lifts the bottom panel and slides through. I follow. The sun is high but almost invisible in the haze above. But its power is still immense, causing steam to rise from the dark earth. I can almost feel it through the thinning soles of my shoes. But I barely notice. I can't believe my eyes. I'm standing beside my brother, staring down into a gigantic black hole in the earth, a huge crevice. It's at least thirty metres wide and a hundred deep. And at the bottom I can see something glistening, a thin piece of silver thread.

"No way," I say.

Markus smiles, "Yes way, little brother."

Down there in the dark, a sparkly ribbon trickles across the gaping hole and disappears either side; an underground stream.

"How do we get down?"

"Over there," Markus points to the left, where stones line the wall, creating a very steep staircase, almost vertical, like a ladder of rock and earth.

We begin climbing down, this time Markus leading the way. The earth is dry and crumbly, but stones embedded into the ground provide solid foot holds to step on and grasp. As we start to near the bottom I can hear the trickle of water and my heart starts skipping beats. The crevice grows much narrower, leaving only a few metres either side of the tiny stream. The water flows across the pit from one side to the other, and disappears into small tunnels either side, just tall enough for a grown man to crawl down. The earth grows softer as we approach the water at the bottom, and the air feels cooler and damper. We drop to the ground and it's hard, stone. We kneel by the water and Markus smiles at me, leans forward and rubs the cool liquid into his hair and the back of his neck. I do the same then sit up, revitalised.

"I just can't believe it," Markus says.

"Can I drink some more?"

"No, we should boil what we drink. Look, I found a gas cooker right over here."

Markus gets up off his knees and steps over to a large rock that sits just beside the stream, against the crevice wall. He rolls the rock onto its side to reveal a hidden compartment, dug in the side of the pit. He pulls the gas cooker out.

"Incredible," I say.

He kneels on the stone beside me and pulls a match from his pocket, lighting the cooker.

I spread my legs out, watch him, "It's just like the one we had," I say. For a second my temporary joy wavers as I remember the bigger picture, but it's about the little things right now, and amidst little things, this is pretty huge.

Markus fills the pot with water and places it on the flame. He pulls a couple of litre bottles from his back-pack.

"Filled two already, plus these. And I have another half. That's four and a half litres we can take. I think we need to find you a bag too, if we really are going to try and cross this desert."

I stare at him and nod, though he doesn't see as he turns to the hidden compartment, rummaging inside it again. I look up at the sky, high above us, the hazy light glancing off the stones that line the way up. A ladder of stone down to an underground stream, it all seems too perfect, and a lead weight digs in, my heart starts to flail.

"Markus, there was even a gas cooker…"

But he doesn't look up, distracted with some matches. It's too perfect; someone's been here and dug out the stream. What if they still come here? I go to grab Markus but he's stopped moving. He's frozen still, holding something I think, but his back is turned.

"Markus," I whisper.

He turns to me, eyes wide. The gas mask in his hand drops to the floor. I see them flash before my eyes, soldiers in masked faces, hear the screams again, feel my insides tearing up again.

I whisper slowly, "Maybe someone else found the mask, thought it might be useful, kept it."

Markus shakes his head, "It's a stream, Bandi, running water. Of course it's them. They control everything."

He's talking like he's seen a ghost, his own death, and I know he's probably just envisioned it in front of his eyes. And then we both go still, hold our breaths; because we can hear a sound.

It's a rumble, like an engine, though I know it can't be. Then there's a squeak. I stare at Markus, who stares at me. Footsteps thud along in the dust, growing louder.

We listen for a few more seconds. There are a few people at least, a cough, muttering. Markus quietly scrambles to put the cooker back. I help him, cover the compartment and go to climb up the laddered stone.

"Markus grabs my shoulder, "We can't. It's too late. We have to hide!"

I turn away from the wall and stare at the stream, watch it trickle down the low tunnel of earth.

"You mean in there?" I ask.

"Where else? Quickly!"

I can hear several voices now. Markus is on his knees crawling into the tunnel, pulling his back-pack after him.

"What if it collapses?"

"Just come on, there's nowhere else." His voice is trembling.

I wait for him to squeeze further down the tunnel, then I get down on my knees and follow. There isn't even enough room to turn around, so I crawl backwards after Markus who has done the same. It's dark and the walls are thick and moist, clay I think. It's cool but claustrophobic, and after crawling for a while I stop. The silver stream glistens ahead, where the tunnel reaches the opening. But we are in darkness, the water trickling towards us as we wait in silence.

There's not much air and breathing is difficult, so I breathe slowly, Markus too. We take small, quiet breaths as male voices grow louder as they approach, saying words but nothing I can make out. There's at least three of them for sure.

Then Markus and I both stop breathing, hold our breaths mostly out of fear, as we hear the sounds of people climbing down towards us. Markus shuffles backwards further and I follow. We both squat so that the stream runs over and around our feet. One of my hands is on the ground immersed in water, the other on the wall, as a pair of boots hit the ground ahead, followed by another, and then a third landing beside his companions. I can only see their legs, black uniforms, all matching, and I know what they are.

"I think someone's been down here," one of them says, his voice thin and raspy.

Markus shift backwards more. Something cold grips my spine, holds it tight.

"Why you sayin' that?" Another asks.

"On the way down, saw some finger marks."

"There's no one round here, only us. And no patrols have visited this spot for weeks. Too many dogs. A waste of ammo," the first soldier says.

I continue to breathe slowly, heart leaping, and we move backwards, extremely slowly, trying to get as far down the tunnel as possible, away from them.

"Let's just fill up some bottles and get out of here, we have to get to the northern camp as soon as we can," says a third soldier, his voice quiet, almost a whisper.

"They'll wait for us," says the raspy voiced soldier.

"No they won't."

One of them crouches and I can see his entire body. His gas mask is pulled up onto his forehead and he's smoking a cigarette. He rolls the rock to the side and reaches into the hidden compartment.

"Hang on, this is wet, and hot." He holds up the pot Markus has just used. "You said it's been weeks. Someone's been here in the last few hours."

The soldier stands and I can only see three pairs of legs again.

Markus whispers over my shoulder, "I can't go any further, the tunnel gets too low."

My heart sinks and I wish the ground would open up, allow me to fall, even if it was straight into the fire of the earth's core. At least I wouldn't be here, pain I can't imagine awaiting me. I'd rather burn.

Something cold touches my shoulder and I peer backwards. Markus' hand is there holding the gun, feeding it forwards to me.

"We should be ready, just in case," he says.

There's real fear in his voice, so quiet and choked. I try to swallow as I take the pistol but I can't because my mouth is too dry. The gun is heavy and cold, feels powerful in my hands knowing what it can do. I hold it in one hand and stare at the metal, then down the tunnel where the soldiers are pacing around, still not collecting water.

"Nothing is missing, but whoever's been here can't have gone far. We should find them, take them with us north. More bodies for the spectacle."

The raspy voiced soldier laughs, "That would make it an execution to remember."

Markus grips my shoulder and I put my hand on his, holding the gun at my side in the other.

But then the soldiers start to climb, and one by one the sets of legs disappear from view. The last soldier stands facing the stone ladder to the surface. He doesn't move for a few seconds, doesn't follow the others. Instead he steps over towards the tunnel opposite us, from where the water flows. He pulls out a match and fires it up, crouching by the tunnel entrance, peering down.

"He's checking the tunnels Markus, he's checking," I whisper.

"Just hold the gun, stay still," he says.

I'm shaking too much. I hold the gun with both hands and wait silently, my brother's tense breathing the only sound other than the trickling and faint drips of water.

The soldier rises to his feet and turns in our direction but I know it's dark, we're too deep in the black. He walks towards us, become a pair of legs again. Then he crouches down, still holding the match, staring down right at me.

I'm about to lift the gun when he grimaces and cries out, dropping the match into the stream as the flame gets too close to his hand. I put my finger on the trigger, start to press.

"Wait," Markus whispers over my shoulder.

The soldier pulls out a box of matches. He's a dark silhouette with the pale light behind him. He slides the box open. But a voice calls out from above, "Hen, what you doing? Come on!"

The shout from above startles the soldier and he drops the box of matches into the water.

"I'm coming, hold on!"

He mutters and curses as he takes the matches out of the stream, the box dripping wet. He pulls a match out and tries to light it, but the soaked wood just snaps in half between his fingers, and he throws the box angrily to the ground.

"Hen! We've just seen the signal lit, they're doing it now! Let's go, we'll get water later! I'd hate to miss a hang-a-thon." Laughter follows.

He rises to his feet and starts to climb, disappears from our view.

"And now we wait," Markus whispers.

I don't hear much; a low rumbling follows a few quiet crashes, and then there's nothing. But still we wait, until the need for air finally drives us out.

"I think we can go now," Markus whispers.

"I'll be careful," I tell him, as I crawl towards the opening.

Once out, we both stand. My back is stiff and we're both covered in mud.

"Let's fill these last bottles and get out of here as quickly as possible," Markus says.

I nod and we boil another pot full and fill the last two bottles. We climb the wall and creep into the house where thankfully the rest of our things are un-touched; the rest of the water, the torch, the rope. They must have never gone into the house but walked around the side.

We gather our supplies. I even find a back-pack upstairs in the house; a black one, but it only has one strap. We take two litre bottles each and Markus carries the extra half.

"Still north?" I ask him, as we ready ourselves to leave.

"I don't think we should, you heard what they were saying. Hang-a-thon? I don't even want to imagine it."

"Then where?"

"We continue east, it's the only thing we can do," he says, his voice sincere.

I nod my head, "Yeah, let's go east."

"What about the factory district?" Markus asks, hesitating.

"We'll just have to be careful and quiet," I tell him.

He nods at me, a newly determined look in his eyes. I turn to the front door and quietly open it; no dogs or soldiers in sight. I glance one last time at the cockpit that fell from the stars, knowing with certainty that it was the best sleep I'll have for a while.

I step outside onto the street and Markus follows. We head south, back the way we came, to the nearest intersection that will take us east again.

I stop as I notice Markus isn't following me. I turn and find him still outside the house, facing away, staring at the ground.

"What is it?" I whisper loudly.

I run over to join him and look down.

"Tyre tracks," he says.

10

We walk on side by side, hunched over, constantly spinning in circles as our eyes dart across the suburban ruins, more alert than ever. The single strap of my bag is diagonally across my chest, over one shoulder, and it slows me down. But that's a small price to pay for the water we've collected.

I remember seeing vehicles on occasion when I was small. I remember the sound they made, the rumble. But we thought fuel was all gone. Neither of us have seen a working car or truck in years. But the soldiers have fuel from somewhere, and their increased power is frightening. They could rip across the wastelands now. They could beat us to the sea.

"What do you think it means? How can they have fuel?" I ask.

Markus shakes his head, "I don't know. But we have to be extra careful not to be seen."

There's a tall round building on the corner where we finally turn east. I rush ahead, spotting a carcass in the road. But it's been stripped of edible meat. What remains is black, full of maggots, rotting, the stench thick and gluey.

I can't be near it so I enter the round building which seems to be an old office block. There are pictures of houses everywhere, and I figure it must be a place they used to design homes. Some of them are huge, beautiful. I can't even imagine what I'd do with all that space. Markus comes up behind me a minute or so later, heading straight towards the back of the building where a spiral staircase leads up.

As we climb I can see that each level of the building was used for something else. The third floor is filled with model cars and the top looks like it was once a place where food was cooked and prepared. The stairs are solid all the way up. On the top floor we look out through empty windows towards the east. Ahead, chimneys and warehouses rise high. Small figures scatter the surrounding roads and alleys; the silhouettes of soldiers.

"Maybe the north would be safer, hang-a-thon or not," Markus says. "We don't even know what that means. There can't be this many soldiers there."

"Maybe, but we don't know," I say. "But from here we can see the path ahead, we can plan our way through."

He looks exhausted; tired from no food, tired from having to hide and search the horizon every second of each day. I lower my brows and hope that my determination will ignite something in him to.

Through the window I follow the road with my gaze. It carries on to the east and curves south before ending in a road block, where at least five or six soldiers are stationed. The factories are on all sides of the road. The car parks are lined with built up walls of debris, a maze of trenches and barracks. Smoke rises from open fires and torches. The sun is lowering in the sky, almost mid-afternoon and I know that by the time we reach the factory district the night will have dropped. But I can see a way through, and the darkness will only help us. Before the road curves to the south, there's a long low building that runs on uninterrupted for a several hundred metres. There seems to be no activity the north side of it. From there it's through the lion's den, but in the darkness I know we can make it. The maze won't be an obstacle but an aid—our passage through the shadows.

Markus is also studying the road ahead. "Have you found a safe path through?" he asks me.

"Of course I have," I tell him, and we leave the window, head down to the road again.

The sun barely brims the sky as we reach the long building I'd spotted from high. We hug the wall and move round to the north facing wall, beginning our long trek alongside it. We move slowly, without a sound. I lead the way and Markus follows. We can hear voices inside, soldiers talking; murmurs and mutterings drift out through the empty window frames. So we stay low, backs to the wall, moving sideways one step at a time.

It takes several minutes to reach the end of the building. From here we have to cut straight across land littered with soldiers. But it's darkened. The sky is a heavy grey and looming towards black. We crouch besides each other.

Markus glances at me, then out ahead again. "I don't see anyone," he says, chewing his nails.

"We just have to be careful. They won't be expecting anyone," I tell him.

"That's true." He looks at me, forces a smile, then glances over his left shoulder. "No Death," he says.

I look over my left shoulder, a chill creeps down my back.

"I think you're good to," Markus tells me. He taps me on the shoulder, "Still only me."

I force a smile back at him.

"So, which way?" he asks.

I stare out from our perch on the corner of the building, looking south-east. There's twenty metres of empty tarmac before us, followed by a small hut alongside a fence, bordering the next area of warehouses and factories.

"We just have to go through that fence," I say, "Then we head more or less straight across, towards the twin chimneys."

I point out ahead at two thin spires that sit side by side, aimed at the sky like fingers, long and thin, eerie in the dullness.

"Between the chimneys there's a warehouse we have to try and get through, apart from that we can stay outside the entire time. There's plenty to keep us hidden."

Markus studies the layout ahead, trying to picture our path. He shrugs. "Ok little brother, you're the one with the sense of direction."

I stare ahead again, perched on my hands and feet, like a runner from the old Olympics. I glance left and right and then dart across the tarmac, light on my toes. Markus is right with me. We duck through a gap in the mesh fence and keeping low, sneak towards a large truck that sits just beyond it, the back of it loaded with beams of steel. We hop on, climb the beams and lie on top of the metal. It's a good vantage and I can see far ahead. There are way more soldiers than there were before. They're everywhere.

Straight ahead of us is a long stone cylinder, an old factory chimney, lying on its side. Parts of it are missing, crumbling, but it's mostly intact, creating a tunnel across the car park before us. It leads straight past a group of five soldiers who are sitting around a fire talking, hardly paying attention.

"They're barely even looking around. They don't expect anyone to try and come through here," I say.

"That's because no one is crazy enough to try."

I throw him a harsh look. He shrugs.

"We can do this," I whisper. "Just follow me. All we have to do is stay silent."

"Like ghosts, I know," he says.

I nod, then start my climb down the other side of the truck. I land in the concrete and squat, begin to prowl slowly towards the fallen chimney. The group of soldiers are about fifty metres away, in the centre of the car park. I know their eyes must be adjusted to the firelight, so surely they can't see far in the dark. It's almost completely black now, the moon obscurred, the sun gone. Markus is beside me, I can hear his jeans brushing the concrete, the quiet patter of his hands. It seems like we're crawling forever, all the while my eyes are fixed on the soldiers, hoping none of them catch sight of some movement in the distance.

We reach the top end of the chimney and duck inside. I can almost stand up. Markus has to bend over a little more. I'm about to open my mouth when he puts his finger to his lips, motioning towards the chimney around us. The echo would carry my voice all the way down, and I breathe out in relief. How quickly this all could have ended, if I'd said just one word.

We begin stepping down through the chimney, a tunnel that keeps us hidden in the dark. There are some gaps in the concrete which we move slowly across, hands low, feeling along the ground to ensure we remain undetected. We pass the soldiers to our left. Their words are muffled inside the chimney. We cross a gap in the tunnel and I peer out, see that we've moved beyond them. My heart relaxes a little, but I know there's a long way to go.

We reach the end, and we're by the factory that the chimney must have fallen from. Half the wall is gone, the pieces all around us, chunks of stone to hide between. I lead Markus around to the right of the building, choosing to stay outside as we'd discussed. There's an old blue van on its side just around the corner, the double doors to the back missing. We crawl inside, lean against the top and rest for a moment.

Markus pulls out his water and I do the same. As I drink my stomach rumbles, and I remember how hungry I am. We haven't eaten in days and I can smell cooking fires, charred meat wafting in the air.

"Where now?" Markus asks.

"I'm not sure. We just have to keep going until we reach the twin chimneys."

I put my bottle away, half empty, another litre bottle still to go. I wait for Markus and then crawl out of the van, back into the night. We move slowly along the factory's south side. On our right, another stone wall runs long and tall, but through gaps in it I can see a large building. It's surrounded by tents, huts, like the ones we lived in, with sheet metal roofs. There are many voices on the other side of the wall. Occasionally a voice calls out and it's scary how close they are. But this side of the wall seems safe, quiet, and slowly we carry on, pressed against the factory's bricks, hearts pounding, my mouth dry as sand again already.

Eventually the wall cuts north and leads all the way around. We slip through a small gap in the stone and find ourselves facing the vast open space, strewn with debris, trenches, small huts and more tents. The large building that seems to be the centre of the soldier's camp is to the south-west now, but only a couple hundred metres behind us. I glance around, try to spot our way through. The twin fingers we're heading for spear up in the distance. There are hundreds of soldiers, more than I ever thought there would be. And I can feel Markus growing fidgety beside me, worked up. My heart rages hard against my ribs.

"I can't see a way through," I say, "I can't, there's too many of them. Too many fires. It's so bright. They'd see us for sure."

I try to swallow but can't. I'm panicking and can't stop. Markus is chewing his finger nails again, eyes flicking around. I breathe out, try to calm myself down.

There's a tap on my left shoulder and I fall back. But still it's not Death, only Markus again, because I'm still in the factory district, surrounded by soldiers, feeling smaller than I ever have. But alive.

"Why don't we try going under them," Markus says.

He's smiling. He points to the right, just a few metres ahead. It's a drain.

"Yes, Markus!" I almost shout I'm so excited.

He smiles at me, shrugs, "Let's just hope we can get it open, and that we can make it through. Who knows what we'll find down there."

I nod, creep forward to the drain. I can't get my fingers into the crack so use my knife, managing to loosen the lid, lift the metal disc enough to get my fingers under. Markus arrives beside me and grabs it too. Together we lift it all the way up, the weight of it straining my neck and back, all the way down my legs. But we can't drag it, the noise would be immense. This is the only way.

We finally ease the cover down, managng to do so with barely a sound. We both kneel either side of the sewer drain and stare inside. It's too dark. Markus pulls the torch out and holds it down low, inside the shaft, so the light it emits isn't seen by any stray pairs of eyes. He flicks it on for only a second and we both sit back defeated. The ladder leading down is gone. Only the top rung remains.

I stare at Markus and he's thinking, glancing around. I spot the end of the rope sticking out of his zip. He sees me do so, whips his bag off and pulls it out.

"Didn't think we'd be needing this so soon," he whispers.

"We'll tie it to the top of the ladder, slide down."

Markus nods and leans over the hole again, begins tying the knot. When it's done he pulls on it, checking it's tight.

"I just hope it's long enough," I say.

"It has to be," Markus forces a smile, gnawing at his nails.

He lets the rope drop and we hear the sound of the end hitting the bottom. It's louder than I expect.

"That sounds like a lot of rope hitting the ground," Markus says.

"Then we can salvage some of it at least."

I grab the end of the rope and hang over the edge. Moving my hands and feet slowly down the rope, I descend. Markus waits for me to get a few metres down before following. We reach the bottom and it's dark, the stone beneath us dry. Markus flicks the torch on and I cut the rope as high as I can. I roll it up and tuck it away, at least ten metres long still. Markus clicks the torch off.

"Back in the tunnels; now this is where we want to be," Markus says.

It's pitch black. All I can hear is our breathing, amidst nothingness.

"Home ground," I say, a smile on my face.

It quickly fades as a sneeze snaps out of the dark. It isn't me, nor Markus. There's someone else down here. Then a light flickers on down the tunnel. A man is standing there, a soldier. He's staring right at us, a rifle in his hands. He holds it up, ready to fire, "Who's down there? Hey!"

Markus and I both drop to the ground. It's cool and it smells like old sewage, but it's dry, just dust. The soldier continues to stand, holding the rifle out at us, blinking in the dark, squinting, trying to see. Then he starts to move forward, slowly stepping.

He pulls a flare from his pocket and I quickly start to feel around in the dark. I pat the ground, the walls, the side of the sewer tunnel. I feel an opening with my hands and reach into it. It seems to be another passage leading off to the left, a tunnel leading east. The soldier is still slowly stepping towards us, and he cracks the flare into a red glow. Markus is still lying on his stomach motionless, and I'm certain the soldier will spot us any moment. I tap Markus on the hand and he looks up, barrel rolls towards me. I grab his arm and drag him into the side tunnel. Here we stand, once again with our backs to the wall, breathing heavily, desperately trying to stay quiet.

"Hello?" The soldier calls again.

His footsteps stop just around the corner. The light of the flare glows brightly and illuminates us too now. I hear his boots shift in the dust and he coughs.

"I need a drink" he mutters to himself, "Alcohol withdrawal. Making me hear things."

He turns and shuffles off back down the tunnel. We wait until he turns the light off and what little visibility we had is gone. We're in total darkness again, with a long way to go. But I know all too well, that darkness is our friend.

11

Markus holds onto my shoulder and we move forwards like that, blind in the dark. I keep my arms out ahead of myself as we take one step at a time. It feels like the black will never end but at least we don't hear a sound, no sign of any more soldiers. After what feels like forever the darkness begins to fade. All of a sudden my hands hit a wall, and I feel around, but it's a dead end in front of me. I look left and reach out, touching cold rust. It's a ladder rung. I wrap my finger around the metal and look up. I can see a faint circle of thin light above, a way to the surface.

"It's either up, or back the way we came," I say.

"Then up we go," Markus whispers, "I don't want to risk going back. If there's one soldier down here there could be many."

"There's probably even more if we go up."

"Let's take our chances. With some luck we're right by the twin chimneys by now."

"Ok," I say, and start to climb.

I hear Markus just below me, his feet scraping on the rusty metal. To my relief the ladder goes all the way to the top, and there I stop and listen; not a sound.

I keep one hand tightly on the ladder and use my other hand, along with my head, to force the drain cover open a crack. It's heavy and it hurts my neck. I struggle to stop the metal clinking on the stone. I peer out at a wall ahead of me but can see nothing else. It's even darker than I expect it to be.

"I think we're inside a building. Maybe an old factory basement."

"Is it clear?"

"I can't see much, but I can't hear anything."

"Let's wait a few minutes, see if anything happens."

I let the drain cover down again and we wait, listen intently. After a few minutes of silence I lift the cover again, peer out, then as quietly as possible I slide it out of the way. It's heavy and I can barely move it on my own, but slowly I manage to move it across enough for me to squeeze out and climb to the surface.

I'm in a large room, in the far corner. There are huge grey tanks all around me and the ceiling is at least thirty metres high. Markus climbs out and squats beside me. It's very dark, the room windowless. A little light comes in through a large hole about ten metres off the ground on the wall beside us. There's also a small window on a wooden door to our left. A faint light flickers on the other side, like fireight.

"Which way do we go?" Markus asks.

"This wall faces east. We have to find a way around."

I glance across the room. The only other exit is a large steel door on the far side, but it leads west, backwards, only above ground this time and surely towards trouble.

"Through there," I point to the wooden door on our left.

Markus stares at me, looking very uncertain.

"I'll take a look," I whisper, as I begin crawling towards the door.

Markus slides the sewer cover shut again but there's a loud crash. I look at him; he's staring at the large steel door on the other side. The crash wasn't him. Someone's coming.

The sound of several footsteps approaches, growing louder.

I look at Markus, frozen.

"Go!" he says.

I push myself up onto my feet and move quickly to the wooden door. I peer through the small window. Before I have a chance to see anything Markus crashes into me from behind and we fall through it.

We land sprawled on the ground and both scamper to our feet, our eyes darting around the room. It's smaller than the previous room and a torch burns on the wall. I spin around and there are several steel beds in front of us. Three of them are empty, stained with blood. The fifth bed is curtained. We dash for it. Markus gets there first and I slip through a gap in the plastic sheet after him. We both freeze. My insides charge and my heart rate doubles. There's a soldier in the bed, his leg wrapped in bandages. I look up at his face and he's staring right at us, his expression blank.

I grab Markus' wrist and we both spin as we hear the door the other side of the curtain kicked open.

"Can't we just do it tomorrow?" a voice says.

"No, he'll die in the night if we don't try and hack it off now."

They're right there in the room with us, at least three soldiers, possibly more.

"He'll die anyway," the first voice says.

"Yeah well, we have to at least try."

"Do we?"

"Shut up and get ready."

I can hear banging, the sound of cabinets opening, the sound of metal clinking.

Markus is frozen stiff, his eyes wet. He knows it's the end. The soldier in the bed continues to stare but I'm not even sure if he can see us. I recognised his face the second I saw him, but his skin is yellower now, even more pasty and ill than it had been two nights ago.

"You ready yet?" One of the soldiers calls.

"Yeah, let's do this."

I can hear them stepping towards us. I know that any second the curtains will be pulled back and we'll be caught—killed. I hold Markus' wrist and I don't breathe, just stand waiting.

"Hang on!"

I spin my head around, almost falling through the curtain in the process. The voice belongs to the soldier in the bed.

"I'm taking a dump. Give me five," he shouts.

"For Christ's sake," one of the other soldiers says, "I'm not helping you with that."

"We'll go for a smoke," says another. "Then we'll be back to take care of that grimy leg."

I hear the door open and the sound of several footsteps as they all leave. The door squeaks shut. Markus and I both turn to the soldier in the bed, my hand still tightly gripping Markus' wrist. We just stand there, unable to say a word.

"You haven't got long," the soldier's voice is calm, quiet, no longer slurred by booze, but weakened by his slowly rotting leg.

"How do we get out of here?"Markus asks, trembling.

"There's another door at the far end of the room. Follow the corridor through there."

He coughs, closes his eyes. Markus and I glance at each other, petrified.

"Nobody ever goes back there. You'll be fine. There's probably a window at the back you can get out through."

"How far are we from the factory with the twin chimneys?" I ask.

"They're right above you."

I look at Markus, could almost smile, but we're a long way from escape.

"Let's go," he says.

I nod, turn to the soldier.

"Listen to your brother little fella," he says.

"Why didn't you just let them find us?" My voice shakes and I can barely get my words out.

"You should really get going. They'll be back any minute."

Markus grabs my wrist and pulls me out through the curtains. Sure enough there is a door at the far end, blocked off with a wooden crate. We move the crate and push through the door. I wait as Markus pulls the crate back across, hiding our exit point. We both turn and run, backs hunched over, light on our feet down the long dark corridor.

We burst through at the end and we're in another large room with high ceilings, but this time there's a row of windows, most of them empty, just over two metres off the ground. The room is almost completely bare, other than some old machinery that looks completely stripped of anything that once made it useful. I put my bag down and Markus gives me a boost up. I grab a window ledge and pull myself up, perched so that a leg hangs either side of the wall. I look out and there's a road that leads north. It looks empty, safe.

Markus tosses me my bag and I gently let it drop to the ground outside. After taking out the rope he throws me his backpack which I toss down beside mine.

"Take this," he says, "tie it to something. I'll be able to climb out."

He throws me the rope and I tuck the end into my jeans. Then I ready myself to jump.

It seems much higher now that I'm up here but I can't hesitate, and I leap feet first. As I hit the ground I let my knees buckle and lean forward, propelling myself into a roll. It absorbs most of the impact but still rattles my ankle bones, and for a split second I lie on my side, before pushing myself to my feet.

On the other side of the wall Markus is still holding the other end of the rope. I search for something to tie it to, something heavy. There's a large metal crate but it's too far away. I can feel Markus tugging on the rope; we only have ten metres to work with. There's a huge rock just beside the wall and I try jamming the rope in between the rock and the ground, pulling on it hard so that it's wedged in.

"Give it a try," I whisper up though the window.

The rope tenses up, and I can hear Markus struggling up the other side of the wall. The rope starts slipping out from under the rock so I grab hold of it, pulling down with all my might. I want to scream, holding Markus' weight almost entirely on my own now. Suddenly the rope seems weightless. I look up to see Markus' face peering out through the window, his hair stuck to his face.

He clambers up onto the sill and sits for a minute, worriedly looking down.

"How the hell did you get off here?"

"Jump and roll," I tell him.

He looks at me with slight disbelief, and I can see he's afraid to jump.

"Come on big brother," I say.

He shoots me an angry look and I know he has to do it now. If I can he can. That's how he sees it.

Markus crashes to the ground, cries out a little and falls into a roll, landing sprawled on his back. I pick him up and we both dust ourselves down.

"It's higher than it looks," he says.

I smile at him, "I know."

Markus packs the rope away and we quickly take a sip of water. I could easily neck the whole bottle but I've learned to be sparing, it's always been like this, more or less.

I look up at the building and see the twin chimneys rising up right above us. The sky is thinning out, a pale light sliding across it from where the sun rises to the east, our way onwards.

We set out along the road heading north, still sticking low, silent as possible. But we move with pace now, all too aware of the growing light, the end of our friend darkness, who helped us sneak right through the lion's den.

We turn east at the next intersection and move along the tram line past the old tram depot, where dozens of yellow trams sit piled beside each other, all of them trashed and broken. Here we finally take a rest beneath the hazy sky. But its bright now, orange and brown dust reddening everything. The twin chimneys rise up to the south-west, Death's fingers, long behind us now.

We drink a couple of sips and catch our breath. Sitting down I feel like I could fall asleep, faint even, and my stomach rumbles ferociously in the silence.

"Why do you think he helped us?" I ask.

Markus shrugs, "I don't know. Maybe it's because we left him alone."

"But he's a soldier, saving us from other soldiers."

"I know. But we don't know much about them. Maybe he hates the other soldiers. He did seem… different somehow."

"He didn't seem that bad."

"Careful Bandi – he's still a soldier. We know what they can do, what they did..." Markus' voice trails off. His eyes are wet, a grimace on his face as he tries to force back the tears.

"I know. But this one saved us."

Markus stares at me, wipes his eyes, smearing the dirt around so that he looks like a panda, "I guess he did."

We sit for another few minutes before moving on again, wanting to get as far from the factory district as possible. I feel weak, delirious in the growing heat. I begin to stumble as we continue along the road, heading south-east now, past endless square buildings that mean nothing—are nothing.

"Markus..." I try to call out but I can barely speak.

He grabs my shoulder, tries to hold me up. I can see he's talking but I can't hear anything, only my heart beat. Bright spots start to sparkle all around me in the air and I feel light, floaty. I stare out ahead and I can see the heat rising like steam off the tarmac. Then I see the panther, straight ahead, perched low and staring at me. I try to point, but as my arm goes up I fall forwards. Everything goes black.

12

I'm running through the dark and the panther, its jet black fur shining as if lined with diamonds, waits for me just ahead. I near and he roars loudly at the empty sky, but I'm not afraid. I kneel before him and look deep into his eyes. I can see deep green waves rolling and crashing, and a calmness swims through me and settles. The panther lies down and I walk round to his side, climb onto his back. He takes off at speed, running straight down the road; nothing either side of us, nothing in front us.

There are faces in the sky. They're only outlines at first but then I can make out my father's square chin, his thin lips stretched into a warm smile. My mother's face is beside him, and they both watch me ride the panther through the dark. I hold onto his fur tightly, and I can feel the muscles in his back stretch and tense as he carries me forwards. I stare ahead and a small shape appears in the distance, straight ahead of us. As we near I can see it's Markus, and he's waving. Then I hear his voice, but it's in my head, calling my name. The black panther roars and starts to run faster, and I lean forwards, rest tightly against his back. Markus calls to me again, "Bandi, please, wake up, little brother..."

I open my eyes a crack and the silhouette of Markus' face appears. The light burns and I quickly shut my eyes again, start to cough. I feel a bottle pressed to my lips and I drink, causing cement-like saliva to wash down by throat in clumps.

I open my eyes again and sit up. We're by the side of the road, in the shadow of a tall tree, its bone-like branches hooking us into shade. Markus is holding me up, a bottle in his hand. He looks relieved, his eyes red, his forehead drenched in sweat.

"Drink some more," he says.

I take the bottle in my hands and it feels so heavy, my arms trembling, weak. I drink a few sips and start to cough. Markus takes the bottle and starts rummaging in his backpack.

"Was saving these for emergencies, and I think this counts."

He holds out his hand and in his palm are a few brownish yellow lumps, but I can't see what they are. My head is spinning and my vision is still blurry.

Markus puts one of the lumps to my lips. "Chew and swallow," he says.

I open my mouth and chew. It's slimy at first but tastes nutty. I manage to swallow and Markus gives me another two to eat. I swallow them both and have another few sips of water.

"Finish that bottle," Markus says, "we have plenty."

I drink the last few sips and look around, remembering passing out—remembering my dream. I can't see the black panther anywhere.

"Did you see it?" I ask.

"See what?" Markus is looking down the road ahead blankly.

"Nothing," I sigh, struggling to my feet.

I sway in the gentle breeze, held up by my big brother.

"How were they?" he asks.

"Strange, slimy. Not too bad."

He seems surprised.

"What were they?" I ask.

"Larvae."

"What?" I almost vomit on the spot.

"I got them from the dog carcass, the one we found yesterday afternoon; maggot larvae."

I shake my head in disbelief.

"I read it in a book. Has protein, carbohydrate, minerals. It's good for you, trust me."

"Why don't you have some?"

"I'll wait till I'm really hungry. They look grim."

Markus picks up his backpack, smiles at me. I can't be angry at him because he's probably just saved my life, though I wish he'd told me before. But I am feeling surprisingly better already.

"You good?" he asks.

I nod, picking up my backpack, slinging it over one shoulder as we begin heading east again, on towards the edge of the city which we should reach by sundown. As we walk I think about my dream some more. I remember the feel of the fur between my fingers, the wind in my hair as the panther carried me at speed. *It brought me back when I was almost gone.* I remember my parents' faces in the sky and my heart drops. If they were there at the end, on the other side, then they're dead for certain.

Though I know it must be true I try to force the thought away, and I know deep down I still have hope, hope they might still be somewhere here, alive, even though I saw them, in the sky at the end, waiting for me.

I step on, following my shadow that falls before me now, as the sun begins to descend behind us. I hope that what I saw wasn't the end. I hope it was just a dream, just my subconscious showing me what I truly want to see; my family whom I miss, and the panther, that's leading me out of danger, away from death.

We move on and pass an old airport. The Statue of Freedom is to the south-west, rising above the buildings beyond the dried up river. The riverbed lays like a gigantic dead slug, brown and limp, curling gently between the ruined bridges. White and green metal strips and bars spike out of the sand, once mighty suspension bridges, connecting our city together. Now the sides sit separated forever, both halves dead without the other.

We head on east, ignoring the roads, cutting across car parks and through alleys and over tram tracks and debris. Entire buildings are missing, only their foundations remain. I think of the bombs that could have caused so much damage, the number of people they surely killed.

Tiny black shapes circle up high in the sky. Markus is walking just beside me and I grab him and point, "Pigeons!"

We cut across a dirt road and into a field of dust. We crouch beside a car and sure enough, dead ahead, five more pigeons sit roosting in the open, less than a hundred metres away.

Markus pats me on the back with force, "I can't believe it!"

I smile at him, haven't seen him this excited in a while. He takes off his backpack and begins digging around inside.

"We can't use our only bullet. We'd probably miss anyway," I tell him.

"I'm not getting the gun," he says, "I have one last surprise for you."

He stops searching and smiles at me, pulling my sling-shot from inside his backpack. I take the smooth wood and hold it in my right hand, pull back on the rubber. I thought I'd never see it again.

"We're eating pigeon tonight," I say, before leaning onto my stomach, and beginning my crawl forwards.

Markus waits by the car and I move on alone, stalking the pigeons, flat to the ground. I push forwards with my knees and elbows until I can see them clearly, four of them, the fifth one now in the sky with the others. I stop and slowly reach inside my pocket, pull out two small rocks, tuck one into the small square of leather that sits between the elastic. I stretch my left hand out holding the wooden handle and pull the rock back with my right. I aim at the nearest pigeon. It's scuttling around. I wait for it to be still, then I fire.

There's a faint thud and three pigeons fly up into the air at once, their flapping echoing across the plain. I stand up, stare proudly at the one bird that lies limp on the ground.

"Got one," I say.

I rush over to the pigeon and I'm about to pick it up when it opens its mouth, raises one of its wings. Markus arrives by my side.

"It's not dead," I tell him.

"Well kill it, quick!"

I approach the pigeon and its wing drops back down. I dive in and grab it round the neck, hold it tightly under my arm.

"What do I do now?"

"Break its neck," Markus says.

I look down at the bird, its tiny red eye is staring at me, and I hesitate.

"Just do it, Bandi."

I glance up at the sky and close my eyes, pull on the bird's neck as hard as I can. There's a huge crack, I feel it resonate through me, and I almost vomit right there, dropping the dead pigeon to the ground.

"Never had to do that before," I say.

"Aim better next time, for the head."

"I did!" I punch Markus in the arm and he wrestles me to the ground. I laugh as he jabs my ribs. I laugh for the first time in days. We're out of the lion's den, and we're eating meat tonight.

We wrap the entire pigeon in material we cut from the car seat. We decide to go a little further, because we can see the second airport in the distance to the north. Our father had told us about the airports, two of them, just beyond the city's fringes. Airplanes used to take people all around the world, then they were used in the wars, for killing, dropping bombs. The airport was one of the first places to be destroyed when our country was invaded. Only the main building remains now, the towers and airplanes all blown to pieces, long gone.

We march on and I know that soon there will be no roads, no cars to hide us. Only dust and sand awaits us—a desert until we reach cover at the foot of the mountains. I can see them on the horizon, dark shapes looming. It will take us a day to cross the plain. It was once rich farmland, where farmers roamed and herded their horses, for hundreds of years. My great-grandfather was one of them, my mother's told me about him many times. She was proud of who he was, what he did, but the horses are gone, and the horse men of the plains haven't existed for years, not since long before the old world came to an end.

We start to collect anything flammable for a fire; some wood, dry shrub, cardboard. The city is far behind us and the sun is almost out of sight. We arrive at an old farmhouse and head into the barn. We leave our bags in there and search the house, manage to find a small candle, some new clothes; t-shirts, extra hoodies and socks for both of us. Markus finds some books to take back to the barn but I stay in the farmhouse a little longer. The walls are painted blue throughout and it feels peaceful. I'm happy to be there, not out in the wastelands of our world, but somewhere that's part of the old world. There's a painting on the wall, a picture of a clown, white-faced with orange hair. He's crying, his painted mouth slopes downwards. There aren't any clowns anymore. I wonder if the artist knew that all clowns would disappear when he painted it, whether that's the reason why his clown is so sad.

When I step outside again a strange sensation rises. It's like I disappeared for a while with that clown in that farmhouse. It remains there somehow, untouched by everything, frozen in time. But I know we can't stay here and freeze with it. Our time moves on.

Back in the barn we build our fire and light it with a match.

Markus rattles the box at me, "Only five more."

While the fire gets going we rip apart the bird, try to cut away the skin and feathers. It's messy work and it takes a long time. I continuously add to the fire to keep it going while Markus skewers the meat. We sit opposite each other and watch the meat sizzle and smoke as blood and fat drips into the flames.

It takes forever for the meat to cook, or it seems that way at least, and I'm salivating intensely by the time it's finally ready to eat. Pigeon's never tasted so good.

We eat without a word, slowly chewing, to give the illusion of a full meal. We suck the bones clean, and when we're done eating, we cook the rest of the meat and pack it away for tomorrow. We have to eat it soon. It won't last in this heat.

Afterwards we just lie by the fire, under the moon.

"I like being on the surface," I say, "I feel free."

"Yeah, but it's just a feeling."

"What do you mean?"

Markus has his hands behind his head, looking up at the barn's ceiling. He shrugs, "We aren't free."

I sit up, "Yes we are. We're out here alone, further than anyone we know has ever gone. And from here we can go anywhere, do anything."

"No we can't. Freedom means we can act freely, make our own destiny. We can't."

His tone is frustrating, I sit up agitated. "Of course we can. It's just us, the whole world out there."

He doesn't say anything for a few moments, then he sighs, "It's not freedom when Death is everywhere. That's all there is, Death. Freedom died a long time ago."

I stare at Markus through the flames. His eyes look paler in the glow. They're wet; he hasn't blinked in a while.

He continues, "Each person should be able to act as they want, go after what they want at every given moment."

"We can," I say.

Markus sits up, "Of course we can't. I want to howl at the moon and dance around this fire. Should I?"

He's right, it's beyond dangerous, but I want so badly to outsmart him, him and his books. All his ideas come from there. They open his eyes, and I start to see that sometimes it might be better to keep your eyes closed. I was happy with our mission, fulfilled by it, but Markus is right. We aren't free—far from it. But maybe at the sea…

After a few minutes I rise up.

"Where are you going?" Markus asks.

I smile at him, raise my head to stars and howl.

"Are you insane?"

I keep howling and he tries to jump up and take me down. I dodge his tackle and keep howling. He falls to the dust and I stop. There's only silence, the fire's crackle.

Markus shakes his head, "You're crazy," but there's a smile on his face. "Next time you do that, I'll be joining you. Death can suck it."

We sleep by the dying fire, there in the barn. We sleep past midday. That leaves us several hours before nightfall to make our final preparations. We have a small strip of pigeon each and a little water. There's a truck outside the barn and we use some old tools to remove the wheel. Then, with a small hack-saw I find in the barn, Markus cuts away at the tyre. He hacks off four pieces which we tie securely to the bottom of our shoes, using the remainder of the rope. Our soles are wearing thin. Now we should be able to cross the desert, even the mountains, with no problem at all. At least not from our feet.

I stalk another group of pigeons nearby and manage to kill one more. We cook it and pack it away, knowing we'll need the strength to make it across the plain. The juices in the meat could save us too, since we only have one bottle of water left.

We rest up after eating and watch the sun fall away in the west, before turning our attention to the east, where the mountains are now invisible, though we know where they sit and the direction we should head.

"We just have to make sure we don't get turned around, head straight the entire time," Markus says.

We pack away our supplies and leave the barn behind. My heart is heavy. The last day and a half almost felt like I was living a real life—safe, with my brother, hunting and eating, talking by the fire—but our journey is far from over. Side by side we march on into the black, with one night to reach the mountains, before the sun rises and we are totally exposed to its deadly heat, as well as soldiers, dogs, and whatever else is out there.

Two thorns emerge from ash and rust, forced out into the sand.
Two thorns not ready to be buried yet.

13

There is no moon in the sky, blocked off by the thick haze above us. I can barely see Markus beside me. He's just a dark shape. But I can hear our footsteps padding along in the dust. The grains of sand crunch against each other and the wind drives over the plain.

"How much further?" I ask in a whisper.

"I have no idea. I don't even know how long we've been walking."

"Feels like forever."

"I wish we could see the moon. Then we'd know," Markus says, gazing up at the black sky.

"Is it just clouds, the haze?"

"I hope so, because if the moon is gone, the end of the world is closer than we think."

I stare at Markus, but can't see his face. I don't know whether it's just his bleak sense of humour or if he really is worried.

He pats me on the back, "You know how thick it is sometimes. We didn't see the sun for almost a week last year, and that was way after the rain clouds had cleared. It's rubble and dust, it comes and goes."

"I know. But it's nice to be reminded. Everything feels different now, since...," I breathe out slowly, hold it in. "It feels like we're in another world, again. New rules."

Markus puts his arm around my shoulder as we walk on, "I know little brother. But it's the same world, and we know how it works. We know how to survive."

As I stare out in the darkness, I feel the panther's emerald fire igniting in my heart and mind.

It doesn't grow lighter nor darker. There is nothing to guide us, no clues, just darkness and desert, cold wind scattering over our forms. We stop and put on our new hoodies, to protect us from the sands. I pull the hood up over my head to shield my neck and the side of my face, and on we move, further into nothing.

I start to lose all sense of self in the dark. We try to keep going in a straight line, but I worry that we are turned around already, heading in the wrong direction. Then we hear it in the distance, dead ahead, but a long way off. The unmistakable sound of gunfire. It's far away but the bullets echo in my head, and I hear screams from before; screams bouncing off the metro station walls; screams of our family; people we knew.

Markus pulls me to the ground and I snap out of it. As we lie beside each other in the sand, lights flicker in the distance as weapons crack and blow. Machine guns and pistols light up the sky to reveal black clouds roaming over and under each other.

"Is it soldiers?" I ask.

"I sort of hope it is," he says.

"Why?"

"Would you prefer two groups of bad guys with guns hunting us?"

"They might be good guys," I say.

"They might also be space mutants or walking, talking armadillos," he says.

I grunt and fight the urge to hit him. "If they are soldiers, what are they doing all the way out here?"

"I don't know. But I'm starting to think they're going to be everywhere," Markus says.

"I thought they stayed in old cities, where they could hunt people."

"Maybe there aren't enough people left in the cities to hunt."

Things have gone quiet; the gunfire at an end. I rise to my feet, help Markus to his.

"It's far off," he says. "We can't turn around, we'll get lost."

"We just have to keep going. Hopefully by the time we get there they would have moved on." I look at Markus, he doesn't respond. "Well?" I ask him.

"Yes," he says, "I nodded."

"Well I can't see you, can I?"

He sniggers and it brings a smile to my face for just an instant.

"We've got to be extra quiet and stay extra low," he says.

"Low and quiet, as we do."

We walk on with increased care, focused on the spot where we saw the flickering light of gunfire. We stay closer together, almost shoulder to shoulder, and for a long while we don't say a word.

We stop fast, our feet hitting something hard, like stone, not the dust and sand we've been moving over.

"What's this?" I ask.

Markus turns to me, "It's a road."

Something starts rumbling in the distance. I turn to face the sound but can't see a thing. I concentrate on my feet, trying to feel whether the earth is moving. The rumbling grows louder, approaching us. I look up and Markus is stepping backwards, away from the deep sound. And the rumble grows to a roar, as giant shapes come rolling out of the black.

Markus squeezes my arm, "Engines."

We both stand solid, dead like the trees. I'm the first to break out of the fear, grabbing hold of Markus and pulling him after me. We run off the road and into the sand, aware enough to head straight ahead like before, so we don't get turned around. We run as fast as we can, slipping and scrambling in our panic. Lights fire out of the dark, appearing from nothing, powerful headlights. We drop to the ground and dust kicks up around us. There are three vehicles; a small cargo truck with an open back, piled with soldiers, followed by two cars. One of the soldiers hops down from the truck and ignites a flare, starts searching around in the dark.

"It was probably a dog or something," he says.

"I'm sure I saw faces," says another, calling from the driver's seat of the truck

"In this dark? There was nothing once we hit the lights," says the first soldier, continuing to turn in circles with his flare.

Markus and I are flat on the ground, just out of the flare light's reach. The headlights are angled away from us. I tap Markus' arm and start to crawl backwards on my stomach, flat to the ground like a snake. He does the same, and slowly we move away in the dark.

"Come on, let's get back to camp. We got a lot of meat to sort through. It's bleeding all over everything back here."

The soldier on the ground is relieved to stop his search. He tosses the burning flare to the ground and hops back onto the vehicle. The engines start and they cut their lights, I assume to save power. They roll off, rumbling in the dark again. My eyes have adjusted to the brightness and I can't see them disappear once the flare in the road dies. But in my head I can feel black-masked forms, faceless, staring at us as they pass, unaware we are here, laying right beside them.

The engines subside with the distance and I sit up. My eyes grow used to the dark and Markus' shape emerges from the shadows, perched beside me.

"That was too close," he says.

"What do you think they had back there, in the truck?"

"Probably some dogs or something. I wouldn't worry."

But I do worry. I think about who it could have been; maybe someone's mother or father, brother. Maybe a whole family, slaughtered in the plain. Maybe they were headed the same way as us, towards the hills, over them and onwards.

"At least we know what the gunfire was," Markus says.

"Yeah," I sigh, "That's something I guess. We should keep moving."

I'm unaware of how far we must go, or how much more of the night remains. We walk for hours, jogging for short periods of time, conserving our energy. As the darkness begins to subside we pass small dead shrubs, the occasional bare tree. They grow more frequent and I know we're nearing the foot of the hills. I can see the land grow steep up ahead in the grey.

Further on we finally come to a stop and take a drink, sit against a small tree for a few minutes. I gaze out ahead at rocks strewn over the plain, small dark shapes close to the ground. We venture on and skip and hop over the jagged terrain. Daylight is near and the ground begins to rise.

Markus and I both stop suddenly. Amongst the rocks we can see something else. It's similar in size and colour but it looks furry, and I can see blood.

"What is it?" I ask.

"I don't know, maybe a carcass."

Markus is scared, he has that look in his eyes. We step slowly onwards and as we near the shape I can see eyes, a nose, blood pooling into the dirt. I pause, ready to hurl my guts, but Markus carries on towards it. Dead eyes stare over at me, black and empty.

"Bandi, it's a lion," he murmurs.

He kneels down and I approach, steadying my breaths, because it's only blood and guts, I tell myself. The lion is a female but only the head remains, the rest of it nowhere to be seen.

Markus moves on a bit and picks something up off the ground, bullet casings.

"This is what we must have heard in the night," he says. "The soldiers were attacking her. They must have taken the body, left the head behind."

"Do you think the lion came from the zoo?"

Markus stares at me, "Probably. What if there are more of them? Still alive?"

I gulp, glance around, my eyes darting over the landscape, searching for anything moving.

"We have to keep walking, there's nowhere to hide out here. We're almost across. Look," Markus points ahead.

Trees grow thicker, the ground rises. I nod at my brother and we both dart off together, at once.

We pass another lion head, just over a small mound. It's a male this time, its mane half torn off, most likely taken for its fur. Bullet casings are scattered all over the ground here as well and we spot another two lion heads, females again, their eyes open, mouths gaping, tongues dangling out onto the dirt. We keep moving at speed, each head pushing us faster, until we're almost sprinting, leaping over obstacles in our paths, bursting through dead thicket and brush, desperate to escape the lion massacre.

The sky continues to grow lighter but a haze still hangs over us, blocking out the sun climbing just ahead, blanketed from view. I'm leading the way but come to a sudden halt. Markus flies into me from behind and knocks me to the ground. We both land in a pile in the dust and I smash my knee on a rock. I can feel my jeans sticking to the blood underneath and it burns. I roll onto my back and hop up, stare out to the east again.

My heart races, "Can you see it?"

I point out to where the ground grows suddenly very steep. It prowls low, as if stalking something. I turn to Markus and he's dusting dirt off his clothes, staring at it too. It's a dark shape, only a silhouette, but I'm sure it's the panther.

Markus comes up beside me, his chest is heaving. I look at him, a huge smile on my face as he continues to stare. I turn back to the panther, but another animal appears beside it.

"I don't think that's your panther, Bandi," Markus says.

I stare hard, waiting to feel the warm green light inside me, the power and strength of our guide. But it doesn't come. My heart sinks, then starts to hammer with fury. It's not the panther at all. It's lions—lions up ahead.

"What do we do?" Markus whispers.

I grab him by the shoulder and pull him down. We squat behind a large rock and watch them. They're still a long way away. I scour the landscape for a way past, any solution. I spot another three lions further along, to the north-east, lounging by a steep cliff. And we thought crossing the plain was going to be the hard part.

"It's no use hiding or trying to sneak by, they'll smell us for sure," Markus says.

"Then we need to hide the smell."

I stay low, spin around, but there's nothing we can use.

"What if we wait?" Markus says.

"Let's move on a little, they're still a long way off and we can see them coming. Maybe we'll find something to cover our scent, or find a way through."

I begin to creep forwards and Markus follows. The lions sit on the rocks, turning their heads occasionally but otherwise remaining still. We crawl through brush and in between rocks and the ground grows very steep. Trees appear thicker and we pass between them, under their empty branches, all the while watching the lions, never taking our eyes off them. I spot a pile of lion dung and Markus taps me on the shoulder, noticing it too. He moves over to it and waits for me.

"This should help at least," he says.

I stare at him, unsure of what he's suggesting. Then he reaches down into the dung with his hand. It's dry and crumbly on the outside but Markus pulls it apart, revealing a softer, stickier inside. He takes a clump and starts to rub it over his body. I stare at the dung and reluctantly pick up a piece as well. I break it apart in my fingers and start to rub it everywhere; in my hair, over my hoody and jeans, even my shoes and the tyre fragment strapped to them. It actually isn't so bad. Nothing compared to some of the stenches I've had to endure.

We continue up the steep hill and listen to the growls, watch the lions open their mouths and roar at one another.

"Do you think they can sense us?" I ask.

"I'm not sure." Markus looks at me, then glances over his left shoulder, "No Death, so hopefully not."

I can't even force a smile because my heart is in my throat, choking my ability to express anything but raw fear. I feel sick and tired, my head is pounding and my legs are weak, shaking. We're deep amongst the graveyard of trees that covers the hills. I can no longer see all the lions, just the three to the north-east by the open cliff. I panic even more wondering where the others have gone, start darting my eyes left and right. There's another roar, this one even closer, bouncing off the rocks all around us, hiding its origin.

"It's too close Bandi," Markus is white-faced, sweat pouring from his forehead.

"We have to run. We have to find somewhere to hide."

Markus nods at me and we stare at each other for a few moment, before hoping up and starting to run. We veer south-east to try and avoid the spot where the lions had been. I glance to the left as I tear up the slope, see the flickering shape of a lion running alongside us, a large female, powering at speed. Adrenaline rises higher than I've ever felt it, and it carries me faster than I ever thought possible. Markus is on my heels. Dry grass is scraping at our ankles as we dodge the trees. The lion is moving closer and I can hear its grizzly growls, the throaty moan, its jaw snapping. It's so close, only thirty metres separating us. Then I see a flash of black drop down from a tree. I hear growling, roars, scuffling, clawing, but all of it behind me. I don't dare turn around. I have to keep moving.

There's a large rock face up ahead, no way through. I swerve to the right, heading south, along the wall of stone. The sounds of battling beasts grows further away, cries and yelping ringing clear but fainter. While running I turn myself into a spin. Now I have to see. Markus' face is bright red. He can barely run anymore. Behind him, I see it through the trees, another flash of black, and I feel power in my veins again. I spin forward and duck under a branch, slide between two larger trunks.

Markus cries out, "There! Through there!"

In the rock face ahead there's a large square of concrete, with a long horizontal slit just a metre and a half off the ground. I launch towards it, reach it in a few seconds. I grab the ledge and pull myself through. Markus follows and we both topple over the concrete into darkness.

We pant and heave, leaning against the wall, sat low. There is no other sound, no growls or roars. We made it.

I look to my left. Markus turns to me, closes his eyes, his head back against the stone.

"Tell me you saw it," I say.

He pants, tries to swallow, just stares at me, relief bringing tears to his eyes.

"I saw it, Bandi," he whispers, "I think I saw it."

14

I stand up and peer out through the slit in the concrete wall behind us. There's no sign of the lions or panther, nor can I hear anything. I sit back down beside Markus, lean against the stone.

"What is this place?"

"I think it's an old bunker," he says. "Maybe snipers used this spot as a lookout point."

I gaze around, my eyes adjusting to the dark. We're in a small round cave, the slit the only way out other than a tunnel leading deep into the mountain opposite us.

"What do you think is down there?" I point ahead.

"No idea, the rest of the bunker? Whatever that means."

I kneel, looking out again. The thin trees stand motionless, hiding anything beyond, obscuring the downward slope we just climbed. At least we're safe.

I stand and Markus rises beside me. He pulls a bottle from his pack and we both drink, the last of our water. My mouth and throat are so dry that even the hot, stale water is smooth, cleansing.

We sit and wait to catch our breaths. I strip off my outer hoody, my head pouring with sweat. The bunker is hot, airless. I lean out, sucking breaths from the open hillside through the slit. Markus stands beside me and does the same.

"I told you it was real," I say.

Markus looks at me, "I don't know what to think anymore."

"I thought you saw it?"

"Well, I saw something. I was scared, running fast. It could have been anything really."

"But it wasn't anything. It was the panther. Why can't you just believe it?"

"All I know is we're safe, but with a long way still to go."

I'm so angry I can't even look at him. But I know to leave it. It's better that way with Markus. He'll make up his own mind when he's ready. But still it's frustrating. The panther is the one thing giving me hope, giving me strength. Why can't Markus accept this gift we've been given?

"Even if it is a black panther, it's just an animal. It's wild. It hunts and kills like everything else," he says.

"Then why did it attack the lion? Why did it appear when we were about to become lion food? That's three times now it's come for us."

"If that's true, then why didn't it warn us about the attack on the station?"

His expression is solemn, but I can tell he isn't expecting an answer.

"Maybe it did," I say. "Only I was too stupid to know what it meant."

I stand up, hating Markus and hating myself—hating everything because the panther first appeared the night before everything changed; before everyone we knew was dead. But I didn't know what it meant then, and Markus still won't believe in it now. So what's the damn point?

The tunnel ahead is dark and down it I go without a word, all that hate I'm feeling plateauing in numbness and a need to keep moving and be alone.

"Wait," Markus calls after me.

I walk on ignoring him, stepping through the dark blindly. I can hear him rustling behind me, packing away his bag, hurrying to follow. I don't wait, just head down the tunnel, holding the sides to guide me through the dark. There's a strange, sweet smell in the air and I sniff as I walk, trying to figure out what it could be. The tunnel starts to grow lighter and soon the rock walls are visible, craggy and dry, the tunnel moving on straight for a while, before seeming to come to an end.

Only the tunnel doesn't end, but curves around to the left. I catch another strange scent in the air; this one more potent, more familiar and fowl. The tunnel grows lighter still, and I can almost see the light flickering, as if from an open flame.

My eyes are fixed ahead, down the passage, and I feel my foot crunch down on something. It falls on something soft and moist. I look down at my feet and there's a shape there. I stare hard in the faint light, trying to make out what it is. Hooves, horns. I cry out, fall back.

Markus comes rushing up behind me, pulls me to my feet and we both stagger backwards, away from the horned creature.

"What the hell is it?"

Markus shakes his head, too afraid to move on. I crouch and edge towards it. The hot stench digs deep, creeps under my skin.

"It's just a goat," I whisper, "Only a stupid goat."

Markus comes up beside me, "Don't ever run off on your own, Bandi."

"I'm sorry," I say, "I just want you to believe me."

"I do. I want to. I just don't want all of our hope to rest on one thing that we don't even understand."

I nod, turn to him, "Let's just keep going. The smell, I can feel it sticking to me."

"We need to watch out. There's a dead goat in here and that could mean something killed it."

I get down on my knees again, beside the carcass, inspect the flesh, searching for a cause of death. I find no bite marks, no sign of tearing claws, but the neck has been cleanly broken.

"I don't think an animal killed it," I whisper.

We move further down the tunnel and it continues to grow lighter. We pass several more goat carcasses, some of them stripped completely, just piles of bones. We round another corner and the source of the light is finally revealed. There's a flame torch on the wall, jutting out from the rock, its orange flame tall and skinny, rising high. On the wall surrounding it, paintings emerge out of the rock, etchings carved in stone. They appear to move, almost dancing in the torch light.

"Animals, Markus. Look!"

There are several pictures all over the wall, drawn mostly in black, with some red, some brown; colours of the earth. There are lions, dogs, cats and birds. The pictures carry on along the tunnel walls and I follow them, follow elephants, horses, a rhino. A little way down the tunnel another torch burns brightly, and further along another still. The tunnel seems to stretch on for hundreds of metres, all the while lined with cave paintings and torch light. Markus and I move carefully along, studying the sketches, crossing back and forth across the dank, narrow passage.

A low murmur drifts out of the darkness, breaking the silence. I hold my steps, listen hard. Markus is still pacing around and I have to grab him and put my finger to my lips to keep him quiet. I hear music, a melody.

Creeping slowly forwards, I strain my ears. Muffled words bounce through the dark towards us. Markus follows just behind me. Occasionally we stop to listen, then carry on, edging closer.

The muffled tune grows clearer, a hoarse voice sings. But I still can't make out any words, or have any guesses as to whom or what it might be.

There's a click behind me and I spin around. Markus has the gun out, the torchlight smears the metal.

"Better to be safe," he says.

I nod and turn back towards the hum, step carefully through the dark as the smell returns; the strange, sweet smell, now more potent.

"Can you smell that?" I whisper.

Markus nods, "It's like flowers."

"Flowers? How is that possible?"

Markus shrugs, "We'll find out pretty soon."

I've never smelt flowers, only had them described. But this smell is stale, smokey and sweet, not the fresh odour I'd always imagined.

The tunnel opens up into another large cave, the ceiling high off the ground, dimly lit by more torches along the walls. In the far corner of the cave I can see a form, hunched over on the ground, smoke rising high around it, hovering into a mist beneath the stone. Markus and I lower ourselves close to the ground and watch for a moment. It's a small man, old and frail, hunched against the wall, facing away from us. He's humming, tossing in occasional words, "Hum-dee-hum, the world is young, in dark we wait, with open arms."

We listen and watch. Markus readies the gun. The man is up against the cavern wall, scratching at it, painting with a stick. He has a flat piece of wood in his hands, the stick in the other, and a pipe burns in his mouth. He's thin like a skeleton, no meat on his bones, just skin, giving him an insect-like appearance. He's dressed in a brown cloak that falls down to his knees, a hood up over his head. He continues to paint, to sing, "And there will be a hum-hee-hee, dum-dee-dum, the war was won."

Then he stops. It's as if he's sensed us. He goes quiet and drops everything in his hands without turning around. I stagger back a little as he stands upright.

"Hmmm," his voice is gargled, frothy, "Garth is not alone, haha!"

Slowly he turns his head, his hooded face curling towards us, and his eyes are fixed on me right away. They're small and beady, black. There's a huge toothless smile on his face.

"Well, well. What is this? What have we here?"

He turns his whole body and takes a step forwards. He puts his pipe to his lips and inhales. As he inhales the pipe glows and fires up his tiny eyes with a fierce sparkle, a diamond glint in the hollow black. He smiles widely, his thin lips pulled all the way across his face.

"Come out of the dark, come say hello. It is rude not to do so! Hee-Ha!"

He lets out a gargled laugh and Markus and I remain still, frozen. Markus' fingers are tightly locked on the trigger, the gun aimed out straight.

I slowly rise to my feet and Markus does the same, keeping the gun locked on the strange little man.

"We just want to pass through, that's all," I say, but my voice comes out weak and quiet.

The man stares and I'm not sure if he's heard me. Then he shrugs, turns back to the wall and resumes his painting, singing to himself once more.

I turn to Markus, "Let's just go. I think he's lost it."

"Be ready for anything."

I nod, start stepping though the cavern towards the man, who continues to smoke and hum by the passage entrance opposite us, the only other way out.

The cavern is lined with paintings of animals as well. I glance at them as I pass but try to keep my eyes fixed on the man, ready to run or fight at any moment. He continues to sing, "There are those who lose, and those who are lost, hum-dee hum, the war was won, with skies of fire and lakes of blood."

Across the cavern something catches my eye. On the wall just beside me, surrounded by small shapes and figures, is a picture of a large black animal. I lean in, stare hard at it, just to make sure. And I'm right, it's a panther.

Larger than all the rest of the paintings, etched deep into the stone, the lines are marked heavy and black. I stop and stare at the picture, point at it so that Markus can see. He doesn't seem interested, continues to edge towards the exit, the small man right in front of us now, just a few metres away. His bare legs and feet are filthy, his hands almost completely black. His skin is as wrinkled and dry as the tattered cloak covering it. The cloak itself is no more than a grain sack with a hood.

I stare at the painting of the black panther and as if reading my thoughts, the man speaks, "He sees the beast, the majestic one, that comes at dawn, and leads the good to the sun, the sea, the right place to be, when all is ending."

I swivel towards him, staring intensely. He continues to puff on his pipe and scratch at the wall, as if nothing has happened. Markus is all the way across the cavern, waiting for me by our exit, waving his arm frantically for me to hurry. But I can't believe the words I've just heard. There could be more and I need to take this chance.

I struggle to swallow, take a step towards the man, "What do you know about the black panther?"

He stops drawing, turns to face me. His beady eyes are wild, erratically darting around. He puts his finger to his lips, motioning for me to be quiet, then stands in silence, as if waiting.

He lets out a wild roaring laugh. I see Markus lift the gun in the corner of my eye. I fall back a step.

"Come with me, boy. Garth will show you how to see, Garth will show you who to be, how to live, what illumination can bring."

He scurries off down the tunnel, past Markus who holds his breath, unable to move, his face white. My own breathing is racy, part excitement, part fear.

"Why, Bandi? Why did you have to say something? We could have gone right past him."

I look at my brother, "He knows something, Markus. I know he does."

"He's crazy, he doesn't know anything. He could be dangerous! We need to get out of here. Let's just go back."

"To the lions? No way, Markus. We have to move on. He won't hurt us, he wants to help us."

I walk straight past my brother and head down the second tunnel after the man. After a few seconds Markus lets out a frustrated groan. Then I hear his footsteps following me down the passage. It's lit with torches again, and a little way down I can see the man waiting for us, with a huge grin on his face, leaning against the rock wall. He beckons for me to come and claps his hands, the crack echoing in the dark. Then he laughs again, puffs his pipe and turns around, heading down into the darkness ahead.

15

I can't see the man up ahead anymore so I speed up, pacing quickly, then accelerating into a gentle jog. I can hear his laughter bouncing off the walls, echoing in all directions, but I never see him. Eventually I come to the tunnel's end. It's blocked by a small wooden door. A white light, a natural light, slips out through gaps in the wood. Markus comes around the corner and I don't wait another second, I burst straight through.

We're in a vast cavern, as if the entire mountain has been hollowed out. At the top of the cavern there's a huge opening, above it a bright but hazy sky. The ground is lined with a thin layer of dirt and growing, absolutely everywhere, are bright red flowers.

"Poppies," Markus whispers.

They grow out of cracks in the walls and on the ground, strong and vivid over everything. To the left of the cavern there are bunches of pods growing on sticks. The man is hunched over the dry things with a tiny blade, slicing the pods open. I move closer to him and can see he's extracting some sort of sap, leaving it there to dry. He moves over to other pods he's previously sliced open and scrapes off some resin. He packs the reisn into his pipe.

"What's he doing?" I ask.

Markus is gazing around in wonder, follows my gaze to Garth. "He's smoking that sap from the dried poppies, that's what those pods are."

"Why's he doing that?" I whisper.

"A lot of soldiers smoked it. It's called opium. I read about it before. They usually use a special lamp that doesn't burn the poppies, just creates a vapour. This old man obviously doesn't have a lamp. He's just smoking it."

I watch the man pack the pipe and light it with one of the torches. He sits and leans back against a rock, puffing away joyously.

"It's addictive," Markus says, "Can make you a little crazy."

The man giggles and sniggers to himself, enjoying the bright light of the cavern. He seems to have totally forgotten about Markus and I, or doesn't seem to care that we're here. The sweet, flowery smell is potent and fresh, something I can't ever remember experiencing; the smell of something living, something that grows.

I turn to Markus and smile, "I can't believe it. How can they grow in here?"

Markus shrugs, looking dumbfounded. I lean down by a cluster of the poppies, touch the petals, run my finger down the stem. It's soft, crisp, and so frail. No wonder they can't grow out there on the harsh and barren plains.

The man gets up from his seat against the rock and moves towards us, barefoot on the thin layer of earth. He begins to speak, "Volcanoes—they stay fertile, long after all else dies!"

He leans down and picks up a handful of the dark earth, lets it fall through the gaps between his fingers. Markus and I both stand to face him and he steps closer, his back hunched low. He's barely taller than me, and I'm short for my age. He offers me the pipe but I shake my head.

"You boys have come far, should be dead, haha! But here you are, alive, still with your heads atop your bones!" He cackles and coughs, spitting into the dirt.

"How did you grow all of this?" I ask.

"Found a box full of magical seeds one day, long years past. The masked ones left it behind, the lions made sure they moved on fast! A sprinkling here and there, and nature cares, did the rest, haha!"

I gaze around again, still completely in awe of a sight I never even imagined I'd see.

The man turns and wanders back to his seat nestled in flowers. He leans back and starts to pack his pipe again. I notice a strange twitch that he has, a sudden ill glint in his eye, not quite right. But it disappears as fast as it came, leaving behind that wide, toothless smile.

Markus and I sit beside him, weary, alert. We watch him smoke for a few moments before I gain the courage to speak again.

"My name is Bandi, and this is Markus, my brother. What's your name?"

I half expect him to burst into song, but he just looks at me blankly and laughs, "Garth is my name. The one and the only, the very same."

I force a smile.

"It's a pleasure to meet you," Markus says, his voice coming out whiny and pathetic.

I shoot him a look. He shrugs.

I turn back to Garth, "We want to know more about the black panther. I think it's been helping us, guiding us."

Garth smokes his pipe, and I get the distinct feeling he's not even listening, gazing up through the top of the volcano, his mind up there beyond the haze.

Slowly he starts to speak, "The beast will come for those in need."

I turn to Markus who nods, telling me to go on.

"I first saw it a while ago, in the city to the west. Since then it's appeared a few times. It's like it's leading us, watching over us."

Garth slowly pulls his focus away from the sky, stares at me hard, his smile gone. "Black panther you say? A magical beast. Bringer of power to those it seeks, staring unblinking in the night, rousing desire, seeing through the body and deep into the otherness."

I glance at Markus, he's listening intently.

A smile creeps across Garth's face, "The black panther holds power of the moon, warden's energy, watchful eyes. The solitary ghost, once, they called it. Comes to welcome night and see it end, awaken the light within the deepest dark," he smokes his pipe, "That is you."

He smiles, offers me the pipe again, "Do you wish to see?"

I shake my head and watch him toke at it, his bony fingers gripping the worn wood, his shrivelled lips locked around the spout.

He continues, "Black is the colour of the creator, from which all is and are born. You and I, petals and thorns. The panther, solitary ghost, wise without words, a most instinctive wisdom."

As he speaks I can see the panther, see its eyes deep inside me, feel its heat and clarity.

Markus speaks, "But it's only an animal. How can any of this be true?"

Garth flashes Markus a hard look, "You are a fool to say such a thing, boy. The panther holds secrets of unseen worlds, but places which are. I have seen them in my poppies, as I offer to you. There is another side, and the panther sees, brings you vigour from his realm. A great blessing, and one that is not granted on many, especially here, now, in this rotted place, haha!"

I feel butterflies flapping upwards, desperately trying to blast out of my stomach. It's elation, a joy I can't ever remember feeling. It's all real, everything I've felt—seen. I knew it from the day I first laid eyes on the panther.

I glance at my brother and I can see he's thinking, trying to make sense of Garth's words. I don't need to think. I've felt it all first hand. I know Garth is telling the truth.

"Garth, Sir," I say, "We're trying to get to the sea, to the east. Do you know a way out of here?"

"The great blue, that sits across miles of sand—ha! It is a sad truth, that even with he, that brings the night, the journey will be longer, harder, than you ever have known, haha!"

"But it is there?" Hope continues to rise in me. I want to run to the sea right now; run forever if I have to.

"I sense many things, see many beings, many places, some up here," Garth points to his head, "some with these," he points to his eyes. "But I do not see waves roll and crash, roll and crash."

My heart falls a little but not knowing is better than being told it's gone. The drunk soldier told us it was there. Markus is still staring hard at Garth, trying to make sense of all the information.

"I will be back, when I feel being back is right to be—ha!" Garth speaks suddenly and jumps up just as fast, hurrying off down another tunnel opening, one that seems to lead into darkness.

I turn my attention to Markus, "All those things he said, it's all true. I felt that power, its eyes, right here," I point to my chest.

"I believe you, Bandi. But this man's crazy. And besides, he said the sea isn't even there."

"He said he can't see waves. We don't even know what that means. He's cryptic. He probably means he can't see that far in his mind or something."

"I think it's pretty clear what it means. You can't choose what you believe. You can't believe him about the panther but ignore what he says about the sea."

"I believe him about the panther because I felt it, exactly as he described it. It's a guardian, leading us to safety, to the sea! And I don't care what he says about waves. I know the sea is there. It has to be."

"Why does it have to be? We either believe a drunk soldier or a crazy hermit? Neither of them are reliable, are they? What about our father? He told us the sea wasn't there at all. Why would he lie?"

I shake my head, desperately frustrated at Markus, "The soldier was telling the truth. He saved us, Markus, remember that? He saw something in us. He was a good person."

"He was a soldier. How can you believe him, and not your own father?!"

"I don't know. But I have to believe it's there, we have to. Otherwise what is there left to go on for?"

"I don't even know why we're trying to get to the sea. What's even there? We have no idea what we'll find."

I stare at my brother, still hopeless, "We'll find cold blue waves, a place to stay—we can live on."

There are tears in his eyes and for a few minutes he says nothing. He claws at the dirt, stares at a poppy beside his shoe. "I hope you're right, little brother," he eventually says. But there's no conviction in his voice. He's saying what he knows I want to hear.

Garth comes rushing back as quickly as he left, throws a bloody goat leg down in front of us. It looks fresh, as if he just ripped it off an animal seconds ago.

"Eat up little ones, you have far to go, across sand and fire, where nothing lives."

"Can we cook it first?" I ask.

"If you must, if you must."

We find an open rock, free of poppies, and use one of the torches to light a small fire, burning the dry stalks. We cut off small chunks of meat and skin them, threading them onto sticks. Markus and I sit either side of the fire and watch the smoke curl up towards the volcano's open mouth and merge into the haze.

We eat the meat and it tastes delicious, much better than pigeon. While we eat Garth just paces around, smoking his pipe the entire time, muttering to himself and prancing about erratically. When we have eaten as much as we can, we cook the rest of the meat and pack it away in our back-packs, wrapped in cloth.

I ask Garth whether he has any water, and he almost drops his pipe with excitement, bursts into laughter again, "We drink to live, live to drink, in mountains deep, is there such a thing? Haha!"

16

Garth charges off down the dark passage again, from where he brought us the goat leg. This time Markus and I follow, leaving our bags behind. We chase his laughter down the tunnel which opens up in a smaller cavern. The remainder of the goat whose leg we've just eaten is bleeding out on the ground in front of us. Further on there are two more goats, still alive and roaming in the caves.

"Are they his goats?" Markus asks.

"Maybe they just live here in the hills. That would explain the lions being here."

"How do you think they survived everything?"

Garth calls from down the tunnel, "They may look silly, like small horned horses, but they are strong, need little to live and they defy all forces! Ha!"

Markus and I are both stunned.

"How the hell did he hear us?"

Markus shrugs, "I have no idea but I'm not surprised. I think I've lost the ability to be surprised by anything."

We carry on down the passage, crumpled into darkness among the lowering and narrowing rock. We move slowly now, calling in the dark, "Garth? Where are you?"

I leap backwards and crash into Markus, stunned by Garth's face suddenly popping up out of the dark, inches from mine.

"We're here," he says.

His grin has returned, and he swiftly darts off round the corner. I run after him, Markus by my side, and we come to a tunnel that drops straight down. Garth is dancing, bouncing left and right, clapping with excitement.

He glares at us, the smile wiped clean off his face, "The way down does not always lead to hell and fire."

For a few seconds all three of us stand there, Markus and I gazing down into the hole in front of us, the only way onwards. Then Garth leaps, straight down into the dark. I grab Markus and stagger back, and the moment of total silence seems long. But then there's a splash, somewhere far below.

Markus and I glance at each other, then back down into the hole. Garth calls up, his voice far away, echoing off the stone, "Come young brothers, the pool is cool, and drink it we can, swim in it we may!"

I take one more look at Markus, shrug, then leap forward. He shouts after me but I'm already falling, screaming, feet first into the black. If we survive this, Markus will have a punch in the gut waiting for me; for being such a maverick, he'll say. But it's all this stuff with the panther; with Garth. I guess I feel kind of invincible, protected. There's magic in our lives right now.

After a few seconds a light appears below me, a turquoise blue glimmer that grows. A second later I hit the water.

It washes over my skin and coats my body. I feel it spread through my fingers and my hair, the dust, sand and lion filth washed away. I kick hard and burst onto the surface. I'm in another large cavern with a high ceiling, the opening I fell through is above me. Garth is floating on his back with his eyes closed, the water sparkling in the dim light, falling through tiny shafts in the cavern roof. The holes are small, the size of fists, but big enough so that light from above illuminates the entire cavern. There's a small beach by the pool with two tunnels leading away, one upwards and the other down into further darkness.

I try rolling onto my back by kicking my feet and splashing my hands. But I start to sink. I've never swam before. Desperately

I push at the water with open palms but I barely move. I start to panic and swallow water, cough. I try to cry out for help but can only splutter as I begin to drop again, down into the deep.

I stare up through the water hopelessly and reach out at the streams of light that cut the pool's surface. My eyes start to flutter. My vision begins to fuzz away. Garth is floating on the surface; I can see him from down below. My eyes fall shut and bright green flames surge in them. I hear the sound of a roar from somewhere else, but I'm weak, sinking deeper still.

A hand grabs my wrist and I'm being pulled up again, the water rushing over me. I burst through the surface and start coughing, as Garth drags me to the edge of the pool. On my hands and knees I cough the water out of my lungs while perched in the shallows. Then I fall onto my back, half-submerged. My legs float as I lie and regain my strength.

Markus is shouting my name, his voice small and far. He's deeply concerned, terrified even. I realise he probably thinks I'm dead.

"I'm alright Markus," I shout, "You have to come down here, it's amazing! Just be ready to swim!"

I can hear him hesitating, deliberating. I watch the opening, waiting to see him come falling through it. A minute later I shout up at him again, "Do it already, big brother!"

That's the last bit of persuading he needs. I hear him scream and a second later his body appears, hands flapping at his sides like pathetic wings. He screams and hits the water with force, the splash flicking high onto the cavern walls. He surfaces and manages to paddle to the side with great difficulty, his chest heaving when he finally makes it.

"If we're going to live by the sea, I'm going to have to work on my swimming," he says.

"At least you sort of know how. I almost drowned!"

Markus looks worried for a second, but then a smile appears on his face, "I'll teach you, Bandi. It's not hard."

We spend the next few hours splashing around; Markus teaching me how to move my arms, keep my fingers clamped shut. I'm not fast but I get the hang of it, learn how to stay afloat. We drink and we swim and all the while Garth just bobs on the surface, occasionally humming or muttering, but acting more or less as if we aren't even there. But I don't think too much of it. I don't really care. Water is my only focus—fresh, cool water all around.

After a while we follow Garth back up to the main cavern with the poppies. The tunnel on the right leads steeply up and it's a long way around. It takes almost an hour to get back up through winding passages and I'm thankful that this time Garth moves slowly so we can follow. He grumbles constantly and never smiles. There's a grim look in his eye and he seems irritable, constantly scratching.

Back in the main chamber the torches have gone out and Garth efficiently lights one with some flint. He uses that torch to light the others and soon the open cavern is lit with a warm and hearty glow, the sun's power weakening above us, the powerful shafts now pale and dull. Markus and I light our fire and sit by it to warm our cool bones. I feel more refreshed than I've ever been, clean—reborn even.

We eat some more of the meat and ask Garth to join us. He pulls some chunks of raw meat off the bone and chews. I can barely watch as he bites the wet flesh, but he smiles and laughs again, his pipe in hand, puffing away on his opium between bites.

"Why do you smoke that all the time?" I ask him.

He leans back on a rock, fingers a poppy, smells its flower, "It gives me great power, boy. I see the other, I see more, between lines, through stones, inside flesh, a more glorious side, haha! Your panther is no stranger there, no, no, he is no stranger there nor here."

He offers me the pipe again and I desperately want to take it, but know I shouldn't. He's helped us a great deal, but I can see he's scarred mentally from years alone, years spent in a haze between worlds, or whatever it is he keeps talking about. I know I don't want to end up like him. But I do want to see the 'other side', whatever that means, especially if the panther's power comes from there. Maybe that's where my mother and father are, waiting for me, maybe it's the place I saw in my dream, when I collapsed at the city's edge. I rode on the panther's back under a calm sky until I returned here, to this side of things.

"What's on the other side of these mountains?" Markus asks.

"Ancient battlegrounds, paths carved in the earth, like rivers, but not rivers, the ruins of war, burn and rot and metal. Then trees that are black, thick and aged, dead and gone, but lost amongst them, many have been."

"Then what?" I ask.

Garth looks at me sincerely, his beady eyes revealing little, "Garth does not know what lies beyond the dead forest. He does not know."

"The sea?"

I glance at Markus, know he wants to hear the same thing I do. But Garth just gets up and walks away. He moves over to the walls and resumes painting, humming.

"Why won't he say anything about the sea?"

"I don't know," Markus says. "But I'm starting to think we should move on, as great as it's been."

"I want to learn more, Markus. He can teach us more."

"I'm not sure you'll get much more out of him. Or you might, but it could take weeks. He's all over the place. Look at him."

I turn to watch Garth and he's smoking his pipe still, standing on one leg, drawing a goat using blood from his own finger.

"I suppose you're right. We know the way and we know what's ahead. We can stock up here first."

The sky above is dark now and I ask Garth if he'll take us back to the pool so that we can refill our bottles. He seems happy to lead us there again.

Second time around, I spread my arms as I fall. I enjoy the couple of seconds of rippling air. It's a new kind of freedom, one I enjoy every moment of, until I hit that glassy surface. It stings for a few moments but I rise up, fulfilled and ready to move on towards whatever comes next.

Markus drops a few moments later, in silence this time. When he emerges I can see he felt it too, that freedom in air, and he floats on his back with his eyes closed for a while, embracing it.

We fill all of our bottles and pack them away. We're about to head up again when I hear a rumble. The ceiling shakes. Small rocks start to fall and splatter the pool, disturbing the shimmer. Dark shapes block the shafts above us. The rays of moonlight from the clear night sky are obscured by something up there.

I freeze, grab Markus by the arm.

He's still fiddling with his backpack. "What?" he cries.

I jump on him and cover his mouth. We lie staring up at the cavern roof.

"There's something up there," I whisper.

The silver shafts of light continue to be blocked off by shadows.

"Lions," Garth says in a low voice, "They can smell the sweet pool. They always come, sniffing about above. But they can't get in, haha!"

Low rumbling sounds above. Growls echo and roll across the rocks, bouncing off the silvery water.

"Let's get back to the fire," I say, "I've seen enough lions for one day."

Garth is spread out on his back with his eyes closed. But like lightning they flash open, the beady things stretching wide, terror I've not seen in him yet. He sniffs the air and glances at Markus, then me.

"It burns!" he screams.

17

Garth charges up the tunnel towards the poppy chamber. Markus and I follow, picking up our backpacks off the stone.

"What's he talking about, Markus?"

"I have no idea, but he looks freaked out."

While running I realise my back-pack feels light and I turn to see the contents rolling back down the tunnel. There's a huge split along the bottom of my pack. It must have caught on a rock. I rush back to grab the bottles of water, my sling shot.

Markus calls after me, "Bandi, just leave it!"

I'm panicking and my fingers are trembling. I stuff my sling-shot in the back of my jeans and stick a few flares and the torch into my pocket but have to leave the rest. I scramble up the tunnel slope towards Markus who's waiting for me wide-eyed and looking desperate.

We carry on up the tunnel but again Garth has disappeared. We can hear his muttering resonating and echoing from all directions. We spin around in circles, the tunnel almost totally dark. We choose a passage that leads upwards and I spot Garth ahead, rubbing the stone wall, whispering. He spins around when he hears us approaching and gives us an eerie stare before speeding off again, skulking low, skinny legs stepping at speed.

We do our best to follow but the tunnel air seems murky, something hangs. It grows intense and sweet, a smokey smell pours thicker and stronger. Markus and I start to cough a little and have to slow down, the tunnel only leading one way now, and I recognise the animals on the walls.

The tunnel shrinks and grows and I begin to feel strange and tingly, light on my feet. Every time I take a step it takes longer for my foot to reach the ground. Markus is stumbling strangely beside me. We can see a bright orange light at the end of the tunnel and all of a sudden I hear a scream. It's a piercing sound, horrific and sharp, like the cry of a dying horse.

We reach the poppy filled cavern and find Garth on his knees, weeping and shrieking, surrounded by flames.

The heat rages around us, bursting up like fiery spears as the fire spreads. Markus and I cower, step back into the tunnels. All of the poppies and pods, everything in the open cavern is alight, smoke flowing up through the old volcano's empty peak.

The flames are fierce, and I start to feel weak at the knees, drop to the stone. The fire shimmers and shakes, turns red and dissolves, and I can't understand what I'm seeing. I rub my eyes and it only gets worse. Pockets of darkness appear in my line of sight, black holes clouding my vision.

Markus has one hand cupped over his mouth and nose but he's struggling with it too, desperately trying to keep his focus. With his other arm he's tearing at his sleeve but he can barely grab the fabric. I start to crawl towards him but fall on my side, drag myself the rest of the way. Together we tear off his sleeve and rip it in two, each of us wrapping half around our face to cover our airways. All the while Garth wails, beating the ground, crying out, "They took them all!"

I struggle to my feet and pull Markus onto his.

"What do you think happened?"I shout.

"Our fire, did we leave it lit?"

I can't remember. Markus shrugs and his eyes are pulled tight, tears are streaming down his face from the smoke. The poppies burn crimson into the night sky. The smoke tumbles down the passages and tunnels. And in the fire I see a face, walking out of the flames. It's masked, black; the rubber starting to melt off it. The eyes in the mask are bright red and the form moves in slow motion, a soldier, with a tank strapped across his back and a flamethrower in his hands.

I scream and my heart beats so quickly I can't even feel the rhythm, each beat blurred into one giant quake of fear. I turn and start to crawl down the tunnel as the rocks fall around me. The animals on the walls seem to pop out and then they start to roar, bark and cry at me. I stumble, falling down the tunnel, moving away from the flames, the melting gas mask still in my head. I look up and the soldier is standing in the tunnel entrance, a horrific silhouette, surrounded by the fire. Markus is falling down the tunnel after me and he takes my hand, his eyes wide. His mouth opens into a scream.

He pulls me to my feet and we scamper off, heading in any direction as long as it's away from the fire. Soon all the roaring and shouting subsides, the flames are far away and the smoke is thin. I become aware of the fact that Markus and I are alone in darkness.

Neither of us says a word but I can't stop scratching, the itch always eluding me. And then I hear a huge thump, and the entire cave shakes. And then again, and again.

The thump grows louder, more frequent. Then it stops.

Markus' eyes are closed, his lips moving. He's jerking his head to the side repeatedly and I wonder what nightmares are going on inside of him.

I push myself up onto my trembling legs and feel about for the walls and then I fall, straight into a rock. But the rock gives way and I continue to fall into total black. I scream but I am nothing, can't feel myself at all. I'm just floating nothing, within nothing, like invisible dust in a field of darkness. I try to open my eyes but I have none. I can think and I can feel but I have no body, have no being attached to my thoughts. All I want to do is scream. But I have no voice. No way of making a sound. It's as if I don't exist at all.

Then things fuse to bright, darkness fading to green, warmth. I crawl down the tunnel, whimpering as I sway on my hands and knees. I approach the pool and it shines like a sheet of diamond. I crawl to the water and flick the cool fluid onto my face. I stare up and long black snakes begin rappelling down from above, gaping pink mouths aimed at me, teeth glistening in savage moonlight. Then I see figures, the shapes of men, sliding down the snakes towards the pool. Hordes of masked soldiers slip down towards the water and I manage to push myself to my feet at last, adrenaline driving me upright. I stagger into the shadows, screaming towards the safety of darkness, a second tunnel leading down. I shout for my brother, I scream his name, "Markus!"

And that's all I remember. Maybe there are some flashes—some faces and smells I recognise but do not know how. But other than that, there is nothing.

A familiar tune causes me to stir, sung by a familiar voice. My mother used to sing to me, and I remember asking her not to anymore. 'I'm too old for that,' I told her. What I'd give to hear her song now. But it's not her voice that patters out of the dark. It's that quiet, raspy whisper, that same melody…'Hum-dee-hum.'

I open my eyes and I'm staring at gigantic spikes made of stone, hanging down from above. I sit up and I'm in another small cave, somewhere new, Markus lying beside me asleep. Garth is across from me, against the wall, humming away.

The cave is lit by a candle in Garth's hand and with the other he's drawing again, etching things into the stone. I stand up and approach him, wanting to see what it is.

There are two stick figures, Markus and I perhaps. Next to the figures he's drawn a black panther. He's working on a picture alongside them but I can't see what it is. He finishes and moves his hands away. There are flames, bright red flames in a circle, a poppy at the centre, scratched in black. He's drawn a gas mask beside the flames. But he isn't finished. He sucks his pipe, his lips pursed like a spout, and he continues to draw, muttering on in the candlelight. Another stick figure takes shape beside the others, this one lying horizontally with crosses for eyes, dead.

"Who's that?" I ask him.

Garth turns to me, his eyes waver, as if his mind is suddenly fluttering back from somewhere far away. The beady things hone in on me, gaze with ferocity, certainty. He lowers his brows, curls his lips, "It is me, boy."

A sickening feeling rises through me and my heart builds to a steady hammer.

I point at his drawing, "Are you, dead?"

He nods slowly, still smiling.

"But why?" My voice comes out weak.

Something in his eyes scares me. He doesn't reply, only turns away, back to his drawings. I sit down again, thinking for a minute and trying to remember what's happened; but I can't. I only remember flames, the soldiers, stumbling blindly in the dark. I panic when I suddenly realise I haven't checked if Markus is alright. I crouch beside him and shake him, calling his name. He opens his eyes and looks up at me, confused. He coughs and I pull a bottle of water from his bag, put it to his lips. He drinks and I realise how thirsty I am as well. I take only a small gulp, remembering the water I've lost; two entire bottles.

Markus finally sits up groggily, "What happened?"

"I don't know," I turn to Garth, "Garth, where are we? We can't remember what happened."

He turns around and comes to sit beside us, crosses his legs. He holds the candle right by his face and those black beady things seem deeper than ever, the rest of his face shrinking around them.

"You stumbled over the dark, magic in your minds, but too much, too much for young souls to comprehend. You were not ready, it was too heavy, for you. But I found you, took you away, to here, deep in the caves."

I turn to Markus, "I saw a soldier walking through the fire, with a flame thrower in his hands. There were hordes of them, rappelling down towards the pool. How are we alive?"

Markus stares at me hard, confusion creasing his face. I realise he has no idea what I'm talking about.

He shakes his head. Tears form in his eyes.

"What did you see Markus?"

He turns away, wipes his tears with the sleeve fragment around his neck. Before the attack on the station, I couldn't remember the last time I'd seen him cry. Seeing him in tears again scares me, but I know not to push him; we've been through so much. We need to find a way out of here, that's the most important thing right now.

Garth is leaning against the wall, scratching his neck. There's blood under his fingernails, cuts opening up on his skin. He doesn't seem to notice, doesn't seem to care. My eyes wander up the walls to the pictures he's just drawn. I stare at the horizontal figure, with crosses for eyes. What does it mean? *Why has he drawn himself as a dead man?*

I glance back towards Garth and he's staring at me, grinding his teeth. I realise then that I can't ever be sure of what I saw, will never know what really happened. The events that had just taken place were forever altered in my mind, changed by the burning pods. The things I saw were visions, hallucinations. Garth had said they were from 'another side', another place. I'm not sure what that means but I'm thankful to be alive, thankful to be breathing clean air again.

Garth smiles at me, blows his candle out, sending us into total blackness.

18

I wake up sweating and writhing, my body shaking furiously in the dark. Markus is whimpering and mumbling beside me in his sleep. I pull a match from my pocket and light it. The cave flashes into life from the tiny flame and I glance around. Garth is gone.

I'm shivering and shaking, my body slathered in cold sweat. I squeeze my knees against my chest and tuck in my chin, trying to contain what little body heat I have. Markus struggles beside me, with what must be terrible dreams. I hold his shoulder and shake him awake, unable to bear his horror any longer. He jumps up startled and cries out, panting fast. We see each other for a second before the match dies and we're in darkness again.

"Are you alright, Markus?"

"Yeah, are you?"

"I'm fine. But I can't see Garth anywhere."

"It's so dark," he says.

"I know, but I don't want to waste any more matches."

I squint my eyes, hoping they'll adjust but it's hopeless. The black consumes us.

"We need to use a flare. I can't take the darkness anymore."

"Ok," I say.

I hear some rummaging as Markus searches for his bag in the dark. There's some shuffling, a click, and the cavern lights up in a deep orange glow. Markus smiles at me but his eyes are sad, his forehead covered in sweat, hair soaked. He's shaking too.

"Now what?" he asks.

"I don't know. I guess we should move on, look for Garth."

I stand up and it's difficult; my knees feel weak, my stomach ill and empty. My mouth is bone dry and it keeps making me cough.

Markus sees Garth's picture on the wall and his face grows concerned. I tell him all about it, what Garth said to me.

He keeps shaking his head, "We need to be careful, Bandi. I'm not sure about him at all."

We drink a few sips of water, just to moisten our tongues and throats. We help each other up and then contemplate which way to head. There are three larger tunnels leading out of the cavern and a very low passage that seems to head down deeper into the earth. We listen in silence, hoping for a noise that will help us decide which passage to take. Markus holds up the flare and we peer down each tunnel in turn. Down the very last one, we see a flurry of movement, a shadow darting across the low light. We both stand still, wait for more movement. I glance at Markus. He takes a step forward with the flare. The tunnel leads straight ahead from the wall on which Garth had been drawing. I sniff the air. It seems cleaner, though I'm not sure if it's just my mind playing tricks on me. Clean air means outside. The other ways smell a little smokey and sweet, damp. That makes me think they lead back to where the fire raged.

"This way," I say, "It has to be."

Markus looks at me puzzled.

"Fresh air," I tell him.

"And a scary shadow…"

But I'm already walking down the chosen passage and Markus has no choice but to follow. My own shadow shrinks before me as he catches up with the flare. We hug the walls closely and tread carefully, avoiding anything that might come charging out of the dark.

Familiar laughter echoes from close by and I stop moving, wait. I can hear him grunting and he sounds enraged, filled with fury. He's cursing in the dark and I hear a metallic click behind me. I spin my head to see Markus standing with a flare in one hand and the gun in the other. I face the angry muttering again but there's silence now. A dark shape that wasn't there before is standing a little way down the tunnel. It's motionless, but I feel as though I can see it rise then cower. Raspy breathing scuttles out of the darkness and the shape moves closer, grows larger, until Garth's twisted face is right in front of mine. He has his index finger pressed against his lips, an eerie smile across his face.

I see the shadow of Markus' arm reach out as if from nothing, the gun in hand.

Garth whispers to me, "Who are you, young soldier? Burning and destroying, taking everything!"

His whisper turns into a scream and he launches himself at me. He claws at my hoody and I try to bat his hands away but he's stronger than he looks, holds me down with ease. He tries to bite my cheek but only manages to nip it, though I still feel the warm blood burst from the sting. I struggle, falling to the ground with Garth on top of me. He's scratching at my torso, his sharp nails cutting my skin, even through my clothes.

Markus shouts, "I can't get a clear shot!"

I manage to kick Garth to the side and roll on top of him, desperately trying to push his head down against the rock surface. He bites my hand and laughs, grabs me by the throat and shrieks and wails, his eyes seeming to turn fiery red. He keeps hold of my throat with one hand while beating me in the side with other. I lose strength and he kicks me off, hurls me against the rock wall. I hit my head hard and wilt to the ground. He dives on me again, this time onto my back.

I hear the sound of metal clatter as Markus drops the gun to the cave floor and charges at Garth. He jumps onto his back and wraps his arms around Garth's neck. I roll out of the way as Markus battles the madman to the ground. I crawl towards where I'd heard the gun fall. The flare is dying on the ground beside me and I feel around for the gun's cold grip. I find it, stare at the weapon, then turn to face them. Garth takes a bite out of Markus' arm and he screams loudly before falling to the ground.

Then the beady-eyed monster turns to face me. He stops when he sees me holding the gun, aimed at his chest. Markus is still writhing on the floor holding his arm, and Garth erupts into his sick, gargled laughter. I stare at his eyes, search for the glint of the man who told me about the black panther. The man who told us about great power, another side. He's gone. A maniac left in his place. I hold the grip in both hands and pull the trigger.

The recoil sends shockwaves up my arms to my shoulders, all the way down my spine. I stagger back and drop the weapon as soon as I fire. The blast echoes down the tunnel and sounds ten times its strength. Garth is still on his feet and he smiles at me. Then I see blood seep through his ragged cloak and grow into a puddle of red. He falls to the ground, like a puppet whose strings have been cut, and I know he's dead. I drop to my knees, try to make sense of everything that's just happened. One thought beats like a drum in my mind: *I've taken a life... I've killed a man...I've taken a life...*

Markus drags himself over to me, away from Garth's limp body and we hold each other as the flare light dies.

"You had to," he tells me, "You had to do it."

My breathing is heavy and rapid and I try to calm myself down, as that one thought continues to hammer. We lean against the rock wall behind us. I can't see Garth's corpse but I know it's there. I can feel his dead eyes watching me, like the icy stare of the dead soldier who appeared at the start of all of this. This time it was different. This time it was I who killed, and my stomach is a storm, one that feels as though it will never die.

Markus speaks to me quietly in the dark, "He was insane, Bandi. He was an addict. He needed his opium," he says. "He blamed us. It's all he cared about. It was him or us."

But it doesn't help. I stare into the darkness before me, "You didn't pull the trigger Markus. I did."

Markus doesn't say a word after that, for a long time. I can tell he's wrestling with his own demons. I keep seeing Garth's smile in front of me, bright in the dark. It's a smile that won't ever be seen again, because of me.

Tears drip down my cheeks but I try not to make a sound, so Markus won't see. There we sit, together but alone in the dark; thirsty, weary, cold. We're more alone than ever before. Our own secret torments prying us apart.

19

After what feels like hours and hours of darkness and silence, I drag myself to my feet.

"We should get out of here, Markus."

My brother stands up beside me and I pull a torch from my pocket. This is one of the rare instances when we really have to use it.

The cave lights up and the beam is still fairly strong, a good amount of power left in the batteries. I hope that it's enough to see us out of these tunnels. I shine the light down the direction we'd been heading before Garth had attacked us. I try not to look at the body as we pass, but it's hard not to. The black and beady eyes drill into me, still open, but lifeless now.

Markus picks up the gun and checks the cartridge and it's empty, sure enough. He packs it into his bag; it's worth holding on to, in case we happen to come across any more ammo, though I know that's almost impossible. Bullets and ammunition are rarer and more valuable than diamonds once were.

I feel terribly weak, in every sense. All the awful things that have happened over the last week, that were locked away, hidden because of our need to survive, seem to all implode within me at the same time. There's been so much death, so much fear, desperation. I feel as though it's finally too much, my murder of Garth the last nail in my spirit's coffin. I think of the fire, the poppies in flames, and I wonder whether it really was us that caused it. If it was, then Garth's death really is our fault. He was fine until we came along.

It didn't really matter that he was an addict. He was all alone in the dark—what else was there for him to do? And he believed it gave him power, and who are we to know? All we know is our home in the city, salvaging, surviving. This journey itself is a new world in our eyes, but it's still here, on this planet, the same one we were born into and have always lived on. The panther is proof in itself of something more, a power greater than our lives, greater than simple 'being.' Maybe Garth was better than us. He was a part of something beyond what we can see and comprehend. And I killed him. But I guess Markus is right—in the end it was him or us.

The soldier's melting face walking through the fire is an image I can't shake, and though it seems that it may not have been real, it haunts my every step. The poppy fumes were sweet, intoxicating, yet look what they did to my mind and to Markus. He hasn't been the same since, barely saying a word.

We stumble on through the tunnel and it leads only one way, through darkness, walls of stone. There are no drawings on the walls here, and I drop my torch when the thought hits me. It rolls along the stone and comes to a rest against the wall. I shudder, almost vomit from the strong sense of eerie that rises in me when I remember Garth's final drawing.

He drew himself dead, as if he knew what was going to happen. How could he have? It's not possible. He spoke of another side, hidden power. Markus says he's mad, nothing more, but Garth knew what was coming. He painted it on the wall.

"What is it?"Markus asks.

"The drawing. He knew what was going to happen. Explain that."

I can barely make out Markus' eyes. There's a faint sparkle of wet.

"He can't have," he says. "Don't even think about that."

I pick up the torch and keep walking, but Markus is wrong. If Garth truly knew what was going to happen then maybe he really did have some power. Maybe there really was some truth to his mad mutterings and ramblings. The black panther is still out there, guiding us to where we need to be, *the solitary ghost*. If Garth could predict his own death, then maybe the panther truly is our guardian, leading us out of danger.

As my spirits lighten, so does the dark. The black fades to a bluish grey and I start to run, Markus on my heels. I run fast across the dust and stone, leaving the misery of the poppies, the death and foul images behind. I charge around the corner and the opening is before me, daylight on the other side. It's a narrow crack in the thick cave wall but I climb up the rocks, squeeze myself between the stones. Markus passes his backpack to me though the crack, then slides through the gap by wriggling on his stomach. The daylight is bright and we squint on the cliffside. We're on the edge of a mountain and the sun is out, setting behind us. We're facing east.

I grab Markus by the arm and we both smile and pat each other on the back, so glad to be out of the nightmare that hung over us in the gloom of the caves.

The cliff drops steeply before us, levelling out into a barren plain. Beyond that I can see paths and dips carved into the earth, wire fences and mounds. Markus sees it all too and we both drop down in order to remain hidden. Our joy doesn't last. I roll onto my back and close my eyes, want to cry in frustration. There's no end in sight, just danger following danger, an endless chain of threat. I know what lies ahead; it's trenches, as far as we can see, an old battlefield. And I know that means there will be soldiers nearby. There always are.

"They're everywhere," Markus says.

I roll back onto my front, lie beside him, peering down as the sun disappears. The haze in the sky immediately seems to thicken and the familiar dusty horizon appears and begins to dim. Markus washes the wound on his arm. Garth's teeth marks are deep in his skin, a chunk gnawed clean off. It looks sore, still seeping. I help Markus bandage it up with some cloth from his bag and then we both take a drink, eat the last of our pigeon meat. It's old and tastes funny but we're confident it will be ok. Our stomachs are strong.

Markus lies back on his bag and closes his eyes. We decide to rest until dark, begin our descent then. I watch the horizon, looking out for shapes moving below but can't see any. There are no birds in the sky, no sign of anything living. There's a thick dusty smell in the air but it's just the haze, I've grown used to it. It's sour and unpleasant but a refreshing welcome after that heady, sweet smoke. I feel a headache brewing just thinking about it.

My head is a weighty stone, my bones like lead. It feels as though Markus and I have been travelling forever, but it's only been about a week. One week since I saw my parents, one week since they all died. I ache for another night in my metro station shack, with a relaxed and happy Markus at my side, my mother and father in the next room. Never again. Any of it. Never ever again. And now I'm a killer. No better than the soldiers I fear so much.

The light dims further and that's when I see it again, coming to welcome the night, as Garth had said. It's a long way away, across the trenches, on the fringes of my gaze, over the old battlefield. I can feel its eyes again, burning bright within me, taking the weight off my bones, lifting my heart and mind.

I turn excitedly, want to wake Markus right away. But he's fast asleep, finally at peace. I know he needs the rest, to heal his wounds. He'll see it when he's ready to.

I turn back and the panther is still there, its fiery, emerald eyes burning as if they were inches from mine.

I leave it all there on the mountain, in the caves. The terror, the pain, I leave it all there, ready myself to move on without it. Something magical is happening to me, something amazing. In the face of everything—all the pain and hurt, the death and danger, the constant terror in which Markus and I must live—there is magic. There's always a hope, a glimmer, and the panther is ours. It's going to lead us, guide us to where we need to be. It's not over yet.

20

I open my eyes and it's dark, starless, moonless. I sit up fast and realise I must have drifted off. Markus is still sleeping beside me and I gently shake him until he wakes up. He looks at me bleary eyed and yawns. I pass him the bottle and he sits up and drinks, gazes around in the dark.

"How are we going to climb down?" he asks, "I can barely see."

"Carefully," I say.

Markus smiles faintly, shrugs.

"We can do this. We've made it this far. Think of the hell we've survived. We just have to focus on what lies ahead, not behind."

Markus nods and I know he wants to be as determined as me, but something is still eating away at him.

"Like always, Markus. I'll lead the way, scout ahead, you follow."

Markus nods and staggers to his feet.

I hold him up, glance over my left shoulder, "No Death, Markus. Not yet."

I turn to face the cliff drop, begin searching for a way around. I can't see any path that looks safe, can barely see anything at all.

"Bandi, here."

I quickly move over to where Markus' outline is standing. He has his back-pack on, ready to move, and there seems to be a ridge leading north, but down off the mountain at least.

"It's a start," he says, and his voice sounds stronger, he sounds ready.

I pat my big brother on the shoulder, "Then down we go."

Hunched low we walk carefully, watching every step, every foot hold. The rock crumbles in the dry earth and huge chunks of stone fall and tumble down from under our feet. I scour for a passage that would take us east, but the drop is still too steep, too high. North remains the only way we can hike.

After a few hours of following the ridge, heading downhill, the mountainside finally opens up and begins to flatten out, allowing us to veer east towards the trenches. A grim smell, one I know all too well, begins drifting up towards us, brought on by heavy winds hurtling up the slope. It's the smell of rot, dead things. I sniff, glance at Markus, who gives me a knowing look, but we carry on without a word.

We pass between two tall pointed rocks that claw at the sky and the stench grows deeper, fouler. The first trenches are just a hundred metres below us now, and we approach more slowly, the night coming to an end. I can see further, the grey battlefield looming low and vast.

There's barely any cover, only rocks, the occasional burnt out tree stump and fallen timber, all of it charred and black. There's just one open area to cross, before we can drop into the first of the trenches. There's a barbed wire fence torn up, blocking our path, and then sandbags piled high around the brim of the trench. I glance around one last time before making a dash for it, stepping lightly as I can.

I leap over the barbed wire but it cuts my ankle mid jump, and I clench my teeth to avoid crying out. I use my hands to vault over the low wall of sandbags and drop into the trench. My chest heaves as I back up against the earth wall, as Markus tumbles down from above, landing beside me.

"I didn't see anyone," I say.

"We should still be careful."

The sun is rising ahead of us and keeps us on course as we wind through the paths, carved in the mud long ago. They're not as steep as they once were; the wind over the years has blown heaps of earth and stone down into the passages. We have to stay low and keep our heads down to avoid being seen, by anyone or anything that might be lurking.

The cause of the smell doesn't hide for long. As we step through the deep, soft earth I spot the occasional hand or foot emerging out from under the ground. There are several bodies half buried beneath our feet. I try not to look at the hands, the fingers, grey and stiff, some chewed by animals. There's a hand with only a thumb left and I end up tripping over it, falling face first into an old boot. I scramble away from the dead limbs, heaving at air but it only makes me feel worse. Moving on, I work hard to keep my eyes up and ahead, watching the way forward. We continue slowly, choosing left or right, sticking as much to the east as possible. Years ago this would have been an ideal spot for salvaging all sorts; weapons, bullets, even food supplies. But anything useful will be gone now, Markus and I know that. Soldiers would have taken it all over the years but that doesn't stop me hoping.

Jagged wires curl and drop down into the furrows, follow their walls with us. We have to duck and slip through gaps to avoid getting cut and all the while the stench of rotting grows worse.

The sun has risen high over the eastern horizon and it's mid-morning now. The haze seems thinner and there's a shade of blue beyond it all.

We finally come to the end of the criss-crossing trenches and I peer over the last edge. A vast plain lies ahead of us, the other side of it far away, lined with black things – trees.

"I don't know how we're going to make it across. It looks like it might take days," I say.

Markus pulls himself up to peer out as well, shakes his head before dropping back down. I land beside him and we sit for a moment. The grim stench continues to waft inside me. My stomach groans but I feel too sick to want to eat. We climb out of the trench, beginning our crawl towards the next spread of earthwork. I take only a few steps before I notice something to the right, a little south. It's a large drop, and I hope it might be an old bunker or something, somewhere we might be able to rest up, away from the dead things. Keeping as close to the ground as possible I jog over, Markus right beside me. But the smell doesn't fade. It grows stronger. I approach the edge of the pit and arch my neck.

I'll never, ever forget what I see down there, as long as I live. The force of witnessing something so horrific rips right through me, from head to toe. I vomit onto the earth, shaking. I vomit again.

"Oh shit," Markus murmurs, "Oh shit."

It's a pit almost fifty metres wide and it's filled with thousands of bodies, stacked up and decaying into each other. Markus pulls me back from the edge and I cough, spit onto the ground.

"Come on Bandi, we're out in the open."

I can't shake the image of black flesh, all morphed together like a giant monster of body parts. The crawling things are everywhere, wriggling slimy creatures, burrowing in and out of contorted faces. Markus leads me on towards the next drop, a passage that leads from north to south as far as we can see in either direction. It must have been the old front line.

We squat in the dirt and I close my eyes, try to picture something else. But anything else that comes to mind is only worse. I try to slow my heavy breathing and put my hand on my chest, think of the one thing that can help me here; those emerald eyes.

Markus speaks calmly, "Our best bet is to follow this trench south. The plain here is too big to cross. We won't make it. Maybe to the south we'll find a shorter path across, or something to use as cover."

We don't hesitate, move on at once. The deep gully carves on in a straight line and we follow it till the sun is directly above us, passing nothing out of the ordinary, just more bodies immersed in earth and sand, more barbed wire and debris.

When the sun is already on its way down, we come to an area where the trench opens up into a large square dip. I stop Markus with my hand; we both freeze. There are footprints in the earth, fresh ones. The marks are clear and defined, unscathed by the wind.

I carefully creep over to them, inspect them closely. There are several, all similar, but I can't tell if they belong to one person or many. They all look like boot prints, large ones, the kind soldiers wear. Markus is glancing around, panicked. I spot something shiny to the left, lift it from the ground. I rub it clean on my jeans, hold it up in the sunlight. The glass glistens, a lens from a pair of glasses. I search around on the ground and find the remains of the other lens, crushed into shards and sparkling amongst the stones and earth. Then I spot the frame, dig it out with my fingers. Tears start to fall down my cheeks as I stare at them, because they look just like the ones my father wore, now bent and twisted, but all too familiar. Markus kneels beside me and sees the glasses in my hands, puts an arm around my shoulder. I sob into his arm as we kneel side by side in the dirt, wishing for our father's guidance, his words. What would he have done?

Markus pulls me to my feet, "I'm sorry, Bandi, but we need to go, the footprints."

I shake my head, try to focus on survival again. I tuck the one good eye glass and frames into my pocket and stand, ready to move on.

There are three dead soldiers lying face down where the trench continues. I see movement on one of them—an arm. So I stare for a while and there is nothing. I know I must just be spooked.

I carefully walk forwards, avoiding looking at the dark forms, trying to keep my gaze up and ahead. I step over one of them and sigh in relief. Then I feel something grab my ankle.

The dead soldier rolls onto his front, his hand gripped tightly round my leg. I scream and Markus falls backwards, thrown by my cry. The soldier's masked face cocks to the side, lifeless without eyes, warden of the end. I try to run but he has a firm grip and I fall to the ground, smacking my forehead on a rock. Blood rushes out from the gash and drips into my eyes, blurring my vision. Other soldiers start rising up from the ground, like the dead coming to life. Markus is backing away on his hands and feet, like a spider caught in retreat, dragging himself to the trench's side. I pull the knife from my belt and stab the soldier in the hand. He wails and releases me. I struggle to my feet.

"Get 'em alive!" one of them growls, and I feel strong arms pick me up from behind.

I squirm and kick and something hard smacks me in the back of the head. I try to look up but everything begins fading fast. Two soldiers corner Markus and he's unable to move. I feel my own hands being tied up, then my feet. I spot my knife glistening on the ground but I can't reach it as I'm carried away, blood still pouring from my forehead. It stings and my head drums harder and harder, the world growing darker with each thrash. Markus makes a final bid for escape, leaping up off the ground and swinging his knife. He manages to smack one of them down with the hilt, a heavy crack to the cheek. That's it though. Four of them circle him and kick him to the ground. They keep kicking him and I try to flail, tear at my hand ties, but I can only whisper, "Markus."

They pull something over my head, a dark hood. It's fastened around my neck. I can hardly breathe. The hood starts to stick to the blood on my forehead and I cough, wheeze. I hear Markus struggling, crying out. There's a final thud. He goes quiet.

"Little rats, how'd they get all the way out here? There's not a town for miles."

"Who cares? Better than catching more deserters. They're young; meat'l be nice'n fresh."

They pick me up by the waist, too weak to struggle, and I'm heaved up over someone's shoulder. Thunder rolls out of the distance, engines approaching, then I pass out completely, don't hear another sound.

21

I wake up to the rumble of engines all around me, like I'm in the belly of a mechanical monster, my body flung side to side, bouncing up and down. I realise quickly that I must be in the back of a truck.

I open my eyes but I'm still in darkness, the hood tight on my head. I pull at my ties, trying to slip my hands or feet free, but the ropes are too tight. They burn my skin. I groan and tussle with the ropes some more, then a whisper shoots up from the darkness, "Bandi?"

It's Markus.

"Over here," I mutter, remaining quiet in case anyone else is around.

I roll towards his voice, hit something cold. I manage to swivel up onto my knees and spin so that I can feel what's blocking my path. Metal bars, a cage of some kind.

"I can't see anything," Markus says, "this damn hood."

"I think I'm in a cage," I tell him.

I can hear shuffling, Markus wriggling around. I hear him knock against something metal, followed by some rattling.

"Me too," he says.

We both sigh, and before we can say another word, the rumbling monster we're within goes silent. The engine clicks off.

I can hear voices outside, several, as well as gruff laughter. The doors creak as they're swung open. A cool wind hits me.

There's the rattling of keys and I shuffle back against the cage, as far from the doors as possible.

"Hello there young one," a low voice sniggers. "Awful long way from home aren't you?"

Strong arms grab me and I'm flung over the soldier's shoulder.

"Grab the other one. Take 'em to the carriages, with the others."

I listen to more jangling keys, then the sounds of Markus groaning and gasping as he's picked up.

The soldier carrying me starts to walk. There are voices all around me, fire's crackling; I can feel the warmth flutter over me in waves as we pass between them. We must be at a one of their big camps, and that's when it hits me. This is the worst thing that could have possibly happened. They have us now.

The soldier carrying me stops and calls to another, "Open it up, come on!"

I hear the unmistakable sound of a trigger being cocked back. My throat is sore and heavy, as if something sharp and bitter was stuck at the very back. I hear the sound of heavy doors being pulled open, then several terrified voices murmuring. The soldier pulls me off his shoulder and cold weak hands grab me and take me, many of them, all weak and clammy.

"Stand back you lot, you saw what happened this morning!"

The murmuring subsides and I'm placed down onto a wooden surface. I hear large doors slide closed and things turn darker still. Then the hands start groping at me again.

"Bandi, are you ok?" I hear Markus cry out.

"What's happening?"

I pull away from the hands, can feel them tugging at my wrist and ankle ties. I realise my legs are now free and try to stand but can't, surrounded by bodies, shapes I can't see, clawing at me. I picture them, savage creatures, dark withered forms, then I feel a tap on my left shoulder.

"It's Death, Markus! I..."

My eyes are tightly shut, waiting for the end. I curl up into a ball, listen as Markus struggles somewhere in the dark. I think of everything we've been through, it all cuts through my head, slicing like blades, each one more painful than the last, all for nothing. *Nothing.*

A hand grabs me around the neck and I hold my breath, embrace the end. But it doesn't come. In a swift motion the hood is pulled away and I breathe the damp hot smell, a sour smell I have not been around in a while.

It's very dark, but I see faces—sad and desperate faces—weak and empty, like ghosts starved of life and a past.

"Bandi!" Markus grabs me from behind and I hug him.

Neither of us lets go. I close my eyes.

"It's Ok, boys, it's alright," a woman's voice says gently.

I look up at a young woman with pretty eyes, but her cheeks are gaunt and scarred, her hair thin and frazzled. She's half-dead from what she's surely been through. Only her eyes show who she used to be, maybe, once. But she's not a monster. And she's not Death.

We're in a rectangular shaped room, no bigger than a bus. It's full of people, thirty at least, all of them grey and frail, all of them quiet and broken.

"Where are we?" Markus asks.

"In a train carriage, at one of their camps. But you're safe for now," the woman says, "They only take a few of us each morning, and they've been already."

"Where do they take them?" I ask.

The woman smiles sadly, "Don't you worry about that, not yet."

I turn to Markus, he looks worried, more so than usual.

"We'll find a way out, we will," I say.

"You keep saying that," Markus replies, "but this is bad..."

I turn away from him and stare at the faces, and realise now that most of them are women, almost all of them.

"Why do they keep you here?" I ask.

The woman with the pretty eyes leans in closer to me, puts a bony hand on my shoulder, "We're all here because they need something from us. If they didn't, we'd be dead."

"Most of you are women, what do they keep you for?" I whisper.

She smiles kindly, tearfully, "Because we are what they need the most. If you don't understand then maybe you're too young."

I glance at Markus and his eyes have deepened, he understands. Her pretty eyes twinkle at me and I realise what she means. It's sickening, and I feel tears trembling behind my eyes, just waiting to fall. But I hold them back.

"What about us?" Markus says softly.

"I don't know," the woman says, "I truly don't know. But you're alive for now. That's something to be thankful for."

Markus grabs my wrist and I face him.

"If they aren't going to, you know, then maybe they want to turn us, make us like them," he says. "It's happened before, it happens all the time throughout history. Armies get boys when they're young, teach them their ways, brain-wash them, so they can be slaves forever."

"But we're not stupid little boys anymore, Markus. I'll never be their slave," I say, "I'd rather be..."

"Lunch?" The voice that calls out is high and scratchy, and is followed by a piercing, demented laugh. It's a wild-haired woman who said it but I ignore her. She's clearly lost it in here, and who can blame her.

"We just have to wait," Markus says calmly. "Close our eyes and wait, for whatever comes next..." his voice trails off and I know he's losing all hope again, just when he'd started to believe we might make it.

"We'll wait, Markus, but not for the end," I tell him. "We'll wait for a way out."

We spend the rest of the day crouched against the carriage sides, picking at the wood, slowly trying to get through it. My fingers are full of splinters. Cuts under my nails bleed onto the wood. It gets very hot during the day and the smell grows worse as unwashed bodies stink in the heavy air, along with the urine, the shit. Most people sit in silence, a few share stories about better days, torture themselves. They focus on the past, not the now. We're all here, trapped, at the soldiers' mercy. We have to get out.

Most of the prisoners came from the cities, were caught fleeing their camps, just like us. Some have been here for days, others weeks. All of them live one day at a time. I can see now that the past gives them hope. That's all they have. But they talk about it like it's a dream, a distant land. They talk to ease their minds as they ready themselves to pass on. Markus listens, watches, and I can see his eyes dull, his chin drooping as the day wears on, as he wears on, ready to accept the end. It's in his eyes, that sparkly green starts to look more like a murky grey swamp.

I refuse to let go, knowing that a power from another world has chosen us, given us a light when dark consumes everyone else, everything else. And I don't intend to forget that magic, not now and not ever. I'll fight to the very end.

I continue to claw, to scrape at the wood, taking it apart one splinter at a time. The air feels cooler, the slivers of light that trickle through the cracks in the wood have dimmed. It's getting late.

Before long, after a day of silence outside the carriage, heavy footsteps approach, along with the sound of something being dragged along the sand. We crawl back away from the doors as they're thrust open. I barely have time to see anything. A flash of moonlight blinds me as a body is thrown into my face, knocking me back.

The doors are slid shut with a force that rattles the carriage, the lock is bolted. I push the body off myself and scramble out of the way. Markus pulls me up and I dust myself off. A woman and a man pull the new woman off the ground. She's barely conscious.

"Stand back," the man says, "She needs air, as much as we can give her."

People step back as much as they can but it's crowded. I'm at the front and I watch as the barely conscious woman opens her eyes.

"You're alright, Kati," the man says to her.

He's on one knee, crouched down, resting her back on his thigh. He ushers the others to move out of the way and helps Kati to the side, where she can lean on the wood.

"It hurts," she murmurs, holding her stomach.

"Rest Kati," the man says.

"I saw the doctor" she whispers, "He's alive. They're using him for an operation. I overheard."

"Thank God he's alive! I thought...it's been so long," Anna, the woman with the pretty eyes, leans down and checks Kati's eyes, her pulse.

"Who's the doctor?" I ask.

The man turns to me, "He was in here, a good man," he pauses, shakes his head, "They took him a few days ago, we thought he'd be dead by now. But clearly they found a use for him which is more than I can say for myself."

"What do you mean?" I ask.

"Rolland was an actor, before..." Anna's voice trails off. Tears fall from her eyes silently. "Kati is dead," she says.

"That's it! Let them come!" Rolland suddenly belts, "They can have me! I'm finished with this place!"

He jumps up, starts to shout, "They fought till there was nothing left to fight over! Now they hunt us, in this poisoned wasteland, rotting in our own filth! And I don't mean the fumes, the smog, the wastes of a war, the end of a world! I mean the filth inside, that lets a man treat another this way! For power, for wealth?!" He starts to laugh, a deep, sinister laugh. "Now none of it matters does it?! None of it!" he screams.

He stares up at the ceiling and spreads his legs, starts to stamp, "I was a warrior! I did my own stunts! Just give me a sword, let me fight you like a real man!"

Markus and I step aside. Rolland beats his chest, starts to punch the carriage walls. His long dark hair is wild, his thick eyebrows cast a shadow over his eyes and he looks terrifying, but so scrawny, so weak even now in his moment of rage, just an angry sack of bones.

Anna tries to grab him, calm him down, but he's in a blinding fury, swinging his arms like windmill blades. He catches her in the face and she tumbles down as he continues his rant, "Filthy rats! Treating us like animals, I'll show you an animal!"

He starts to roar and scream and his eyes are crazed, his lips are cracked and blood has started to cling to his beard. Some of the women are crying as he hammers repeatedly on the carriage door with his head and fists. Blood drips from his hands and his forehead but he doesn't stop.

Before long I can hear hurried footsteps outside, several of them, along with shouting.

The door is dragged open and a gun is fired into the air. We all hush and Rolland looms in the open doorway. He stands bare-chested; the moonlight greys his skin even more, sharpens and shines the blood on his face and hands.

"What is this?!" a soldier cries.

I step back by the edge of the door so that I'm mostly hidden, but can see everything. Seven or eight soldiers have surrounded the carriage, all of them with guns or rifles in their hands, fully masked and fierce. I gasp as I watch them all, the faces from my nightmares here in front of me.

Rolland stands to my left, looking even smaller. He takes a step forward.

"Don't move again, or we'll grab you, gut you, and tear you to pieces," one of the soldiers says.

"You can't treat us like this, dumping where we sleep! You're monsters! You're cowards! Face me, man to man! You're soldiers! Fight me! Fight...."

A blast echoes in the night. A bullet slides out of the dark and slips through Rolland's skull. A pellet of red pops out the back of his head and the bullet burrows into the wood behind him. He crumples to the ground and all sound is sucked away for a second, before the silence erupts into chaos as everyone in the carriage charges for the doors screaming and wailing.

I'm pushed out of the carriage by the bodies rushing from behind me. I fall in a heap as legs kick and fall over me at the foot of the train. Guns are going off all around and bodies go limp in mid air and then crash to the silver sand. I manage to crawl back under the carriage and peer out, desperately searching for Markus. I spot him backed against one of the wheels, a little to my left. I scramble along under the train and grab his arm. He pulls away in shock but then turns and sees me. He rolls under the carriage beside me. We lie for a moment before I shuffle to the right and begin crawling along the tracks, low as I can under the heavy train above us. The wailing is over, the screams have subsided. I glance to my left and can see the dozens of bodies all in a heap; the soldiers walk amongst the dead, checking them.

"Men aren't going to be happy about this," one of them says.

"They rushed us! What were we supposed to do?" says another.

"If any of them got away..."

"How could they?"

I crawl as fast as I can, the rocks cutting my knees and hands, but I don't care. We're out of the carriage—we're free. Markus is just behind me. I can feel his hands brush against my feet as he edges forward and the end of the train is up ahead.

A voice calls out from behind us, "Hang on, didn't you catch a couple of youngsters this morning?"

Markus taps me on the foot and I realise I've stopped crawling. The thump in my chest rises again.

"Yeah, we caught them in the trenches, savin' them for a special night. Why?"

"I can't see them."

"What do you mean?"

"They're not here! No boys!"

We reach the end of the train and peer out. There's a tent up ahead to the right. It looks dark and isolated; safe for now. To the left I can see the main camp; firelight, voices and smoke drifting out of the faint glow.

"Find them! Find them!" The soldier cries, and the few remaining by the carriage start to run, searching.

"Under the train!" one of them calls.

I don't wait another second. Staying as low as I can, I sprint out from under the train and head for the lonely tent. It's less than a hundred metres but it feels like I'm running forever, thinking that each and every second will be the one when they spot us. But they don't.

There are some crates beside the tent and I duck behind them. Markus slides along the dirt, coming to a rest by my side. We both pant furiously. I lean back and close my eyes, trying to steady my breathing.

I turn to Markus, "We can't go into the desert with no supplies. We should check inside."

Markus nods.

I turn and crawl towards the tent, noticing a strange smell in the air. It's pungent, but something I don't recognise.

There's a very dim light coming from inside and I slow down, silent as I can. I lift the tarp covering the doorway and peer inside. There's a bed in the middle of the room, surrounded by old medical equipment. The dim light comes from a lantern hanging over the bed. On the bed a man groans and squirms. There are white and yellow sores all over his skin. Another man emerges out of the shadows at the other end of the tent. I almost tumble backwards from the scare. He's wearing a white coat and he's limping and coughing. It must be the doctor. He leans over the body with his back to me, his form just a silhouette.

Suddenly he turns and heads straight towards the doorway. He stops straight as he sees me. My heart rises to a furious thump again and I'm paralyzed, unable to move.

"Who's there?" his voice is hoarse and weak.

I can't speak. He takes a step closer. Markus crawls up beside me and we both stand up slowly, trembling.

"Please," I say, "don't tell the guards. We'll go now. Please."

The doctor squints at us, standing there in the tent opening, frozen still. He takes another step closer, "It can't be… can it? Bandi? Markus?"

22

I step out of the dark and look up at my father's face. Tears start to trickle down my cheeks and I rush forward to hug him.

"Stop," he says loudly, "You mustn't come closer."

I freeze, study his expression. He's thinner than before, the life eroded from his face, wrinkles are longer, deeper. There are sores on his neck and hands. He coughs, a dry and pained croak. Markus rushes up beside me.

"What's wrong?" I ask.

He collapses to his knees and begins to sob. He stares at us and I can see he's smiling, in disbelief that we've made it this far. And I can't believe it's him, my father, here after so long—so many days and nights spent thinking he was dead.

I rush towards him again, unable to stand back any longer. I want to feel the safety of his arms around me, smell him and cry into his chest. Markus rushes with me and we grab him, squeezing him tightly.

He holds his hands up and covers his mouth. "Boys, please, you can't," he cries, wriggling free and stepping away from us. "And stay back from him too," he says, pointing to the soldier on the bed.

"Are you sick?" Markus asks.

My father nods as he leans against the metal shelves at the back of the tent, still holding a piece of cloth over his mouth.

"It's infectious, something new," his voice comes out muffled from under the cloth. "Cover your faces. You have to leave, now."

We do as he says and pull our shirts up over our mouths.

"But we finally found you, after all this time," Markus says. "We can't leave you. Of course we won't!"

"I can't believe you made it this far, both of you. I can't imagine how..." his voice trails off, he has to gather himself. "I wish we had time to talk about it all. But they'll come soon—the soldiers—to check on me."

"We're not leaving without you!" I sound desperate, my voice more shrill than usual.

"Boys, it's too late for me. Whatever this sickness is, I have it now. The only reason they kept me alive was because they thought I might be able to help them cure this. But I'm not a doctor, not really. And now this has become my end. I caught the sickness hours after starting work on this soldier. This disease is aggressive, and it will take you too. That is why you can't come any closer."

"We'll find a cure! You're a scientist, it's what you do—what you did," Markus says.

My father puts his finger to his lips, "You must stay quiet, please. I wish it was that simple. This soldier here, he was taken ill only a week ago, and he's barely hanging on. With the right equipment maybe I'd have a chance, but here, in this world, it's just not possible. I don't have any of the things I need."

My eyes feel frozen, heavy. I'm unable to react, numb to it all. It's too much, and I start to glance around, searching for a weapon. I can't leave my father again. I can't. Markus squeezes my arm, I can hear him snivelling beside me. My throat aches, my chest is tightening. My heart feels brittle, constricted in a giant snake's coils. Markus falls to the ground and buries his head in his arms. Seeing my father is too much, seeing him and having to leave again.

"When the soldier comes back, we'll kill him," I say, "then we'll get you out of here."

My father is shaking his head.

"We're not leaving you here! It's simple. We'll all die if that's how it goes. But we aren't leaving you. Is there anything sharp?" I start to move around the tent, looking. Markus is still on his knees.

"Bandi, stop, please," my father says.

I ignore him and keep searching. Empty glass vials; we could break them, but the shards would be small. There isn't much else, just some tubing we could use to strangle one of them. Markus is up as well, searching with me.

"Boys, I know this is hard," my father's voice is choked. "Please stop." We turn to him and he continues, "You have to keep moving, you have to go right now. You've been here too long already. I'm dying! And if you stay here and try anything, you'll die too."

His words knock me down. It's the truth I can see but try to ignore.

"You have a chance here—a second chance," he says. "This sickness, it's killing all the soldiers. Hundreds have died. It keeps spreading. It might be from the water, or in the air, I don't know. I haven't been able to find out. But it gets into the blood, that's how it spreads."

Markus and I stand side by side silently watching him, taking him in. My father takes a step towards us, so he's just a few metres away.

"Look at you two, you're both young men. It's in your eyes. You're not boys anymore," he wipes a tear away, "Your mother would be so proud."

Markus starts to cry. I choke it back.

"Where is she?" I ask.

I think of my dreams, I saw them both in the sky, thought I knew what that meant. But now my father's standing before me. Maybe she's alright, maybe she's also alive.

But he shakes his head. "I don't know what to tell you. We were separated in the attack. I never saw what became of her. There was so much chaos, screaming, smoke, bullets. They caught me, held me and were about to finish me, but I told them I was a doctor. It kept me alive."

"We were there," Markus whispers, "We saw them and knew they were coming. We just wanted to get some meat, to make you proud..."

"I am proud," he says, his voice suddenly calm and level. "Your mother and I are both more proud than you can ever imagine. Living in this ruined world hasn't been easy, and you've never complained; always helped, done what you could to keep us alive, as well as yourselves. And now here we are, hundreds of kilometres from the city, and you made it here alone, against all odds."

"We haven't done it alone," I say. "We have a guide—a black panther. We're following it east, towards the sea."

My father stares hard for a second and weakens again.

"I know you told us it isn't there, but we met a man—a soldier," I tell him. "He was dying. He's seen the sea, to the east, he told us. And he was a good soldier, I know he was. He could have let us die but he helped us. He had a picture of a girl he loved. Like the one you always carried of mother."

My father stands, staring at us hard, his brows pulled low and stern. "Listen to me, boys, I have to tell you something," he swallows, choking back a tear. "I lied to you. I lied to you for years. I told you the sea was gone because I didn't want you longing after something that was out of reach. I didn't want you thinking the sea was out there, so that you wouldn't dream of something better than what we had. I thought it would help you to be content with the life we lived, the only life your mother and I could give you." He starts to cry. "But I was wrong. I was wrong to stop you from dreaming and wrong for lying. The sea is out there, of course it is. And you've already made it this far. I know you can make it the rest of the way. I'm sorry! I'm so very sorry!"

My father weeps and Markus and I just stand there, sniffing at our own tears. I want nothing more than to rush forward, embrace my father, feel his strong arms around me. But we can't. He's sick—he's dying. *I can't believe he's dying.*

I'm speechless, devastated, my lungs are choked of air and that weight bores deep inside me. The snake's grip tightens round my heart. I don't care that he lied, I don't care about any of it. I just want him to come with us. The tent is my entire world; my father, brother and I are all that exist.

"We don't care that you lied. We just don't want to leave you," Markus says.

My father smiles sadly at us and nods, then he rises to his feet. "The guard will be back any second; they never leave me alone for long. You must go now. Find the sea."

"We can take him, the guard," I say.

"Him alone, maybe, but what about the rest? There's hundreds. We'd all be dead in a few minutes. Please understand, you can live on together, the two of you. Don't throw that away for an impossibility."

Markus and I still can't move, glued to the spot. My father goes to the back of the room and returns with a satchel. He puts a few flares in it and a flask of water. He's careful not to handle it, keeping the rag wrapped over his mouth.

"It's clean. It's for the soldier here, but he hasn't touched it yet. It's not much, but should be enough for a few days if you're careful."

He slides the satchel along the floor but neither of us move for it. There are footsteps outside; boots on the sand. Markus picks up the satchel and pulls it over his shoulder.

The footsteps grow nearer; I can't take my eyes off my father. I want to implode, fall apart inwards and disappear, all of us together.

"I love you, my sons," my father says.

"I love you." My words come out as a whisper.

"Me too," Markus says.

"And your mother loves you too; both of us always will, wherever you end up, whatever happens. Don't you forget that."

The footsteps are too close now. I can't concentrate on escape, seconds away from losing my father again.

He frantically waves us over to the side of the tent. Markus grabs me and we dart across the tent and duck behind some boxes. A soldier bursts in. He's wearing his mask but I can tell he's suspicious, glancing around.

"Who were you talking to?" he asks.

I'm trembling, my bones are rattling and shaking. I'm exhausted, weak, and I can't handle everything going on inside my head and heart.

The soldier pulls a pistol on my father, aiming it at his head. "Prisoners have escaped; boys, two of them. You seen 'em?"

My father shakes his head as if he's not been listening, in a daze. "What, sorry? No I haven't. Your comrade," he motions to the sick soldier, unconsciously breathing on the bed, "He doesn't have long left. I was just putting him at ease, helping his soul pass."

"You a bloody priest now, Doctor?" he lowers his gun.

"Could you get me more water? He's dehydrated, his lips are cracked. It won't save him, but it will ease his end."

"Waste of water if he's dead already," the soldier says.

"But his pain is excruciating. Imagine it was you?"

"I'd let my comrades have my share, like a true soldier, a true man!"

"Suffering does not make one a man."

"Easy, Doctor, if you weren't infected I'd come over and beat you senseless for that. Stop all this high and wise nonsense. It won't do you any favours."

Markus squeezes my arm. His face is panicked, his lips all twisted. I start glancing around, looking for another way out. We could try slipping under the tent's side, just behind us, but he'd see the movement. The tent is so small that it's a miracle he hasn't noticed us already.

My father suddenly speaks, "Then could you bring some water for me?"

I watch his face from the shadows, those warm blue eyes that always made me feel better, the thin lips that would stretch across his wide face as he smiled, and I knew everything would be alright. I stare at him knowing this will be the last time, but at least this time I know, though in a way it makes it worse.

Suddenly Markus is heaving me up. I notice the soldier is gone and the way out is clear. We move straight for the tent's opening and peer under the tarp that blocks it. We can see the faint outline of the soldier marching away towards the main camp. I turn one last time, finally empty of tears.

My father smiles sadly, but his eyes are alive, telling me everything will be alright.

"Always trust each other. Always love each other. Stick together through all that comes your way. You're brothers—family. Believe in that, no matter what." His voice is calm, it gives me strength, as it always does.

I nod, raise a hand slowly. "Goodbye, Father," I say.

"We'll make it. And we'll build an army. We'll find you again," Markus cries.

My father raises his chin proudly, "Just make it to the sea first. If stories are true, you'll find safety there."

I peer under the tarp. The soldier is on his way back, slowly stepping towards us. There's no time to ask what he means, what these 'stories' are. We both stand and take one last look at our father before darting off into the darkness.

23

We run hard and fast and the sand is dense under our feet. Nobody follows us. Either they don't care that we're gone or they've given up. It doesn't matter which, I'm just happy to be free of their grip; but we're alone again, Markus and I.

I try not to think about my father, sitting there dying. I try to focus on our escape, on getting across the sandy plain by day break, when they may send patrols again, trucks and cars that will thunder over the sand at speed and catch us in no time.

Something dark looms in the distance, black jagged shapes spiked high towards the moonless sky. The sun is close, its power starting to fight over the craggy fingers on the horizon. The hot brim is dead ahead and I know that means we're heading east again. I've heard it from my father too, now. The sea is there—he said it. We're not just following the words of a soldier. We're following the words of our father, the greatest man I know. My feet plod heavily and sand seeps into my socks. *My father is the greatest man I know*. The thought won't leave me, and I know Markus and I will be back one day. Back to save him, no matter what it takes. Bandi; *man warrior*. It's in my name, and I'll kill them all if I have to.

My lungs heave and finally we have to stop. We bend over, hands on our knees, panting and coughing in the grey. The tall and jagged figures are close now; trees, black and burnt by fires years ago. I picture the flames that must have cloaked the land here, smoke leaping up towards the sky and blocking out the sun. Fumes thick and poisonous, that then came raining down after, killing all that was left.

I'd never seen a forest before, but I knew what they once were; green and lush, filled with birds and flowers, more colours than I've ever seen. Markus says that in the time before, we lived near a forest just like this. Our parents would take us for long walks on Sundays. Markus would collect leaves and give them to me. I'd run them between my fingers as I sat in my pram, laughing under twisted branches.

It all feels more distant than a dream. Those are days I can't remember, can't understand how they ever could have been. It seems like a myth, a fantasy. Seeing the charred skeletal remains makes it even more so. How could something so dark—so dead—have ever been something beautiful?

I rise up and Markus takes a few strides forward.

"At least the trees will give us cover," he says.

I nod. "I can't believe it's a forest."

Markus shakes his head, "*Was* a forest. I don't know what to call this."

I stare at the black branches, cracked and broken. As we move forward the ground softens, black and white sand grows lumpy and thick. It smells like burn, bitter and earthy. The air around us feels empty, as if we're walking through a ghost. It grows colder as the sun rises, a strange sensation.

"It's ash," Markus whispers.

I bend down to sniff the ground and run the soft grains through my fingers. Markus is right. We're not trekking over sand anymore. A thick layer of ash covers the ground, flaky and light. As we step we kick small piles into the air. I watch the clumps break apart and float up and swirl between the tree trunks. The trunks are wider than any trees I'd ever imagined. They rise up as high as some of our city's tallest buildings. Above them the sky has turned silver, blackening the trees further, as they delve down towards us, deep into the ash-sealed earth.

"Something doesn't feel right," I say.

Markus looks at me, glances over his left shoulder and shrugs.

I force a smile, and on we go; no Death yet, our father's words still fuelling us forth. I have a strange feeling that our journey is coming to an end, though I don't know what that means.

We continue to walk forward and the haze thickens above us, the dead forest grows darker. Our footsteps send puffs up into the air. They rise like balls of smoke, as if our feet are re-igniting the flames that tore down the green so long ago. White flakes begin to fall, tumbling towards us, dancing through the web of branches. I look up at the sky, watching the white fall down from the gun metal above.

"It's like snow," Markus says, "Do you remember snow?"

I shake my head.

"When it was cold the rain would freeze. It fell to the ground as snow. You could make balls out of it and throw it. Father and I made a snowman once," he begins to choke up, goes silent for a few seconds, "You put the hat on its head."

He reaches down and picks up a handful of ash, tries to push it together and tosses it towards me. It explodes into dust as he swings his arm.

I watch the ash come down for a few more seconds, then move on through the trees, Markus' footsteps behind me, plodding softly along.

The air is so bitter that I can taste it on my tongue, feel the stench pouring in through my pores. It's the remains of all that burned, what lingers of the flames. My mouth is dry, the air growing colder as the day goes on. My head begins to ache and I know I'll need water soon.

We move from tree to tree and nothing changes. The forest goes on and on. I notice Markus' footsteps have stopped, my own are the only sound. I turn and see him sitting, leaning against a charred trunk, staring up at the flakes that tumble even thicker now, blanketing the sky above.

I sit beside him and close my eyes for a second.

"We're going back for him, you know," he says, his voice crackling.

"Of course we are."

I open my eyes. He's looking at me, his thick brows low, and I know he means it.

"We need to find somewhere to rest," Markus says. "And we need food, more water too."

He pulls the flask my father gave us out from the satchel and passes it to me. I take a last sip, swirl it around in my mouth, swallowing it slowly. Markus takes the last few drops and we hop up, carrying on, trudging hard, knowing we need to move quickly or we'll join the trees, dying here in the empty grey.

Hours pass and still nothing changes. I grow weak but stagger on with Markus right beside me.

A shape looms up ahead, a low square—I'm sure of it. A building?

It's just beyond a few tree rows. We couldn't see it earlier through the thick ash that continues to drop from above.

"Can you see it?" my voice is quiet, raspy, my throat completely dry.

Markus shields his eyes, "What could it be?"

I rush forward, keeping low and crouching beside a tree just in front of the building. It's a cottage, half burnt to the ground, the roof completely blown away. A staircase rises up into nothing, a second floor also completely gone—burned away. The dust of its remains surrounds us.

"I don't see anyone," I whisper.

"Let's be careful anyway," Markus says, "Fast and silent."

"Ghosts," I whisper.

We move forwards on hands and feet, like panthers. We crouch by the west wall of the cottage and move along it to the right, around the corner. There's a hole in the wall here and I stop to carefully peer in. It's dark and I have to wait for my eyes to adjust, shielded by my hand from the falling downpour. There's one large room inside; any walls that may have once separated the cottage are long gone, burnt away like the rest of it. There's no one inside, just the stairs leading up and a small table in the centre of the cottage. I slide through the gap and Markus follows. It's a relief to be out of the ash storm.

We dust ourselves off and I follow Markus over towards the table. There's a can of peach juice, and a tin of lentils.

I glance at Markus, my heart is charging, and I grab the can of juice, holding it up. In black— in what must be charred wood—someone's written on the can. The writing is thick, rubbed on with a finger. I turn the can in my hand revealing all the letters around it, the word, 'Poison.'

Markus takes it from me and studies it.

"It has to be a trap," I say.

"It looks un-opened. What if it's a trick? If it was poison, why would someone write that on it? Maybe they want us to think its poison. Maybe its fine?"

I stare hard at my brother, shaking my head, "Who would have left it here?"

"I don't know, soldiers?"

"It doesn't seem like something they'd do."

"No, it doesn't."

I pick up the lentils. There's a skull drawn on the side. I show Markus and he takes it, shrugging. "We should take them, who knows how long before we find anything else. It's not worth the risk yet, but later on it might be."

The grim reality hits me hard but I nod in agreement. It might be a trick but if things get really bad we may have to put it to the test.

Markus slips the tins into his bag and we look around the rest of the cottage. There's no basement and nothing else inside. We move up the stairs and they lead to the open second floor, where the staircase carries on up towards nothing. We stare out into the forest but the ash fall is even wilder and we can't see far. We move back down the rickety stairs, out through the front doorway that leads east, or at least what I think is east. It's been a while since we've seen the sun.

As we walk on the ash doesn't wane. I grow weaker, our pace slows and still the dead forest goes on and on. Small dark figures loom ahead, not far away, delirium setting in.

We stop and sink low to the ground, crawling through the ash, our clothes coated in black and white. The figures are not moving. I squint through the falling flakes, staring hard. Soldiers—at least three or four—one of them kneels and the others stand around him. My heart thuds heavily. We lie completely still and nothing moves in the forest. The figures stand frozen.

"Are they..?" Markus whispers.

"I don't think they're alive, they're like...statues," I sigh.

Markus stands up slowly and I follow. We move towards the small band of soldiers till we're only a few feet away. Their faces are grey, expressions of agony and desperation smeared onto their un-masked eyes and mouths.

They're made of ash. Long dead and somehow upright. Their eyes are open but gone, hollow and empty like stone. I take a few steps forwards and reach out, touch the soldier closest to me. As my outstretched finger reaches the figure, it explodes into dust, the ash falling, disappearing into the blanket on the forest floor.

I turn to Markus who moves beside me and crouches, staring at the sullen forms.

"They must have been here for years."

"What could have done this?" I ask.

"I don't know. In the wars they used some horrific weapons, capable of turning entire cities to dust."

Their arms are twisted towards the sky, writhing in pain. They deserve it, for all they've done. Rage rises within me. I try to picture their pain as they fled, only to die, here in this charred forest forever. I hope it hurt, I hope they could feel their hearts burning.

I burst into raging tears, charge forward and kick another one of the soldiers into nothing. I charge at another, swinging my arms until there are none left and no trace they were ever there.

I fall to the ground panting and Markus grabs me from behind. "Save your strength," he says.

My chest is heaving, "I just *hate* them so much! They took *everything*, and even now they're all that's left, they're *still* taking!"

Markus stands up and pulls me to my feet, "There will be a time, Bandi, a time for us to fight back. But now we have to keep moving, otherwise we'll die here, like them, and become piles of ash. And then *they* will win."

I shake my head, tossing out the anger and gaining back my focus on the task at hand.

I walk on with new vigour, plodding heavily as the forest darkens towards night. *There will be a time.*

The monstrous trees go on, row upon row of dark empty graves, scratching and clawing at the sky. But the sky grows heavier, sending a smog down below that thickens the haunting air. Breathing becomes harder and still there is no end in sight.

Time thins and vanishes, there is nothing here. I begin to a feel a thud in my head and my vision starts to blur, images blending into one another, the dim light between the trees flickering gently. I know I can't hold on much longer and I keep waiting for that cold tap of a long dark finger. But it doesn't come, still only Markus walks beside me, Death is out of sight for now.

I whisper to myself, "Not yet."

A dark shape finally stirs the forest ahead, another building, barely visible.

"Markus," almost no sound comes out of my mouth.

I hiss loudly, two sharp bursts, and point out ahead. Too weak for stealth, I push myself up and stumble along. Desperation drives my thoughts, nothing else. I fall into the building and use it to hold myself up, Markus beside me. It's all too familiar, the feel of blackened walls. We reach the corner and move around, tumbling inside through an all too familiar sized hole. There's near complete darkness, but I know the room I'm standing in immediately. We're inside the same cottage, the very same.

My heart sinks and specks appear in my eyes, but it's not the ash rain, we're sheltered here at least. The specks flash more violently, thickening and taking over my head, my sight turning completely dark. I cry out, hearing my own voice echo, growing more distant. Then I fall, lose all feeling—no pain, no thought—just black emptiness.

I can hear a tapping, rhythmic creaking. I open my eyes slowly as I listen to my brother's frantic, cold breaths. He's sitting in front of me, leaning against the cottage wall. There are shadows around his eyes, the light of a flare casting them deep into his face. He's holding his knees up against his chest, tapping his foot and rocking back and forth.

Even in the orange glow his cheeks look pale, like he's seen a ghost. I sit up slowly, my head still hammering ferociously. There's something in front of him, the tin of peach juice, casting a long thin shadow along the floor towards me.

"What is it?" I ask. "Markus?"

He shakes his head, "I had to. I *needed* to."

"What are you talking about?"

I'm trembling. Frantically I crawl towards him. I lift up the can of juice and a powerful wave passes over me. The can is open, half the contents gone.

I stare at Markus, tap tap tap goes the sound of his foot, growing louder.

"Markus," I whisper. "What did you do?"

24

I reach out and grab my brother, pulling him towards me and I bury my head in his shoulder.

"It's Ok," he says. "I think it's Ok."

I pull my head back and give him a hard stare before picking up the can. I hold it up to my nose and sniff it. The scent is sweet, syrupy and rich. My mouth is salivating and I glance at Markus, who has a slight smile on his face. He nods, assuring me.

His eyes are grey, his cheeks pasty white. But maybe the juice is Ok. It's too early to tell. I'm still shaking, shivering, and my stomach is tied. I feel I could vomit any minute and I don't wait any longer. I put the can to my lips and tilt it. The sweet peach nectar comes pouring over my tongue. I swirl it around and swallow before taking another big gulp and flashing my brother a smile.

"Have the rest," he says. "I had half. We need it now, or we'll never get out of this forest."

I slowly sip the rest, feeling the sugar surging around my veins, charging my body with new life. I smack my lips between swigs, moving and swishing the liquid up around my teeth with my tongue. I save a final sip and hold it out for Markus.

He shakes his head. "That's yours."

I lean against the wall beside him and sip it down, breathe slowly out, closing my eyes.

"If it kills you, it'll kill us both," I say. "Always together, like father said."

"It'll be alright," Markus whispers.

And there I sit, eyes closed, feeling stranger than before, but stronger. I hope—wish—that the strange feeling is just in my head.

"It's getting lighter outside. We should move out soon, while we're feeling strong." Markus has a skip in his voice. "The juice won't keep us going long. We'll save the lentils for later."

The flare begins to die and the cottage goes grey again. The cold feeling returns without the rich glow. Markus is on his feet, smiling at me. But it's a sad smile. His face looks gaunt. I feel like I can almost see his bones through his skin.

"Are you alright?" I ask.

"He tries to widen his smile, but it only assures me something's not right. The peach juice—what if?

A howl breaks out of the deathly silence. Markus drops to his knees and shoots me a horrified glance. We both scramble up beside the cottage opening, perched either side of the empty doorframe. Another howl echoes through the trees, this time louder, and another. I slowly peer out and can't believe my eyes.

I get tighter against the wall. Markus is staring at me.

"Wolves," I murmur.

There are at least six, circling the cottage, sniffing the ground. Markus peers out for a second, rests his head back against the doorframe. "What do we do?"

I glance around. "The stairs!"

I dart towards them and creep up to the top. Markus follows, heavy on his feet. A step snaps halfway up and Markus falls, crying out. The howling continues, growing more frequent. I scurry down and grab Markus' arm, pulling him up through the crack in the splintering wood. He grimaces in pain from a large cut on his thigh, but we can't treat it now. We move up and out into the open and lay beside each other, using our arms to push us towards the edge. We look down at the pack of wolves—I can see eleven of them, scuffling about in the ash, turning in circles, snapping their jaws. They bite and growl at the air, but they don't advance. They stand back, around thirty metres away from us, waiting for something.

One of the eleven wolves is larger, almost twice the size of the rest. I can hardly control my breathing, feel my head growing fuzzy again as I watch the giant beast start to slowly skulk towards us. It stands just below, a few metres from the cottage door. I grab Markus' hand, squeezing tightly. There is no strength in his grip, none at all.

The behemoth in front of us howls and all of its companions hush, the forest grows silent. Then the leader rises up onto two feet, and a face—a human face—looks up at us from beneath the jaws.

"Show yerselves little wans, or me brodas and I will tear ya ta shreds."

He isn't a wolf but a man, with a wolf pelt tied up over his shoulders. The head of the pelt is his hood and its paws run down over his arm. I glance at Markus and we both slowly push ourselves up. We look down at the man and he stares at us hard, pulling a huge machete from his back.

"Come down little wans," he says, "tell me what brings ya to me forest."

We both nod vigorously and move down the staircase, hopping over the broken step. We don't say a word to each other, too afraid to speak. We step out amongst the trees and the man is waiting for us, machete still drawn. The wolves are lying down on the ashen bed just behind him. They're calm, almost friendly.

We stand side by side and the man stares at us, looking us up and down. His eyes are a sharp blue, silvery and pale, almost glowing in contrast to his dark skin. A knotted, black beard scatters his cheeks, hanging in tufts off his chin. He's covered completely in grey and black fur, the coats of many wolves. Long black dreadlocks hang down from under his wolf hood. The ears point up sharply and the upper jaw hangs down to give him a brow of teeth. His eyes are fierce, but somehow kind. He lowers his machete and takes a few steps towards us.

"You be brodas," he says.

Markus and I nod.

"You have da same eyes, you share dee same story, like my brodas and I," he holds his arm out, motioning towards the wolves; his pack, his *brothers*. "So tell me; where two young brodas like yerselves come from?"

"A city to the west," I say weakly, "Our home was destroyed. We're heading east..."

"Towards the sea," Markus finishes.

The man studies us for a moment, "And what do ya think you will find at da sea young brodas?"

"We don't know," I say.

He walks towards us and we step out of his way as he passes into the cottage. We follow him and the wolves stay outside, watching the forest.

Standing in the dim light, just beside the table, he finally stops, sits and crosses his legs on the floor.

"What are ya names?"

"I'm Bandi, this is Markus."

"Seet down young wans. Tell me yer story. How did two such as yerselves make it so far? Let Farkas, guardian of da wood, in on yer marvellous tale."

We tell him our entire story, from our life in the city, to the day of the attack. We tell him about our journey so far; the escape through the city; the mountains; Garth. We tell him about being captured and finding our father, and the sickness.

Farkas listens carefully, his head bowed. The silver light of the forest drifts in through the open doorway as morning passes towards noon. His face is scarred, wrinkled, aged from years among beasts. When we talk about the sickness he looks concerned, shakes his head.

"A sickness risin in dee west, where da sun sets, where da end began. It will spread no doubt. It always spreads."

He looks at Markus uneasily, asks him to come closer. Markus steps forward and Farkas touches his forehead with the back of his palm, shakes his head.

"Your big broda always so pale?"

I shrug; Markus looks worse in the daylight, pasty and drained of any colour.

"We drank a can of juice we found in here."

Farkas stares at me sternly for a moment, "You should not have done dat."

"Why? Is it poison?" I ask.

"Ah, that I don' know. It's a game I'm playin', a game of chance. Does wan take dee risk? The masked wans neva know."

"You poisoned it?" Markus' voice is weak, barely a whisper.

Farkas shakes his head, "No I did not. But who knows weder it be tainted. Many tings from dee old world are. That's da game of it."

Markus steps back and shrinks to the ground, tucking his knees under his chin and cradling his legs. I sit down beside him, struggling to swallow Farkas' confusing words.

"I painted dee words, but it's just a game. Is it a trap, is it a trick? Is dee juice safe, left out for all ta see? Or is it bad to dee bone, for da bone. Does it rot life away?"

My heart falls freely into a deep emptiness, hurtles my stomach forward. Farkas, the wolf man, wrote the words as some kind of experiment. Would those who find it heed the warning, or think 'it must be a trick.' The can was unopened, but could be too old and long unusable. It could be our end.

Markus' ill appearance leads me to think one way. But then again I drank it too, and I feel fine, or at least alright. My head is spinning and my stomach is in knots. But it could just be my mind playing games; exhaustion, dehydration, no nourishment in my blood at all. I clench my fists, but my grip feels weak, and grows weaker as I realise it is so.

Farkas becomes concerned with the cut on Markus' leg; staring at it, tilting his head and grumbling. He kneels down by us, swinging a bag off his shoulder. The bag is also made from wolf fur, and from it he pulls out some bandages and a flask of water. He unsheathes his machete and cuts open Markus' jeans, slicing open the upper leg where the blood is. He rinses the cut with the water and the sticky clumps dilute and wash away. The gash underneath isn't too deep, but stretches up the side of Markus' right thigh from the knee. Farkas wraps the bandages around the cut; soft, white wolf skin. He ties it up with some string and stitches up Markus' jeans. All of this he does with great speed, but perfect accuracy. Then he moves up to Markus' shoulder, where Garth's bite is looking worse, pussy and yellowed around the scabbing centre.

Farkas grunts, "Does not look so good."

He takes out some matches and begins to run the flame over the point of his machete, heating the metal. I glance at Markus and he's terrified, because we know what's next.

"This will hurt a great deal, but will save yer life. Hold yer little broda's arm, tight now."

He grabs me and closes his eyes. Farkas places a strip of wood between his teeth. Markus bites down on it and I don't dare look, closing my eyes too. Markus' scream shrivels my heart, but it's over quickly as he falls unconscious. Farkas holds him up and then gently rests him down, wrapping up the wound in fresh wolf-skin bandages. The blood on the machete glimmers as Markus pours with sweat.

"Good as new," Farkas smiles, "He's just out from dee pain. Big broda's a brave wan."

Farkas goes out and sits amongst his wolves, gives them all water. Markus realxes into a gentle sleep. I hope it was the cut or the bite; some of the ash could have gotten into his blood. I try to convince myself. But it keeps slipping into my mind—maybe it *is* the juice? Then there's the other possibility that scares me beyond all hope. *What if it's the sickness?*

Later on, Markus wakes up some time in the afternoon. His arm still hurts and he's as a pale as he was. But he sits up and manages to drink water that Farkas shares with us.

"Where do you get all this water from?" I ask.

"In dee mountains, deep under da stone. Da same mountains where you met dee ludacrous poppy man."

He tells us his story—or at least part of it. He lives in the forest with his pack of wolves, roaming the trees. He never talks of before, as if it were another life, another person. He talks as if his life began here in this ashen forest, born among wolves.

"Da first ting I remember is dee eyes. Dem circled me and dee piercin' blue shot straight into me soul. I knew den, I was wan of dem, born again."

The panther's eyes appear in my mind, like the time I first saw them in the distance, but also within me, deep inside. I stare hard at Farkas and he stares back, as if he knows, as if he can see something in me.

He continues a moment later, "Dem live on instinct. Dem remain as wan. Our own kind gave dat up long ago. There's nuttin left but dee urge to kill and destroy. Dem be machines inside, filled only wid cogs an wires. Da power of da beast is dee only pure ting left."

The black panther; our own animal companion. When we had no one else it came; the ever elusive panther that eludes us still. It's yet to come and guide us out of this forest, but it will come back when we need it, it always does. Our brother.

Night has fallen and the cabin has gone dark. Farkas cleans his own wounds and we listen to the wolves outside as they watch over us, barking to one another; communicating. I know that this man before me, of all people, knows about the power of the beast.

"There's another thing we haven't told you, the reason we made it this far, the reason we always knew which way to turn."

Farkas watches me intently, Markus too.

The air grows still and silent, "We've had a guide, a protector. It's a black panther. I first saw it in the city, the day before the attack on our home. It comes when we're lost, showing us the way. It always comes at dawn or dusk, in the haze. It's never close, always in the distance, but I can see its eyes inside me, in my soul. Like how you see the wolves."

Farkas stares solemnly, his pale eyes flicker bluer, opening up oceans from his past.

"Dee bond between da soul of dee human and da soul of dee beast is stronga dan all else. Especially now, when all oder bonds be burned. You follow dat panther young brodas. You follow him whereva he leads you."

Farkas leans back and stretches his legs. I can barely see his face anymore, only the glint of his eyes. I wrap my hoody around myself tightly, noticing it's turned very cold.

The enormous man-wolf rips a pelt from his back and tosses it to me. "Get some sleep. My fallen broda will keep ya warm. It's a long way to reach dee oder side of me wood."

I settle down, Markus beside me. We pull the wolf fur over us, it's soft against my face, and I feel instantly warm and safe.

Farkas goes outside to sleep with his own brothers. I turn to Markus and whisper, "I think we're going to make it."

He doesn't reply so I sit up to look at him. I know he's pretending to be asleep, taking deep breaths on purpose. He's always done that, when he's angry or sad.

I lie back down and can't shake all the awful things we've been through. I hold back the tears and try to relax my eyes. My mother and father's faces won't leave my head, and I ache for them both, more than anything I've ever needed. Everything grows darker inside me, the hope I had subsides; but the panther's emerald eyes keep the hope burning, won't let it die.

25

"Wake up young wans."

I open my eyes and Farkas is leaning over us, speaking softly. "We cannot stay in wan place for long."

"I thought these woods—your woods— were safe. I thought the danger was behind us." Markus speaks nervously.

Farkas shakes his head, "Be no safe places anymore. Dee masked ones are always trying to stretch dem power to da east. Dem won't stop till der's notin left, till evertin is dead and burned, den dem will turn on eachoda, and der will be truly notin left."

He passes us his flask and we both sip, sitting up and crossing our legs. Farkas sits opposite us and keeps his eyes on Markus, remaining quiet but uneasy. I look closely at Markus and I'm sure he looks worse; weaker and paler, if that's even possible.

"You talk as if you know what's going to happen," Markus suddenly speaks up.

Farkas shifts his weight, tilts his head. His dreadlocks are so long they brush the floor as he leans to the side.

"Let me tell you wan last story, before ya continue on yer marvellous journey. Dem came from dee stars long ago. And after livin among us for a while, leavin behind relics of dem past, dem retreated below dee ground. From down bellow dem watched as we blew eachoda apart; as we killed dee sky and dirtied da waves. We burnt everytin' up till dee air was a poison, dee sky blacker dan dee hell below dem.

"Dem gave us a chance, left clues of der wonders; pyramids dat pointed to dee great outa space dem came from. Dog faced, dem laughin' at us now, causin' dee earth we walk on ta tremble.

"Dem been playin since dee beginning, chosin' our leaders, havin' dem lie, pull a mask ova our eyes. Behind it all it was just anoda game. So now I play games too, wid my brodas, and I fight dee end; what else is der ta do? I defend my forest, and we brodas—you brodas—we live on. And till we all fall, burn away like da rest of it, dem can laugh on. Dis game ees not ova yet."

Farkas stares sternly for a second, then smiles for the first time, exposing a warmth I didn't know he had. I know his heart is good and pure. He's fierce because he has to be, and alive because of it. He's adapted to live on, like Markus and I have to. We've made it this far; stealthy, silent, like shadows—panthers.

A huge smile stretches across my face and for a second I feel strong again. But a howl erupts from outside the cabin and Farkas' face turns grim, "Time ta go! Quickly!"

I jump to my feet and pull Markus up.

"What is it?" he asks.

But Farkas is pacing out the cabin doorway in a storm, and the howling continues, several more wolves joining in.

Markus almost falls straight back down and I have to hold him up for second to steady him.

"Are you alright?"

"I'm fine," he says, annoyed I asked. "Outside, come on!"

We rush out into the ash and the early dawn sky is grey. The wolves are circling, growling and grunting. Farkas stands to the right of the cabin, staring out to the west. A thick smog has set in and we can't see far through the milky haze. The bitter stench rises, twisting my empty stomach.

We run over to stand beside Farkas as he continues to stare out through the columns of trees. "Dey're on dem way!" he says. And my heart thuds heavy and fast once again.

Farkas goes down on one knee, his face level with ours. He swings his bag from his shoulder and pulls out a white, wolf skin wrap. He unravels it to reveal two small blades inside. He passes one to each of us, and I hold the dagger up in front of me. The metal is old, doesn't shine, but the blade is sharp; both edges and the tip. I feel the handle, open up my palm. It's made of bone, carved in the shape of a wolf head; fangs and ears, sharp eyes.

"Just in case," Farkas says.

"What is it? What's happening?" Markus cries out weakly.

Farkas sniffs the air, bends down, listens to the ground and then sniffs the air again.

"I can smell dem, many of dem, dead walkers. I can smell dee black of dem hearts."

I stare out at the rows of trees, black and monstrous, now more than ever. The blanket of white is thick, the smog heavy. I tuck the blade into my belt, readying myself. The wolves line up beside us, hunched low and ready to attack, gritting their teeth menacingly. Shapes begin to appear out of the white, emerging out of nothing. They appear like the dead, black-masked silhouettes armed with guns and clubs. They march towards us in a long line, silent, floating through the mist swirls – at least twenty soldiers.

A familiar heave in my chest returns as I struggle for air, my breaths too quick to control. I steady myself as they march on, moving steadily, rigidly locked in tight rows.

"Soulless, heartless, all dats left. Let dem come!"

Farkas rises to his feet and strides forward towards the advancing enemy, swinging his machete through the air. He howls at the early sky and the wolves all begin to howl and bark, their snouts turned upwards.

Farkas turns back to Markus and I, "It's time for you ta go little brodas. Dis is not yer fight. Look fer dee trees marked wid da claws of dee wolf. You will find supplies der; wata, food. You go on now, follow dee panther, and you will find where ya need to be. Ya will fight on."

"Thank you," I say.

He nods, holds out his machete, pointing to the east. "Go! Maybe I'll see you in anoda life, a better wan, or maybe in dees wan. Maybe dee end is not as soon as I tink. Now go, be gone wid ya, der's gona be too much blood fer young eyes!"

Markus and I turn immediately, charging off the way Farkas pointed, trampling hard across the ashen forest once again. But this time, hopefully on our way out.

Behind me I can hear yelping, growling, ferocious cries. After a few gun shots ring out into the mist there are no more, only the sounds of slicing blades, loud cracks as club and wolf meet head on. I can hear Farkas roaring like a beast and I have to stop and turn, need to see the fight. The ash blows up into a powdery cloud as I skid and swivel to face the battle.

Wolves circle and dive at soldiers, chewing and biting at their legs. Clubs ram down upon fierce and furry heads. The battle goes on beside the dark shape of the cottage, framed by the bands of tall trees. I watch Farkas' large silhouette slide through the ash, slashing his machete left and right, soldiers falling at his feet.

A hand grabs me weakly from behind, "Bandi, what are you doing?"

I turn to face Markus, "We should help them."

Markus shakes his head, "We have to go, there's nothing we can do. They'll be Ok."

I turn and watch, counting the fallen forms. There are many, some soldier, some wolf. But I'm too far to tell them apart; just dark shapes on the ground, reddish on the white and black speckled ash. Farkas fights on, swinging his machete with such force, continuing to roar and howl as he cuts through soulless flesh, until only a few remain. But most of his wolf brothers lie dead.

The remaining wolves dart off after three soldiers that begin to flee, back towards the west. Farkas follows, hunched low like one of them, his long arms almost touching the ground as he hurtles off through the trees.

"Bandi, look!"

Markus points out over my shoulder, as two of the fallen shapes rise up from the ground, peering around wearily. They stand up—soldiers—and slowly start to run in our direction. They've broken the line, the wolves are gone. We're on our own.

I spin around so quickly I fall into a momentary daze as I begin to run, following Markus who struggles on ahead of me.

The ash fall has completely stopped. I glance up at the sky, at black branches criss-crossing over me, but now below a clearer sky. The haze has thinned, the sky washed with a little blue. The sun still isn't visible; its circular outline is out of sight. We have to move straight or we'll be lost. And the soldiers continue to head our way, moving quickly to escape the wolves, unaware they're even chasing us.

I start to glance around for a solution. Trees are all that surround us, row after row. Large trunks rise up, the perfect spot to hide. I hiss, two sharp bursts, and Markus spins around while continuing to run. I point to a tree as we pass it and duck down by its roots. Markus nods and turns, throwing himself down behind another tree to my left. I crouch on my feet, pulling up my hood. I press my back up as close to it as I can. Eyes closed I wait, listen to the footsteps growing closer, heavy boots pounding down over the ash. I picture the dust clouds; their masked faces. I hold my breath and sink lower.

Slowly I peek, as footsteps thud right beside me, passing right between the two trees Markus and I are crouched behind. They're right there, moving slower now, one of them dragging his leg and limping along. Their breathing is hoarse and heavy. One of them coughs but they don't say a word. They don't see us. They carry on forward, heading east. I look to my left, seeing Markus' pale and pained face. He blows out a huge puff of air and leans his head back against the charred wood.

We wait a while, watching the soldiers grow small until they are nothing more than black beetles on the horizon.

Markus crawls over to me. "We should go now, while we can see them. I'd rather be stalking them, knowing where they are."

I nod and hop up. "Fast and silent."

"Ghosts," he whispers.

Markus begins to rub his hands onto the tree, rubs the black over his face and hands. I do the same, following his lead, till we're both completely covered.

We move off side by side, running at first, then slowing as we start to catch up. The soldiers are walking now, struggling with fatigue. I start to feel delirium again.

The forest grows neither lighter nor darker. It all remains the same. My legs grow weaker, my vision spins a little more. As we move on I become less and less sure we're still headed east. There is still no sun to show us the way.

I scour the trees for Farkas' sign, but none are marked with claws. There are thousands of trees, the chances of us finding one are non-existent.

Walking on we eat the lentils; I cut the tin open with my wolf dagger. The fluid inside is the best part. The lentils themselves are hard, transforming into a dry paste in our mouths as we chew. It doesn't matter, I feel better after. I can see that Markus does to, surer on his feet, his injured leg seeming less of a problem.

And then I see it, a third shape on the horizon, stalking on all fours. I know straight away its no wolf.

I grab Markus, pointing at the panther in the distance. He almost falls from the force of my excited grasp, peers through dazed eyes. It's showing us the way east, showing us the way out of the forest.

"Can you see it?"

Markus squints but his eyes are so bleary with sweat and weakness that I know he can't see a thing. He can barely stay on his feet.

I watch the soldiers continue to drag themselves after the panther, heading the same way. I wonder if they can see it, hoping they can't. I hope they get lost in here, never to come out. I want them to end up like the ashen statues we saw, nothing but dust, ready to be blown into nothing by a slight breeze. But the air is still for now and we follow our panther brother towards the sea again, this time two soldiers in our way.

"But not for long," I whisper to myself.

26

The panther appears from time to time, always far ahead, glimpsed through trees, beyond the soldiers. They stay on course; by chance, or maybe they know, maybe they too are following its steps.

Noon passes and I begin to feel weak again, my mouth bone dry. Markus looks weaker than ever, the whites of his eyes are yellower than usual, even against his painted face. Those terrible thoughts return to me again: the sickness, the poison, his wounds.

"Can you keep going?" I ask in a whisper.

He nods but doesn't say a word. The soldiers remain about a hundred metres ahead. Every once in a while they turn back, but only for a second, perhaps to be sure they have escaped Farkas' wolf pack. We keep close to the trees, using them for balance as much as concealment. We move tree to tree, I count my steps between each trunk; eleven, ten, eleven.

After a while the distance between them grows larger. The forest is growing thinner. I tell Markus and he seems unsure. But I continue to count; eighteen, seventeen, twenty. I can see a sheet of light ahead, and the panther flashes between the branches for the last time before disappearing into the brightness. And soon the soldiers are there too, breaking out into the open, the forest's edge.

"We made it," I whisper to Markus,

"Not yet, little brother."

We move forwards carefully, approaching the last few trees staying low to the ground. The soldiers have stopped just beyond the final row, a great plain beyond them, turning into hot yellow sands in the distance—a desert.

Markus and I lie by the roots of a large trunk just inside the tree line. The soldiers sit, take off their masks and lean back against some rocks. The sky is smoggy but silver in the deep afternoon light that burns from the other side of the forest, casting pale thin shadows over charred bushes dotted across the plain. The fire that once raged here looks as if it spread far beyond the forest's edge, all the way to the desert beyond. The black earth stretches on for miles.

"It's like being by a volcano," Markus says.

"It looks dead, like hell," I whisper.

"At least we're out of the forest."

"How do we get past them?" I ask.

"We could move down the tree line, and come out further along."

I shake my head. "No, they'll be out there. They made it past Farkas, we have to stop them. Something tells me soldiers don't usually come this far. This isn't their land."

"Because who would want to come here?"

I stare out at the bleak path ahead of us. Like tar it sits, the spiked shapes of burned out brush strewn all over the flat.

"I don't want to run away, not this time."

Markus looks at me, sees the menace in my eyes. He nods, "Ok, we'll wait till night. Then we'll cut them down, for everything they've put us through."

"For mother and father," I say.

"For us."

Markus and I stare fiercely at one another for a moment, then settle down into the forest floor; watching, waiting for the darkness, our old friend. In its gloom we'll be shadows. We'll take everything they have. Then we'll kill them.

The two of them soon settle down, coughing in the evening air. Markus and I watch silently, lying on our stomachs behind the final row of trees. The land blurs into the smog on the horizon and before it nothing moves, nothing climbs towards the sky. The total silence feels heavy and sad. The soldiers barely say anything to each other, the occasional low mumble rolls towards us but we can't make out the words. The sun finally disappears behind us, somewhere to the west beyond the city from where our journey began.

After endless hours the night has fully set in; the soldiers have fallen into a deep sleep, snoring gently in the dark. A silver patch in the sky lights the plain, the moon struggling through thick cloud and dust.

"We'll take what we can and kill them only if we have to."

"We should kill them anyway," I say.

Markus shakes his head, "You shot Garth. How did that feel? What are you going to do now, slit their throats while they sleep?"

"We can't leave them alive. They'll tell the others and come after us."

Markus shakes his head, "Only if they see us."

I stare out ahead, listening to their snores and gripping my wolf blade in my hand. "Which they won't," I add.

I imagine slicing a throat, visualise the red sliding out like spilled paint as the body quivers and dies. My fingers weaken around the bone handle and I tuck the knife into my belt.

I turn to Markus. "Only if we have to. We have all night to get away. Hopefully they'll die out here anyway. They look weak and injured enough."

"We'll search them and then go, straight ahead," he says.

I nod. "Not a word from now on."

Markus points to the soldier on the left nearest to us. I point to the one on the right, facing us on his back, a couple of metres beyond Markus' target. I crawl forwards, my knees and hands sinking into the ashen floor that grows thinner as I move on beyond the trees. I meander to avoid the scattered shrub and rocks. I move past the first soldier as Markus creeps up behind him and waits for me to get into position. I move slowly, one limb at a time, slowing my breaths to silent gasps. I move around my target so that I'm facing Markus, and crouch behind the soldier. I search him with my eyes first, avoiding the empty stare of his mask. His snoring has grown louder and his coughs irritate my scattered nerves. His chest has slashes across it, his black uniform is open; blood congeals on the frayed material. My breathing quickens and my hands tremble. I close my eyes, trying to focus and remain calm. There's a small revolver on his belt. The ammo straps on his chest are empty and the only other thing I can see is his torch sticking out of his left trouser pocket. His club is set down on the ground. The handle is wooden, the length of an axe. Fastened to the top, with barbed wire and rope, are several large shards of jagged metal, spiked in all directions. The metal shines dully in the pale glow and the blood washed over the spikes appears black, glistening and moist, covered in clumps of ash from the forest floor.

I slowly move around to the soldier's right, kneeling by his side as he continues to face the smoggy sky. I reach out, take the club and move cautiously away, quickening as I get further. I drop the club carefully in a ragged mess of twiggy brush. Just in case.

Markus does the same; quietly moving before crawling back out of the dark seconds later. I creep over beside him and he points to the soldier's left pocket. Around the pocket the material is wet, something inside is seeping out.

Markus looks at me, asking with his eyes. I nod and ready my knife, hold it to the soldier's throat as Markus reaches slowly towards the pocket. His ghostly face is torn with fear and his hands are trembling. He moves his hair out of his face and tries to steady his breaths.

But his hands tremble like branches in the wind and he pulls away, leaning back and shaking his head. He crawls backwards and away, motioning for me to follow. But it's probably water in the pocket. We need it. The plain ahead looks endless, hot and dry.

I turn back towards the soldier and lean down by his pocket. He rolls onto his right side. The movement jolts me. I lean back, holding my breath. He tucks a hand under his head, mutters, and my heart thrashes about, rocking my stomach and my head. But then he settles down again, returns to the quiet hum of his snores. And I can see the top of a flask now, poking out of his pocket slightly.

"Bandi, don't," Markus whispers sharply in the dead quiet.

I ignore him and reach for the water. I narrow my hand into a point and clamp my thumb and fingers around the lid. I pull gently and my grip fails as my hand gently brushes the soldier's side. A black tunnel flies momentarily through my head and I almost pass out, my heart in overdrive.

Still the soldier doesn't move, doesn't wake.

I reach in again, this time cupping the lid, ensuring my grip won't give. I pull but the flask won't move, so I pull harder. Finally it starts to jerk out, a millimetre at a time.

I pull harder.

I gasp as the flask pops out and flies straight from my hand. It sails through the air; the second seems like an age. It clocks the soldier right in the ear and he fires awake with a wail.

I reach for the flask as the soldier flails around, blind in the dark. The other one jumps to his feet, calling out, "There, right beside you!"

I roll onto my front and propel myself up onto my feet and forwards. Markus is running backwards and spins round once he sees I'm following him. The flask is in my hand.

A force jolts through me as I'm jerked back, a hand grabbing me by the ankle.

"Got him!"

The flask flies out of my hands, smashing into a rock on its way down. The water explodes out in a silver spray, splashing over the dead earth.

I don't have time to think about it and I pull my dagger from my belt. The soldier pulls me towards him and I swivel onto my back, stabbing at him, catching his shoulder.

He wails, "You little sod!"

Markus pulls me up from behind and we charge off, our sore feet thumping across the dirt.

The soldiers are up and after us, their snarls and grunts are getting closer. I glance over my left shoulder, two of Death's masked minions hurtle towards us, and my legs start to wither. My breathing is raspy, my heart exhausted and pounding.

One of the soldiers jumps to the left, avoiding a rock.

The crack shatters the plain.

A gigantic flume of smoke bursts up into the sky, dust scatters, sending the soldier to the stars. The blast knocks me forwards and all goes dark, silent.

27

The bells in my ears keep on clanging. I keep my eyes closed and scream, but there's nothing, no one; just bells, bellowing endlessly. Forcing my eyes open, I lie spinning in the dark. I spit dirt from my mouth, squint and struggle to see. There's smoke everywhere, and dust. My thigh is agony and I hold it, feel it's wet—bleeding. As I sit up and stretch my leg, something stabs into me, something in my pocket. I reach in and pull out a hand full of blood, and shards of glass—the lens and glasses—shattered and destroyed. The one thing the soldiers didn't take from me, but not something I can worry about now.

I cry out in pain as I roll onto my front and begin crawling around, searching for Markus. There's coughing just ahead of me. Markus is on his hands and knees, gasping for air. There's blood on his cheek but he seems alright.

On go the bells, and I mouth the words, "Are you OK?"

Markus' eyes turn wide, as he looks at something behind me. I spin and pull my dagger from my belt again. The soldier lumbers towards us, falling now. I take a step back, standing beside Markus, his dagger also drawn. We both run forwards, thrusting our blades into the falling body. Our charge knocks him back and he falls. We land on him, our blades spearing from his chest, pinning him down. He's still, dead, as the bells slowly ring out.

I fall to my knees and Markus falls onto his back. We both pant and struggle for air as the smoke begins to clear. We cough vigorously, my chest a fiery pit. For a few minutes we don't move, don't say a word. Then finally I stand and step towards the soldier. I glare at his masked face, his neck crookedly falling back. I rip our daggers from the corpse.

They slide out easily and I turn, holding one of the blades out for Markus, offering him the handle. The soldier's blood coats my hands, and I stare at the red. This time I don't feel a thing. I don't feel sorry at all. Soldier's blood is on my hands, and I'm glad. I feel satisfied. Stronger.

Markus takes his dagger, and I heave him up by the wrist. We peer through the smoke, searching for signs of the other soldier.

"We're in a mine field, Bandi." His eyes aren't afraid, just defeated and deeply sad.

"We'll just have to be supremely careful."

I try to sound assuring, though my voice trembles. I picture ourselves flying up, exploding into pieces – one bad step, that's all it would take.

"Follow my footsteps," I say, spinning in the smokey dark.

"Which way?"

I have no idea. The blast knocked us up and the smoke hides any signs. I stare through the thick grey, searching for a beckoning glow. It isn't there, only dark mist churns. Closing my eyes, I search for it from within, turning slowly in a circle, searching, searching. I feel something pulling me, something warm and familiar. I stop and open my eyes.

"This way," I say.

It could be my own head forcing me to find a solution. But I have to believe it's something more. I step forwards, small steps, always looking down. And the smoke continues to clear. The plain ahead is basking, laying long and wide. I step lightly, on the balls of my feet, and Markus follows, tight on my tail. We move along like that, as one.

I scour the ground, looking for signs of anything that could be a mine; a trip wire, loose sand or earth. We stick close to the rocks, where planting mines would have been harder. But still it's too dark to move quickly, and we step slowly on till dawn finally brings us a comforting glow and a clear direction in which to head.

We slip carefully over patches of barbed wire, moving along tightly stuck to one another, eyes on the ground. We walk lightly, easing our feet onto the earth before planting our full weight. The sun slowly rises ahead of us and it begins to grow hot, sweat starts to seep from my forehead. Every part of me wants to speed up, cross this desert as quickly as possible. But the mines from wars long ago are our chains, holding us back. Speed would only tire us and make us thirsty. And we have nothing left to drink.

I try to remain focused on the task at hand, navigating through the mines. Small patches of loose earth show us where the bombs are buried, thin tripwires and metal hooks poke out of the jet black ground that now sparkles with vigour.

Soon the mine field comes to an end. We walk for a hundred metres without seeing any signs on the ground. We move on side by side; relieved to be alive, but feeling dread towards our bleak outlook.

"What now?" I ask.

"We keep going, I guess."

We stop for a moment to scour the horizon. Through the distant glare, the thinning smog of the plain, I see a tall shadow, pointing up towards the sky.

"Can you see it?" I point.

Markus stares hard, shielding his eyes with both hands. "What is it?"

I shake my head, "I don't know. But it's something."

"And that's good enough for me."

I smile and turn, continuing to plod over the dust. And black slowly starts to turn golden, the fire's dominion coming to an end, replaced by hard sand beneath our feet. We aim for the tall shape on the horizon, casting an even longer shadow in our direction. As we near it, stumbling weakly, I can see it's a building of stone with a tower climbing high, still intact. It's the only structure anywhere for miles.

Behind us the forest looks days away, a wide, craggy heap in the distance. Ahead the desert grows on, and we continue towards the only thing we can see. The lonely tower to the east.

It's almost noon when we reach it. We lie on the warm sand and stare out, watching for movement. There's none.

The wind picks up and brushes sand over the flat. The grains hit me like tiny needles. Markus takes off his hoody and wraps it around his head, leaving just a slit for his eyes. I quickly do the same, but still have to squint to stop the sand from scratching at my vision.

The building is long and grey, with a tower rising up from one end. The desert is pebbly around us, sharp on our hands as we lie pressed to the ground. Atop the tower an iron cross rises even higher. It's a symbol I know, one I've been told about and seen before. The building ahead is an old church.

"How can it still be standing?" I ask. "Everything else is gone, destroyed into nothing."

Markus shrugs. "Religion was a big part of the old world. It meant a lot to people. It's one of the main reasons wars were fought and people were killed in masses."

"Why did they care so much, to fight wars over it?"

"I guess it gave them something to believe in, when everything else was miserable and hopeless."

I stare for a moment, trying to imagine believing in something so much that I would kill those who didn't.

"Why don't people believe anymore?" I ask.

"Some people might," he goes quiet. "I know Szilvia did. She had a gold necklace with a cross on it. She'd put it on whenever she went above ground to salvage."

I raise my eyebrows. "You didn't talk to her, but you know that?"

"Shut up," he says, but he smiles, though sadly. "She was nice. It protected her. If only she wore it in the metro station. Then maybe…"

I shrug, "It's just a symbol."

"Yeah, after what happened—the old world ending the way it did—who could believe in a God," he says.

The wind subsides, the desert is silent as the church tower looms, its shadow a stump in the high sun.

"But believing in something does help," I say. "We have the panther. Look how far we've come."

Markus turns, stares at me for a moment, then nods, "Maybe you're right. Maybe that's why people will always find things to believe in. Something beyond what we can see."

I turn away. I know what he's saying. He's still doubting whether the panther is real but I swallow my anger and try to forgive my brother. I'm too weak to argue and know he's even more so.

"Shall we take a look? Maybe we'll find water."

I try to sound hopeful, though doubt is hanging hard inside me.

"Churches have always been sanctuaries, for thousands of years. Maybe they still are."

"It's not like we have a choice." I open up my arms, glancing from left to right at the emptiness around me.

"That too," Markus whispers.

We rise up in the hot silence, confident we're alone, and stumble on towards the church's large wooden doors that sit tight and tall ahead.

28

The doors are worn but still strong and solid. There is no handle and I try to grip the crack between them with my sore fingers. They're clamped hard together. I continue to scratch and claw, desperate to prize them open.

Markus pulls out his dagger, slides the blade into the crack and pushes hard. Still the doors won't budge. I squat in the dust and slide mine in below his. We both push on the dagger handles and the door creaks but still doesn't budge. We move around the side of the church and look up, searching for another way in. The wall is solid stone and windowless. At the back I spot a single opening, high off the ground.

"There," I point up, kicking the dust as I slide to a halt.

The window is circular, the glass bashed in. Tiny colourful specks gleam on the sill, scattering flecks of blue, red and green onto the sand at our feet. I begin to climb the wall, using the gaps between the large grey stones as footholds and hand-grasps. I move up with ease, a few stones at a time. Grabbing the window ledge, I push up with my feet, scraping my knees against the stone until I can see through the window. The ledge is littered with pieces of stained glass; the cause of the scattered colourful rays. I squint to block out the spray of light and settle my knees on the stone. Some of the glass crunches beneath my jeans, slicing through. I groan as I slowly move my hands forward, careful to avoid the shards. I pull my hoody from around my head and place it down, covering the ledge in a protective layer to crawl across. My face is sore, blistering from the sun and sand. My eyes stream and my vision blurs as I steady myself.

Kneeling on my hoody, I peer down into the darkness. A circular spotlight, obscured by my shadow within it, is the only light to fall inside. Dust floats amidst the rays and I struggle to see what's down below.

The church looks bare, the floor littered with splintered wood and rubble, not much else. A stone altar is below me and I can see objects shining faintly on top of it.

I swivel my neck and look back outside, down at Markus who's looking up at me, squinting.

"It looks empty. We should search it—rest here at least. It's been a while since we slept."

Markus stares blankly and removes his hoody from around his head. He steps closer and begins to climb, struggling to grip the stone. Sweat pouring from his forehead has made the black across his face run, revealing the sickly skin in streaks beneath it. We need to find supplies. He won't last much longer, that's a sure thing.

As he nears me I reach down, grabbing his arm and holding onto the window frame with my other hand. Markus reaches the ledge and pulls himself up so that he's looking in, right beside me. I shuffle my knees backwards, let my legs hang and lower myself with my arms. I turn my head as I dangle, flat against the stone. The altar is right below me, a wide slab littered with gleaming objects; gold.

I drop, fall onto the metal that clatters around me. I lie for a second with my eyes closed.

"Bandi," Markus whispers from the darkness above. "Are you Ok?"

His form is silhouetted, high above me, surrounded by a circle of white hot light. I sit up and squint till my vision adjusts. Standing, I move forwards to look over the objects; candlesticks and small statues of a man on a cross. Sadly the candlesticks are empty and I shake my head, annoyed I expected anything more. There's a smell of burn inside, a hot dryness that feels heavy and harsh. I catch Markus as he drops down and we both turn to investigate.

"There would have been rows of benches here once, probably all taken for firewood, or to build more useful things," Markus whispers.

The church is around thirty metres long and twenty wide, the whole building one large chamber. The main doors are in front of us, almost totally obscured by a large barricade of various tables and benches, heavy things.

"The benches are right there," I point to the barricade, "There's your something 'more useful'—keeping people out."

Other than the altar, the rest of the church is bare, scattered with broken pots, burnt pages and other useless trash.

I notice a trap door in the corner, a square wooden panel on the dusty floor. Again there is a key hole but no handle, no latch to tug at. I try with my blade briefly but move on, eager to look around the barricade and see what I can find.

Cautiously I step towards it. Markus follows just behind me and together we inspect the old furniture, hoping to find something useful.

Three benches are propped up, making a wall against the doors. A low table sits just behind, chairs wedged under it, locking it all tight. There are chains on the door too, huge bolts, locking anyone inside with no hope of escape, without a key.

Under the table there's a large rug draped over something, and I pull the heavy wool away. Markus grabs me as I lurch back. A sharp smell bursts out from under the rug and hits me. There's a body underneath.

"Why couldn't we smell him before?"

Markus drags me up weakly. Both of us almost crash down again but we steady ourselves.

He leans in towards the body, "He's been dead for a long time. Most of the flesh is gone, the worst smelling parts."

The body looks like a man and he's mostly bone. Even his clothes have started to rot away. He's dressed in thick wool, which seems mad in the roasting heat.

"He's dressed for the cold."

Markus shrugs, "Maybe he died at night. It gets cold at night."

"Or maybe it wasn't always so hot here."

Markus is sitting now, leaning against a table leg beside the body, eyes closed. He nods, barely moving his head.

"What do you think happened?" I ask.

"He must have barricaded himself in," Markus' voice is drained. If we weren't in total silence I wouldn't hear a thing.

"Why would he barricade himself in?"

"He was probably hiding."

"From what?"

Markus finally opens his eyes, stares blankly at me and motions towards the door. "From everything out there. I guess he thought..." Markus loses his voice, tries to swallow painfully. "I guess he thought this church could be the sanctuary it once was."

I think for a moment, as my brother's eyes once again flicker shut, about this man here all alone, living his last days out, waiting to die in the cold. He didn't have a brother to keep him strong—to be strong for.

I turn my attention to searching the body. As I lift an arm I almost drop it, sent into a sudden panic as I notice the hand is gone. I check the other and it's also missing.

"Markus," I whisper.

He opens his eyes, then kneels beside me, taking the arm by the wrist. He examines it. "You can see where the bones been crushed, not a clean cut."

"Who do you think did this?"

I glance around, suddenly feeling a darkness creeping inside me, sitting, waiting.

"Him."

Markus is pointing out over my head, up high towards where the tower opens up. A dark shape, dangles from a beam at the tower's peak. It swings gently from side to side.

"Is it..."

"Another body," he whispers.

"Do you think this man hanged him?"

"Maybe he threw himself off, once he cut this poor fella's hands off."

"You think?"

Markus shrugs, "Without hands, this one couldn't climb out; not the way we got in. He wouldn't have been able to move the barricade either."

I glance around, envisioning Markus' story. The withered form stalks from left to right, as he bleeds out over the floor. I scour the ground, noticing dark splashes of blood, now brown and crisp on the stone.

The cruelty is terrifying and my breaths begin to charge. I shake my head, "It's not right."

"It's why things got so bad, because people did those things."

I lower my eyebrows, feeling anxious and sick. "How could anyone?"

Markus stares at me hard, confused. "We killed men. We let everyone die. All for what—to get to the sea? To save our own lives?"

I can't believe what he's saying. "How can you compare what we did to this? What's wrong with you?"

He just stares blankly and shrugs, "Once you're a killer, it's not a big step to this."

"We killed a few soldiers, who've killed so many. They deserved it! Those people all died because of them! It wasn't our fault!"

Markus just stares at the ground, "Who are we to decide who deserves what?"

"Markus, what are you talking about?" I take a hard step forwards, grab my brother by the arm and, gripping him tightly, I pull. "What's wrong with you? Tell me!"

He falls to his knees. His eyes look empty. "We killed them all! I killed them all!"

I step towards him. "What the hell?" I grab his shoulders and shake them. "Snap out of it!"

He starts to laugh maniacally. "What are you doing?" he says, pushing me back.

"Stop it, Markus. You're acting insane."

His eyes turn fierce and he jumps to his feet. He steps back, glaring at me, his teeth barred. I move away further, my heart racing and sweat pouring down my face.

"Just calm down," I whisper, "Don't be so dramatic."

That pushes him over the edge. He cocks his head, raises his eyebrows and runs at me. He swings his fist and catches me in the jaw. It knocks me back a little but I don't fall. I leap at him and tackle him to the ground.

We both clatter to the stone and he grips me with his thighs and pins me down. He draws back his fist, but he stops. His arms go limp and he starts to cry. I push him off and he collapses, rolls up into a ball and cries, "We should have been there!"

I kneel by him and grip his shoulder as he shakes. "Then we'd be dead, too," I say. "We're just tired. It's time to rest up. We'll figure out what to do later."

My tongue is bleeding and I spit, adding more blood to the stained ground. I stare up at the limp form of the hanging man, and a little joy lands inside me as I say the words, "I bet he has the key to the front door, and also to that wooden hatch we found."

Markus doesn't say anything as I stand up.

"I'll be right back," I say.

An ease flutters through me, hope's welcome return at the prospect of supplies. I just have to figure out how to get up there.

I drift my gaze up the walls, up to the beams, along them to the tower where ropes hang, leading straight up to the dangling figure. I tuck my dagger into the back of my belt and jump up onto the table, along the benches and up onto the top of the door frame. Staring up at the long wall of grey stone above me, I take my first grips, plant my foot and begin to ascend.

29

It doesn't take me long to reach the beam at the top of the wall. I pull myself up onto it and squat, facing the way ahead—a long thin plank of wood crossing the entire length of the church, supported by beams branching out to the sides. I slowly rise up onto my feet so that one foot is behind the other, and begin stepping carefully along.

"You're almost there," he calls up. "Just please don't fall."

Markus is on his feet, watching me nervously. If I lose my balance I'm dead, but I try not to focus on that and edge further along the beam. At last I reach the other end, so that the circular window we entered through is just across from me, but out of reach. I firmly grip the stones that jut from the wall and begin my climb up the tower, to the next beam above.

The wood criss-crosses all the way up to the spire, and once I'm onto the first beam, it's just a case of grabbing the next and pulling myself up one beam at a time. My hands blister and sting on the dry wood that creaks below my feet and growls under my hands. So I move quickly, never staying put for too long.

I reach the fifth and final beam, squat upon it, looking up at the body hanging just above me now, from a heavy iron clasp that probably used to hold a large bell. I slowly rise up and reach high, trying to grab the body. It looks like it was once a man, dressed in a robe, now skeletal and dry, dust more than anything else. It's lighter up here in the tower; slivers of yellow nestle in through cracks in the roof tiles. The man hangs peacefully, glazed in warmth up here. It's a shame I'm going to have to cut him down.

The other end of the rope to which he's tied, hangs down along the tower wall just in front of me. I take it and wrap it tightly around my hands. I pull as hard as I can but the rope won't budge.

With my eyes I follow it, up along the wall and out across the open tower just below the roof. There it's tied to an iron bar, looping down to where it's hooked around the dead man's neck. I do the only thing I can; I climb the rope towards the very top.

I grasp it between my feet and use the stones as hand holds. I move up like that, till I'm level with the hanging man. I let go of the wall with one hand and pull out my wolf dagger. I aim, pointing the tip, then swipe at the rope.

It tears, hanging on by a thread, and I give it a final slice. The body drops, hurtling down towards the ground, where it explodes in a cloud of dust and bone.

"Markus?" I call down, loud as I can.

"I'm Ok! Get down here."

I hug the wall and slide down along the rope to the beam again. I hop down till I'm on the final plank, the one that leads all the way along to the top of the doors. I feel like it's all over, like I've made it. I move along the beam quickly this time, too quickly; my balance wavers. I slow down, watching Markus examining what's left of the hanging man.

"He was a priest," Markus whispers.

"How do you know?" I ask, stopping just above him.

"The robes, they have crosses stitched on them."

I continue to move along, "You find anything..."

My foot misses the beam, and down I fall. I cry out and grab desperately at thin air, hooking my left hand onto the wood as I tumble down. My back pops and jerks as I swing by one hand, my weak fingers slipping.

"Markus!" I cry, as my hand finally loses all strength, and I drop.

All sense of gravity goes as I tumble, turning in the air.

I hear Markus' shouting fade to nothing—am I dead?

The crack hits me like a tram, smack on the shoulder. Everything is white, and I'm sure this is the end; something so simple, a lack of concentration. I gasp for air, there's no room in my chest. But I'm breathing—still breathing.

I roll over and flail my arms, desperately trying to push myself up to see what's happened. I grab at a leg, push a body off of me—Markus.

Dazedly, I try to sit up, struggling to balance. I stare at the beam above and it spins like a propeller blade, so far away. Surely I should be dead. And I realise it wasn't the ground I hit, but Markus, my brother who rushed out to try and break my fall. I turn, the world still a dusty spiral. Putting my hands on my brother, I steady myself, "Markus," I call, tapping him, holding him round the shoulder.

Finally he coughs, kicking into life, but there's another gash on his head and I notice blood on my hands.

I kneel, putting his head on my lap and lay him on his side. He shakes and trembles as I call to him. "Markus?"

All he can do is groan, his eyes closed, pain shutting him down.

"My leg," he groans.

I rest his head down on my hoody and inspect his wound—it looks fine. I go to pull up his jeans and he moans in the dark as I touch it.

"I need to see," I tell him, sliding the torn material up to his knee.

The leg is swollen, twice the size it should be, his ankle bone barely visible. The heaviness in my stomach grows, settling in deeper. This could be the end of everything. Markus can't go anywhere like this.

I wrap him in the rug we pulled from the handless body. He drifts in and out of consciousness; his head also took a smack as our bodies collided. The priest is in pieces, parts scattered over the dirt, fingers and feet, larger bones broken in half. The head is obliterated to dust and bits of hair clump to shards of skull.

I find a small knife tucked into the old robe and run my finger over the golden cross that's stitched onto the heavy material.

I sit beside Markus and curse our luck—no key, no supplies. And my brother's ankle might be broken, but I don't want to think about that. My head is still spinning, a draining ache grows constant and strong. I lean against one of the benches, close my eyes, and hope that when we wake up things will be better, somehow. They can't get any worse.

30

My dreams are full of screams and dark shapes. I walk a black desert, all alone, and I can't find Markus anywhere as I call his name, eluding shadows; searching and never finding what I'm after.

I wake up with a jolt, covered in sweat, and the church is dark, but lit with a delicate silvery glow. It's the moon. I slowly stand up and move towards the window, spotting the white sliver sitting high in the sky, clear for my eyes, for the first time in what feels like forever. I watch for a while, until I hear Markus scuffling restlessly, his arms gently flailing.

I return to his side and gently shake him awake, ending his nightmares. He blinks wearily, and I help him sit up.

"How's your ankle?"

"It hurts."

I gaze at him hopefully, searching for a sign of improvement. But his eyes are still yellow, ill, sad.

"I'm sorry, about before. I don't know what happened. I lost it for a second," he says.

"It's alright. I think after everything, we're both allowed to lose it once in a while."

He chuckles but it turns into heavy coughing. I tap his back until he goes quiet.

"I couldn't find a key," I tell him.

He coughs again, clearing his raspy throat. "That's because I have it."

I jerk my head up, fixing on his eyes. He smiles slightly.

"What? How?"

"I picked it up while you were climbing down, along with this letter. Both were inside his robes."

Markus pulls a ring of keys from his pocket; the iron jangles as it hits the dirt. Then he pulls out a piece of paper and unfolds it.

"I haven't read it yet. Where's the satchel?"

I grab the satchel from beside the handless body and toss it to Markus. He pulls out a flare. "We won't need this out there."

I nod and Markus ignites the flare, illuminating the letter in a fiery glow, revealing black letters scratched onto the page.

It reads:

'Lord have mercy on us all, in these, the final days. The black army marches over everything, skies torn with the darkest of metal, the thickest of smog, whilst fire carves away the living, ripping all that is good and green from our world.

'This, our last sanctuary, I protected till the very end, which is nigh, creeping around the desert's edge. Even here I could not escape the inevitable end, and for long I waited. They came in the night, the first travellers in a long time. But they were not from the vast army of masked soldiers—they were others, a sign from you, a message?

'What choice did I have? What else could I have done, my Lord? For you, it seems, are long gone. This waste at our feet is the end, brought on by your own creation, and as souls bleed into the earth, they bleed on empty ears. Horrors I have seen have revealed the truth – you left us long ago.

'Tell me it is not so. Send me a sign of might, or of beauty? Perhaps I have waited long enough now, perhaps I am writing to only myself, perhaps my words will heed no answer, no true purpose, other than to declare my own end.

'The travellers are an offering to the dark army. They cannot escape, cannot leave. And they tried to, so many times. Hurt them—I had to. For without them, surely I would be hacked down in passing, like everything else. Now it is too late, and I cry

out for mercy. The evil is too vast, too powerful, and it has taken me with it.

'He bleeds below for my survival, his cries strangle my heart, choke the life, the good. So it is time for me to pass, whether it be to heaven or hell. It no longer matters, only escape matters, and I can see just one road that leads out of here.

'Faith dies here with me, for no souls of grace still roam this land. I stepped outside for the final time last night and saw what had become of forests, saw no sun in the sky. I heard screams eminating from all directions, drifting through each other in skies lit with gunfire, rising smoke and cracks that would have scarred the heavens.

'Faith dies tonight, in my hands, and I take it gladly, for it belongs not in such a place. I will not wait for the horseman, for molten rock to fall from the sky. I will not be dragged away! I leave on my own terms, here and now.

'This blood on my hands will be the last, for I cannot fight the ill that surrounds me. The deeply disturbed feeling in the air has consumed its final pure soul. Let the end come. You turned your back on us, rightfully so. And as I write this letter it dawns on me, we are in your image, our eyes and minds were bred by you, my Lord, yet here we are, cutting each other down.

'It dawns on me now, as I write of all that has happened here, on this final page of my life – perhaps you, my Lord, were never really here at all.'

The flare starts to dim and Markus gives it a shake before resting it on the ground.

"I guess you were right," I say. "Sounds like he cut off this one's hands."

"Yeah," Markus says. "And he couldn't deal with what he'd done. As well as everything else."

"He gave up on his God?"

"He felt alone—completely alone. He felt like he'd been deserted."

"He could have made friends with the travellers, rather than killing them."

Markus stares at me and shakes his head. "I guess the fear was too much. Fear of the soldiers. He thought giving them others would save his own life."

I stare at the letter but can barely see the words without the flare light. Thankfully dawn is close by, the sky outside is draining of darkness.

"What worries me is that he keeps saying 'travellers'. Where are the others?"

My eyes move slowly over the ground, hovering above the wooden hatch. I glance at Markus and he's nodding. "We'd better be careful," he whispers.

We crawl over to the hatch with our blades drawn, Markus dragging his injured leg through the dust, carving a trail. He pulls out the keys.

"There has to be supplies in there, otherwise, I don't know what we'll do," I say.

Markus fiddles with the keys. "I just hope we don't find anyone alive down there."

"That would be impossible," I say.

He shrugs. "I would have said the same about a lot of things that have happened since we left the city. But they happened."

He jams a key into the lock. It fits but won't turn, so he tries another on the ring. It's far too big, and I wonder whether it's the key to the front door.

After a few more tries he finds the right one and the lock clicks as he twists the key. The sound echoes through the large empty space, up to the tower. We both go still. I listen to my thumping heart, sure that whoever is down there can hear it too, if they're alive.

I slip my fingers under the wood and slowly pull the hatch open. We both peer down, eyes pulled tight as we struggle to see into the pit. The stench burns the inside of my skull, and I fight the urge to vomit. But it's too dark to see what's below.

Silently, I creep back to the barricade and grab another flare. I crack it and hold it up to the opening, but the light's not strong enough. The depths of the pit remain unknown.

"Drop it in," Markus whispers.

I let go, watching it sail down.

Dark shapes—hands and faces—emerge out of the dark and sit in the red flarelight. Twisted expressions look up at me, black and withered, agony tugging at their eye-sockets and cheeks. I sit back, panting with a sudden fear, our breathing sounding monstrous in the dead silence.

"I think... we found them," Markus mutters through quick breaths.

"What about supplies?"

"I can't see anything, just...*them*."

I peer down again, beside my brother. "Look at their clothes. They're like soldier's uniforms, but different. They're green or brown, I'm not sure."

The faces are starved and moaning for a death that came long ago. Bending closer, covering my nose, I scour for useful items. I ready myself for the worst, which I can't decide on—finding nothing at all, or having to go down there amongst the rotting bodies to retrieve something, which would likely kill me anyways.

I slow my breathing and listen to the silence. Markus coughs, but there is something else in the air. A distant hum, and it grows louder.

The hum transforms into a rumble, and Markus and I stare at each other, eyes wide, the endless fury in my heart picking up again.

I shake my head. "No, it can't be."

Markus glances around, trying to pinpoint where the sound is coming from. It's unmistakable, a vehicle, something large and heavy. It accelerates slowly and quietens as it slows down, rumbling across the desert, getting closer.

"Maybe they won't stop," Markus whispers.

There's no time for risking that. I jump up on tip-toes, run over to the barricade and begin tearing it down.

"What are you doing?"

"They'll try to come in through the door, we need a place to hide, out of the way."

"What about down there?" Markus is pointing down the wooden hatch.

"You can, if you want."

Dirt and sand crunch against stone outside as the truck pulls up and finally stops. I hear several voices as doors open. Feet hit the sand. I slide the table over to the corner of the church, gently pulling it onto its side. I leave a tiny crack between the table top and the wall, a crack to peer through, then drop the rug over it. Markus crawls over on his knees, bringing the satchel with him. We crouch down behind the table, shielded from the door, listening to the soldiers explore the church exterior.

The doors rattle, something is hammered against them.

"Locked tight, solid."

"There's a window back here, bit of a climb though. And a tight squeeze."

Voices call out from all around us, muffled from the thick stone walls, but everywhere. We're completely surrounded.

"Let's just blow the door!"

"Shouldn't we save the explosives?"

"Something tells me this'll be worth it."

"What about the window?"

"Bollocks to the window. I want to see fire."

A few of them start to laugh. Markus and I stay crouched behind the table, in almost total darkness, where we're safest. Gunfire hits the doors and the wood splinters. We hold our ears, close our eyes.

Then comes the blast. The force of it passes through the table, knocks us back a little. Markus groans and I cover his mouth, staring into his eyes with desperation. I'm pleading, but I don't even know what for. There's nothing we can do.

I peer out through the crack and fall silent as a large figure steps in, looming strange in the doorway. The figure turns to the side, revealing his masked face. It strikes rage in me, no longer fear, and I hold the handle of my dagger. But Markus reaches over, taps my arm and shakes his head gently, holding his other hand to his lips. Then I notice the silver fur on the soldier's back, still dripping, stained with red. Farkas' pack—*they couldn't have, could they?* But I control my emotions and fire back to the now, our seemingly hopeless situation. But we won't ever give up. There's always been a way so far.

Several footsteps echo in the church now, and I peer out through the crack again as they walk past us, trampling over smokey bits of wood and shattered chains. They're all cloaked in bloody wolf skin, draped over their black uniforms, and headed straight for the altar. Four of them.

"What have we got?"

"There's a dead one over here," the voice comes from nearby. "And bits of another." The soldier is to the left of us, out of sight from behind the table, so we wait.

"Nothing! All useless!" There's a loud smack as the soldier punches the altar with a gloved hand.

"I found something," another soldier calls. "It's a trapdoor. Too dark to see inside, get yer torch."

The flare must have gone out. I gently push the table forwards to see all four soldiers crouched around the hatch and peering down. Our one chance.

I push the table a little more until the gap is large enough to crawl through. Grabbing Markus by the arm, I slip through. We edge along the wall, Markus doing his best to crawl without pulling his injured leg over the debris. Agony's rubbed all over his face.

"Gregor!" I freeze from the soldier's sudden shout. "Get in here, we have a job for you!"

The soldiers all start to chuckle and I jerk my head towards the door as a voice calls out, "Alright, I'm coming!"

There's another soldier outside and we're completely out in the open. I don't have time to think, trapped in no man's land, half way between the table's safe cover and the door. Footsteps outside grow louder and I unsheathe my blade. I use it as a mirror, holding it up around the door's corner and watch the soldier heading my way. I ready myself for one last fight—one final battle for my brother and I.

But Gregor stops, coughs and calls out, "Hang on, let me take a leak first." He veers off to the left, out of sight.

"Hurry up!"One of the others shouts.

We get low to the ground, in case one of the other soldiers looks up. Markus grabs my arm and aggressively points to the door, his eyes torn, begging me. He's right, we can't hesitate any longer. I grab my big brother by the hand and yank him up, out through the door and around the corner. I flick my head to the left as we pass under the large stone arch and see Gregor the soldier, standing there, peeing against the church wall. He looks up, sees me, and turns, going for a pistol in his belt. I skid in the dust, sliding towards him. His gun goes off but the shot misses me and I plunge my dagger deep into his stomach. He swings at me weakly with a fist, then falls to the ground with a thud.

"Gregor? What the hell are you doin'?"

"Two live ones," he groans. "Get out here!"

I'm panicking, not a clue where to head. I spin around; Markus is limping along, heading straight towards the truck.

I dart after him, swing the door open and jump in as Markus struggles around to the passenger side. It's a large truck with a covered back, like the one we were transported to the train yard in. And the keys are in the ignition.

Two of the soldiers come rushing out of the church and see their friend lying dead against the wall. They look up as I turn the key, kicking the engine on. They shout, "Get them! Shoot them!"

One of them pulls a rifle from his shoulder, takes aim and fires straight through the glass. The other charges at us, and soon two more appear outside, armed with pistols and clubs.

"I don't know what to do!" I scream.

Markus grabs the gear stick, "Push the left pedal!"

I have to sit on the very edge of the seat and point my toes to reach. The gear stick locks in.

"Now hit the gas, the one on the right!"

I hold down both pedals, hanging off the wheel with my hands.

"Let go of the left one, but slowly!" Markus screams.

I release my left foot and we fire off, blasting forwards with a jerk. I can't see anything and guns go off, hitting the metal doors. Something hot flashes over my hand and I release the wheel, crying out in agony. Blood pours out of the graze and Markus has to grab the wheel as I continue to push down on the gas. We hit a rock and almost flip to the side, but cool wind blows through my hair as gunfire fades away and shouting grows quiet. The rumble of the heavy engine, firing high, is for once a comforting sound. It's our rumble now.

31

We go on like that, in first gear, rolling loudly over silent sand. We try to move into second gear at one point, but the whole truck just chugs off and skids to a halt. The engine won't start straight away, so we make the decision not to try shifting up a gear again, carry on at twenty kilometres per hour, which is fast enough to get us far away from the soldiers.

As I look out over the dashboard, I see the sand stretch out till it fades to sky—nothing. The needle on the fuel dial is sinking fast, maybe through a leak or a bullet hole. But I just keep my foot down—we'll take this ride as far as we can and see what comes our way.

It grows hotter than I've ever felt, and the sky is clean, a pale blue; wisps of fog and a pink dust scatter the atmosphere. The sun climbs high ahead of us, moving up over the truck as noon passes.

"Just hold the wheel straight," Markus says. "I'll check the back."

Markus struggles round in his seat, grimacing as he knocks his ankle. He cuts the tarp that covers the back, so that he can see inside.

"There's guns, clubs, some knives..." Markus goes quiet.

"What is it?"

"Nothing. I just thought… don't worry."

I know he's seen something back there. "What is it?" I ask again, trying to turn my head to look back, but I'm all the way on the edge of my seat, perched rather than sitting. I look hard at Markus, searching his face for answers. He's rattled, more than usual, and tears form in his eyes.

"What is…"

I don't finish my words; we hit something and the truck slides off to the right, spinning around. I'm bounced against the steering wheel and thrown into the door, hitting the window. Then all is silent.

I open my eyes; Markus is leaning forward on the dashboard. He lifts his head and looks at me, his forehead is cut open and bleeding. A flume of smoke rushes from the engine. I lean forward, looking for the door handle and blood drips onto my hand. I can feel it on my head, hot and wet. I cover the gash with one hand, jerk the door handle with the other and fall out of the truck on to the hot sand.

I land on my knees and the ground appears redder; it's been darkening as we've moved east. My ear drips with blood and I cup it, watching the splashes fall onto the sand. I lean onto my palms but have to rip them from the surface—hot as a cooking pot on a fire. I stagger to my feet and dazedly limp around to the other side of the truck, to where Markus is struggling to get out.

Bullet holes are strewn across the metal. It's a wonder they didn't hit us. I pull on the handle and Markus leans on to one of my shoulders as I ease him down onto his one good leg.

"You alright?"

He nods.

"Let's get in the back, see what's there and get out of the sun."

"Hold on," he says, but I'm already climbing back into the truck.

I lean across onto the driver's seat and turn the key in the ignition. But there isn't a sound. I close my eyes and twist a few more times. It's dead. Here the truck will stay forever in the baking sun.

I lead Markus around to the back and we unzip the cover. We climb up and begin looking over the weapons, searching for things we can salvage.

"Hang on," Markus says, more harshly this time.

I wonder what the hell his problem is, but spot a flask and pick it up. It's heavy, full. I turn and toss it to Markus, who's looking very worried for some reason. When he catches the flask he holds it up and smiles. He unscrews it, sniffs the contents and smiles even wider. He takes a big gulp and passes it to me. As I swallow days worth of dust and sand are eroded off the inside of my throat by the warm water. I pass it back to Markus and we take it in turns like that for a while.

"I wish it was cold."

He shrugs, "Yeah, but people who lived in the desert always drank their water hot. The body can absorb it quicker that way."

Leaning back, satisfied and strong, that's when I notice it, in the corner. And I know why Markus looked so upset when he peered into the back, why he's been so hesitant about me searching around. Among all the weapons there's a machete, the handle carved with the many faces of wolves.

"It can't be," I whisper, slowly leaning forward, raising the giant metal blade. It's heavy, thick and encrusted with blood.

"I didn't want to tell you, not till later."

"Well, you should have. Now we've crashed, and the truck is broken."

"But we have water," he adds.

I nod, trying to calm down. We need to stick together. My brother meant well, he just wanted to save me the sadness. His momentary insanity in the church feels like a bad dream. This time it's my fault—my fault we crashed—because I always have to look. I always have to know.

"I'm sorry," I tell him.

I look over at my brother, who sits hugging his knees, and he looks like a lost boy, the scared, quiet kid I remember from years ago. It settles in me, a defeating realisation—maybe that's all we are.

He's crying, the fading black on his face is wiped further, as more streaks of pasty white appear beneath.

"If he—someone so strong, with an army of brothers—still couldn't survive, then what hope do we have?" Markus whispers.

I feels tears roll down my own face and the words barely come out. "I don't know, Markus. I don't know anymore."

I move over and sit beside him in the truck's shadow. We cry as we did on the day of the attack in the tunnels we once called home. This time our tears are for Farkas, the wolf warrior, who saved our lives in the forest they call 'dead', where we too could have joined the trees. But our tears are still weakness, like the ones we cried at the very beginning, whilst listening to the sounds of our world being gunned apart. Our journey has taken us so far since then, and still we are the same, still we are weak in the face of it all.

I try to fight the thoughts. "We have to keep going," I say. "We can't give up now."

He listens, but shakes his head, exhausted and weak beyond anything we've ever known. I ache to the ends of my fingers, to the core of my bones. It's a deep ache that's been with me for so long I wonder if it will ever leave.

"What if we don't deserve to go on," Markus whispers, "What if I don't."

I stare at him, put my hand on his shoulder. "Of course you do. I need you. We can do this, but only together. Till the very end, like father said."

Markus looks at me and nods through teary eyes.

Before looking over the rest of the items in the truck, we take another drink, saving half for later. The sun is still high and roasts us under the tarp. I poke my head out, hoping for a breeze, but it's even worse. The heat slams my face.

Most of the guns are broken or empty, and there are no ammo boxes or grenades. There's a rifle with one bullet inside, a few extra rounds are in a tool box by the spare wheel. We find a medical case, full of make do bandages; animal skin, food packaging, torn clothing, anything that can be wrapped around a cut to stop the bleeding. There's also a box of matches inside, with a few left, and a torch. I click it on to see if it works, and the electric beam flashes yellow as I turn it off again. Some luck at last.

Markus wraps a bandage around my head, covering the gash that's finally stopped bleeding. I bandage the bullet graze on my hand and help Markus tie a cloth around his head.

"Like a ninja," I say, smiling.

In a backpack we find a few flares which I add to the satchel. I reach into the main compartment, feeling something wet. The object is wrapped in cloth and deeply soaked. With both hands I lift it out, revealing a bloody rag.

"What is it?"

I lay it down and open it up. Rich, red meat lies inside, cut fresh from an animal.

I stare at Markus, uneasy, because I know what it must be.

"We have to, or we'll die."

I nod. "I know."

The sun begins to lower, creating a shady patch at the front of the truck, so that's where we build a small fire. We use the handles of clubs and most of the materials from the medical box, lighting it all with a match.

We slide the wolf meat onto the end of a bayonet, like a skewer. We take it in turns holding the meat above the fire, turning it slowly. I feel so guilty for what we're about to do, but the meat smells smokey and rich in the flames.

Markus can see I'm distraught and reassures me. "Put it this way, if one of these wolves found you dead in the woods, they'd eat you with no hesitation."

I nod, and I know he's right. Normally things like this don't bother me; I've eaten a lot things to survive.

"It's not that, Markus, they were his brothers."

"Believe me, Bandi. If Farkas was here, he'd be ramming it down your throat."

We chew the meat slowly and it tastes dry and stringy. The pack had been starving. As I eat I think of Farkas, his wolves that gave their lives. And now because of them we can go on, for at least another day.

Swallowing is hard, our stomachs used to no food at all. We sit for at least an hour, eating the meat for need, not want. This is protein we haven't had in a while. Maybe it will numb the ache, the pain I've been feeling.

There isn't a lot and we eat it all, deciding it will only rot if we hold onto it. We also have a desert to cross, with no end in sight. In our current state we wouldn't last half a day. The meat might give us an extra few hours. *What good will that do us?*

It all seems so futile. But we're holding on.

32

We strip the tyres off the truck and re-enforce our shoes again with the thick rubber, cutting larger pads this time, so that we stay on the surface of the sand should it grow deep as the desert rolls on. Markus struggles to his feet and grimaces as he takes a few steps.

He hits the ground and I sit beside him, grabbing two clubs from the back of the truck. I hack away at the wood till the handle comes free. I tie the two wooden pieces either side of Markus' calf, running down towards the foot, using shoe laces from a spare pair of boots found in the truck.

Markus stands up, surer on his feet with his new splint. But I can see in his eyes, he knows this is only temporary. If he walks his ankle will only swell further, ballooning with more pain.

I stand up, turn to the truck and begin cutting along the tarp that hides the back. I jump up onto to the wheel so I can reach the top, slicing all the way along the metal frame. I do this all the way around until the tarp comes off with one hard tug. Then I take a hammer and begin banging against the metal frame over which the tarp had clung. I hammer till sweat pours from my head, till the metal finally weakens and breaks away. I do the same on another bar, so I have two long pieces of thin metal.

I place the metal poles on the ground, parallel to one another. I cut a piece from the tarp, one I measure with my eyes, placing it in between the metal bars. I pierce through the material with a blade, threading a pole either side of the rectangular piece, reinforcing the bars with the other shoelace and thin strips of material I cut from the remainder of the tarp.

I hear the sound of metal on metal, and look up to see Markus on his knees, hacking off one of the other tyres. He pulls off the large piece of rubber and drags himself over to where I'm sitting. He tosses the tire fragment onto the dust in front of me, "We can use it to reinforce the bottom, give it a base. It can slide along the sand, like a sled."

I stare at the tyre, then up at Markus, shielding my eyes towards the sun. "Good idea," I tell him, taking the rubber.

It's like the old days, when we'd help our father patch up the water channels, repair shelters or build new ones. Markus and I know how to use tools and the stretcher we make is a nice example. We cut two pieces of tyre and fold them inside out, strapping one to each of the metal bars. We take the handle from the medical box and tie strings of tarp to it, wrapping the other ends tightly around the frame. The stretcher looks strong, though I hope we won't need it, at least not for a while.

"He'd be proud of us," Markus says.

I smile at him, nodding towards our creation. It'll be heavy but it could save Markus' life. He's my brother and I owe him everything. When I fell from the beam he saved my life. He's hurt because of that, so no matter how hard and how much it hurts, I'll do my best to save him too.

The sun is falling to the west, its fiery reign coming to an end, at least for the night.

"Soon we can move on. I can't wait for it to cool down," Markus says.

"We should finish the water now, rest up, then we'll go."

We take the last few swigs, savouring the liquid, wetting every gap between every tooth and enjoying the feeling that will soon seem like a dream. We take one last look around in the truck, but find nothing else. We pack the torch, some flares and some strips of tarp and bandages into the satchel. I pack away the empty flask too and tuck the matches into my pocket. I lift the rifle, hanging it over my shoulder. It's big and heavy, and I wonder if it's worth taking at all – it can't save us from the desert.

Markus picks up Farkas' machete, stares at the handle and runs his eyes up the blade. "We can't leave this here."

He plants it in the ground, using it for support like a crutch, and we move off across the sand. The sun is falling behind our backs, our shadows rolling out before us, reaching farther and farther. But we move slowly as Markus hobbles and groans. I drag the stretcher along, and it's heavy but watching Markus' struggle assures me he'll be on it before long. Then it will be up to me to fuel us on, dragging us from this sandy hell.

Weakly we stagger on, sweating in the late afternoon sun until finally it disappears, allowing the cool night to sink in. We take our hoodies from our faces once more and pull them down over our arms to wrap up in the grey cold. The moon doesn't rise and I search the sky, only to see the night's first stars. Only last night I'd finally seen it, and the sky is clear enough. It should be out above us now. If the moon is gone, the omen is bad, and I shudder at the thought. Maybe this is just that night, a night when the moon does not rise. Those nights happen every once in a while, it's all to do with science and space things I don't know much about. The moon was a slim curve last night so maybe it will return tomorrow, after one night of hiding. We can only hope.

We sit down, perched on the stretcher, back to back. I stare out to the east, Markus facing back the way we came. I look over my shoulder and the church is completely out of sight by darkness and distance. The deep blue night swallows us whole, and after a few minutes I help Markus up to his feet and we move on.

I walk beside my brother, supporting him with one arm and dragging the stretcher with the other. Markus limps along, still holding Farkas' machete, planting it firmly in the sand with each step and pushing off it.

As we travel on I can feel him weakening, the weight he places on my shoulder grows. Our pace slows. We take fewer steps and Markus' breathing is raspy and pained. The sand remains hard and the land rises at an angle, then falls again in sharp folds. We traverse them slowly, our feet dragging over the curved wrinkles in the dust, lit up only by the stars.

The night grows on and my head is shot with blasts of pain. My fingers begin to tremble and my knees shake. Markus grows heavier, the weight on my left shoulder is dragging me down. I move forward hunched low, now bearing the weight of myself and my big brother.

He whispers to me, a pained sound, too weak to utter anything more. "I can't," he tells me through short breaths. "I can't."

33

Markus collapses to the ground panting and heaving. I squat beside him and put the back of my hand on his forehead. It's moist and hot; even in the cold desert night. I inspect his leg, pressing gently on the swelling. He groans and I pull my hand away. It's gotten worse. I can even make out the dark blotches of bruising, clear in the evening darkness against his drained, white skin.

That's what worries me though, the fever in his mind is what's killing him, not the pain. I inspect his face as he lies on his back, eyes closed. I search for sores and blisters; like the ones the soldier had—the one my father was looking after. The skin is dry, scratched and torn around the eyes from sand and wind, but there are no signs of the sickness on his face, other than the paleness. Not yet anyway.

I try to think back, counting how many days it's been since we were there, with our father at the train yard. I count at least five days, though it's hard to say—we've barely slept, and each day just passes into the next, one horror after the other. I'm sure it can't be the juice, otherwise I'd be suffering too. The sickness, I don't know enough about it—what signs to look for. My father said the soldier had been ill for about a week. Markus is close, maybe the sores are coming soon. I choke back tears, kneeling there at my brother's side.

He opens his eyes and squints at me. "I'm sorry, little brother—for everything." Tears dribble down to his ears as he watches the sky, coughing and struggling for air.

"Stop saying that, Markus. It's not over yet."

He looks at me and shakes his head gently, "It is, Bandi. Look at where we are, I can barely move. We have nothing—no water, no food. When the sun comes out it'll kill us, if we make it through the night."

I stare at him, feeling my own eyes filling up, but I shake my head, refusing to listen.

"Do you think you have it, the sickness?" I ask.

He just continues to stare at the stars, ignoring me. "I wonder if we still get to go up there, when we die."

He goes silent, and I watch the sparkling dots with him, alight so far away. Maybe soon we'll be there, with our father and our mother. At least finally we'll be together again.

Markus rolls onto one side.

"What is it?" I whisper.

He starts to shake, crying achy tears, his sobs drifting far in the silence. "It's all my fault. All of this. Everything that happened is because of me…"

He cries and cries.

I put my hand on his arm, "Of course it's not, don't say that."

"You don't even know! I dragged you all this way, and you don't even know!"

"What are you talking about? You didn't drag me anywhere. We made it this far together. We're still alive because of each other."

Markus finally turns and looks at me strangely. The blue in his eyes is invisible. They're black and empty. Unease rises through me as I wait for his next words.

"If it wasn't for me, we'd all be alive..." His voice trails off as he turns away, unable to look at me any longer.

"That's not true! You saved me from the fall, you dragged me up when the soldier knocked me down—you came back for me, again and again. We escaped savage dogs, lions, caves of fire. We've been captured and escaped, passed through hordes of soldiers time and time again. We only made it this far because we're together. Markus, you saved me, over and over again!"

I'm kneeling to his left and he stares at me. "All those things—all those horrific things we've had to face—listening to our home being blown apart; the screams of our friends; the people we lived with; our family. Those we love and wanted to love. All that came afterwards. Because of what I did, Bandi!" He looks away. "It was me who took it. I took it!"

"What are you talking about? Took what?"

Markus reaches down into his pocket, pullling out something small and shiny. He places the round object in the sand, drops it by the chain it hangs on—a small, golden pocket watch.

I lift it up. It spins on its chain, dancing and flickering in the starlight. The glass is broken, the metal scratched and worn, the tick-tock long silenced.

Markus curls himself up and cries on the sand, tear drops falling and clumping in the dirt. I feel my face crumpling up but I try to stay level headed.

"I was just so angry, at the way that he was and what he used to be. I wanted to make him feel my rage, so I took it. I never thought he'd lead them straight to our home. I never thought he'd do that, no matter how bad he was. All because of a stupid watch!"

He won't look at me, presses his eyes with his hands and chokes on the air. "In the caves, when the poppies all went up in flames, I saw him, his wrinkled face. Before that I tried to convince myself it wasn't all my fault. But he appeared there, in the fire. He laughed and told me it was all because of me—because of what I'd done."

I hold my brother close as he sobs in the night, and certain things fall into place. It wasn't the sickness, nor poison, not anything that happened along the way. It was guilt that had been killing Markus and draining all his strength. His body wasn't dying. It was all in his a mind.

"It's alright, big brother. You couldn't have known."

I look away, trying to push back the tears that won't stop pouring now, dropping onto the sand.

Facing Markus again, I take his hand. "It's not your fault. It was his. That's what happens when you hold onto the old world, it makes you crazy. He cared so much about the watch because it reminded him of who he used to be. He was nothing now, and he couldn't stand it. What you saw in the caves doesn't matter, it wasn't real. It was all in your head, the guilt made you see those things. But it's time to let go of that guilt, Markus. He was holding onto the old world, and doing that destroyed any chance he had here. You told me that, Markus. You did. *He* killed those people, destroyed our home, because he couldn't let go. If you don't let go of your guilt now, then you'll be killing *us*."

My brother stares at me and goes quiet.

I pick up the watch, standing tall over him. I take the chain and swing it round and around so it spins above my head. Then I let go and the watch flies high and far, disappearing into the night.

I kneel by my brother and take his hand. "It wasn't your fault. It was his. Only his."

Markus stares thoughtfully for a few moment, then whispers: "It doesn't matter now anyway. This is it, Bandi, the end of everything."

I stand up and pull Farkas' machete from the ground where it's planted beside us. "No it isn't. Not yet."

"I can't keep moving. My ankle, it hurts too much. I can barely stand."

I lean down, starting to dust down the stretcher. "We brought this for a reason."

Markus stares at me, can see in my eyes that I'm not giving up now. Not until I can no longer stand and open my eyes. He drags himself onto the stretcher and lies on his back. His eyes flicker shut. I take the handle and set off, heaving Markus along after me. The tarp stretches tight, holds strong, as my legs ache with each step and a dizziness rises through me, made worse by the thump in my head. The night goes on and I gasp for air, moving forth one step at a time, gathering my strength before each stride. I sit and rest every so often, gazing back at the long drag marks running jagged along the sand from my staggered march.

I whisper to Markus but he doesn't respond, only his gentle breathing tells me he's still alive. I know he doesn't have long, but the sands ahead appear endless, and for hours I struggle on, but still nothing finds us, only more sand, more emptiness.

I cry out as the aches in my legs swell to unbearable. My thighs and calves pulse vigorously, and on my hands and knees I crawl on, still dragging Markus behind me. My eyes begin to fall, and the thumping in my head knocks sickness through me, an urge to vomit. My body trembles. My eyelids tingle and burn, fluttering closed again and again. Finally I fall in the sand, face first.

I drag myself forwards. With one hand I grab sand, pulling myself and pushing with my knees. In my other hand I still hold the stretcher, but I can barely grip the handle and it won't budge at all. I cry out as pain fires up my arm and down my back, the ache too much to bear. I lie there on my stomach, one hand reaching out, weakly holding the sand, eyes looking out to the east. Finally, they won't stay open anymore and I drift away into darkness.

In a black tunnel I walk, alone and scared. I scour the corners along the edges, but I'm alone and I move on. A voice hums in the background, a familiar tune. But I can't see Garth anywhere, only hear him, and the tunnel carries me forth in the only direction it can, so I let it take me.

The jagged ceiling falls lower and the walls close in. As the tunnel tightens, I have to get down on my knees and crawl. Ahead I can only see darkness, and on I creep, for what seems like forever. The humming dwindles and after an age of total black, a pin prick appears ahead of me, a grain of white light.

The grain grows to the size of a pea, then a fist. I crawl faster and faster, the tunnel ceiling cutting my neck, the ground slicing my knees. The white light is powerful, but feels hollow and empty. It continues to grow before me until finally the humming stops. I hesitate to move on, waiting for a moment, the total silence unsettling and eerie. Then a roar sounds in the deep, a growl that tears through me. There's a flash of hot green and a frenzy of flames.

I open my eyes.

34

Straight ahead of me the sky is brimming with a bluer darkness and in front of that, a dark shape looms. Hunched low, it stands up and turns to face me, hits me with its eyes, bringing me up on to my feet.

I take a step towards the panther and it watches me. I break into a run as it turns away, and immediately I fall, straight onto my knees. I wail, knocked flat by the pain for a second, but I rise up on to all fours, stalking on like the beast I'm after.

I claw forwards in the sand. The panther keeps on moving, stalking over the dark, the warmth of its eyes hidden.

"Please, you have to help us!" My throat tears and scratches as I scream.

I scramble on, kicking up swirls, coughing and wheezing. I fall this way and that, delirium, my head repeatedly smacked with a tomahawk, burrowing deeper and deeper.

But still the panther continues to move away, skulking towards the east where the sun's glow grows over the horizon, dimly lighting the low edges of the sky, until the gold shimmer finally breaks.

The panther stops, turns and faces me. Eyes ablaze it roars, and I feel the power ripple and surge through me. Our eyes meet and the panther goes still, bows its head, before turning away again, breaking into a run and disappearing. Something tells me this is his goodbye, and I watch him charge into the light ahead and vanish.

I beat the sand and cry out. "Come back! We need you now, more than ever!"

My voice falls away into a croak, and the heat begins to rise. I crawl on, following the panther, his footprints in the sand. They lead me straight towards the sun, and I follow them half blind, half dead. I crawl on all fours, my arms and legs both giving way, my vision blurring and fading.

The trail of panther prints ends, and I search desperately for a path to follow. There is nothing to lead me, just rusty sand, smooth and untouched.

I beat the ground and claw at the final print, swiping it away. I punch the sand again, finally defeated and Death not far away. The sun has revealed half its face and I wait for the tap on my left shoulder, holding my breath, but it doesn't come. I glance back, expecting to see a shadow behind me, a masked face. But there is no one there. I turn all the way around to take a good look but I only see the stretcher lying in the sand, with Markus' still form on top of it a way back. Unconscious and waiting for the end. Finally it's here, so I stare at the spot where the footprints ended. I stare hard and then strangely, the sand appears to move, sinking away and falling into an invisible hole beneath the ground.

It makes me dizzy and I fall onto my stomach, holding my head as the tomahawk cracks on. I reach out, flailing at the sinking sand. I gather all my strength, raise my fist up and hammer down hard.

My hand breaks through.

The sand around me gives way, so that I'm up to my shoulders in the grains, my hand freely grasping at air underneath.

Adrenaline kicks in and I focus, pulling my arm up and out, before pushing up off the ground. I dig around the hole and the sand collapses, opening up a huge deep gap in the earth that delves far into the ground. I stare firmly, but my vision is failing, and I struggle to stop the swaying as I tremble.

Something silver flutters down below, silver lines jingling and sparkling. My heart seems to freeze, a familiar glow returns, this time stronger than before. An emerald fire that will burn forever.

I race over to Markus and grab the stretcher by the handle. Something new flows through me, those flames, and they give me power when I have none. I pull the stretcher along to the hole and roll Markus onto the sand. I take the empty flask of water from the satchel and begin tying together strips of tarp, making the longest rope I can, tying the other end to the top of the flask with the lid pulled off. Lying in the sand, face down, I begin to lower it until I hear a gentle splash.

I drag the flask along the surface, imagining the fresh, cool water flooding inside. Then I raise the flask up, feel the increase in weight from the water now inside. I take it and put it to my lips—the fluid is clear and shining. I pour it over my head, rub it around my gums and sip a few times. I feel better right away, so I turn my attention to my brother, who continues to breathe, but still doesn't make a sound. He looks like a ghost.

Gently, I flick water from my finger on to his head, dab it over his closed eyes and on to his ears. He coughs and mumbles something, so I tilt his head, letting the water wash over his lips. He opens his mouth and I pour some water in. He lets it sit for a while, then finally manages to swallow. I feed him sips till he holds up a hand. I help him sit up and turn him around, so that he can see the hole.

"The panther came, while you were unconscious. It led me here, to this very spot. And look what I found!"

Markus smiles wearily, but it's the truest smile I've seen since the final afternoon in the city, when we ran free in the streets, unaware of the hell that was coming.

We watch the water and I notice the silver threads down below are all in a line, as if the water is drifting in one direction.

I look up at Markus, my eyes wide. "The water is flowing."

"A river? We need to get down there."

I nod. "Yeah we do."

I begin scrambling around, guaging what we have and what we can use. I dismantle the stretcher, pulling apart the ties. I twist them around each other, making them stronger, so that they can hold our weight. Markus watches me as I take the large piece of tarp from the frame and fold it up, making a harness. I cut slits in the harness and tie strips to them, readying myself to lower it.

"Give me your dagger, I'm going to need it," I say.

Markus passes me his blade, lifts the machete from the sand and climbs into the harness, so he's sat on it like a swing, his legs dangling down into the pit. The passage down is just wide enough for us to fit, and slowly I begin lowering Markus.

He disappears into the dark as I kneel, slowly releasing more of the rope, begging fate to hold it intact. It grinds against the edge of the pit as sand crumbles away and falls down in clouds of dust. Markus coughs down below and the rope is running out.

"How much further down?"

"I'm not sure," Markus calls up. "I think I'm close, I can hear the water."

I ease the rope down a final few inches, my arms exhausted. "That's all of it. Can you jump down?"

I feel the rope shake as Markus holds the wall and readies himself to drop.

"This is going to hurt," he calls up.

I feel his weight disappear, followed by a cry of pain a second later.

"You alright?"

I drop the harness and peer over the edge. Markus is sitting down in the gentle flow of water, clutching at his leg.

"I'm fine, it was just a couple of metres," he calls up, and I watch as he looks around. "You have to get down here, there's a whole passage filled with flowing water!"

He splashes, looks up at me and laughs. A huge smiles spreads over my face. The panther came—it came again for us and showed us the way, when there was no way to be seen. It came at dawn, brought on the glow of a new day, lit with hope. It walked me to water when our lives were bleeding out. It saved us again.

I rise up, smiling and take one last look at the sun that soon will be flaming away. I look over my left shoulder and smile to myself. "Not yet."

I lift Markus' dagger and slide mine from my belt. I step up beside the hole and lower myself down, stabbing the blades into the well's walls. I drop down, holding the dagger handles; spread myself so that my limbs are planted on all sides and holding me in place. I pull down on the daggers and the sand moves a little. I release my knees, let my weight drop and the daggers give way, slicing down through the tightly packed sand. I slip down the well at speed and stop with a huge splash, hitting the surface of the water. It's cool and I let myself fall back so that the stream washes over all of me. I spread my fingers, moving them around in the flow. I sit up and Markus is just in front of me, in a low tunnel that branches off from the well.

He points behind him. "It leads to another well, and that one leads to another two. It's a whole network of wells, all connected by these rivers."

I drink from my hands and rub water all over my face. "Who do you think built these?"

Markus looks around, admiring the walls. "This has to be from the old world. To build channels of water in the desert where there is no water to be found. There had to have been a river at some point, maybe thousands and thousands of years ago. All that's left is this water, deep under the sand."

"The wells must have gotten buried over time and forgotten." I stare at my brother. "Only the black panther knew they were here."

"He could smell the water."

I nod, continuing to drink, feeling alive again, fresh and full of fire.

Markus pushes his hands over the walls. "It's clay, that's why the sand is so red. There are probably wells like this all over the place, we just wouldn't know where to look."

"We found this one and that's all that matters!"

Markus smiles at me and nods. He reaches down and splashes me with water and I flick some back at him. We laugh together in the gentle flow. It's been a while since I heard it, the sound of Markus laughing, and it's music to my ears.

35

We explore the passages that lead from one well to another, all spread out under the sand. It's dark. All the wells are blocked from the surface, hidden and covered in tightly packed sand. There's an entire network of water channels dug deep so many long years ago, when a village once sat here on the sands; nomads, tribesman. Markus has read about them.

As the day wears on we fall asleep, lying down on our backs in the water. When the sun reaches its peak we crawl into the passages, out of reach from the deadly rays. I watch the water glisten as I drift into a deep slumber, peaceful at last; no soldiers, just an empty rest and a chance for my body to recover, my mind at ease.

When I wake up it's dark and Markus is still asleep at my feet. I crawl out into the first well and stare up at the sky. I smile at the moon, a slim bone in the sky, hooked upon the vast black above. Not gone. Stil very much alive.

It's cold now; my clothes are wet and there is nowhere dry to hide. The water flows through all of the underground. I huddle down beside Markus who sleeps peacefully, his eyelids still and dreamless. Beside him I warm up enough to fall asleep again, waking only to the sun glancing off the stream and into my face.

It's almost noon when we rise. My headache has faded, leaving a fuzzy feeling behind. We spend the rest of the day drinking, keeping refreshed and discussing what to do next.

"We should stay here for another day or so, keep drinking and growing stronger."

"It will give my ankle time to heal."

I nod at Markus, thinking of what lies ahead, envisioning the endless sands that stretch on as far as I could see. We're far from safe, but I can't help but feel we've almost made it. I can almost sniff something in the air.

Day erupts into a furious night as the wind picks up above, whistling as it swirls down the well and skims over the streams. We sit by flarelight and look up at the hazy skies. When the storm picks up even more we block out the tumbling sand with the tarp, digging the corners into the clay walls on all sides. Underneath it we sit, bare foot, soaking our aching toes and our scabbed soles.

"Tomorrow evening we'll leave, heading straight east. We don't stop till we find food or shelter, or till we die in the sand. Either way, we give it one last push."

His eyes are lit, no longer smeared with guilt and pain. Hearing him speak like that only fuels the emerald flames inside me, and they grow just a little more. A smile slowly spreads over my face and my big brother smiles back. He's finally back—here with me—all of him. I know nothing can stop us now, we're so very close, edging towards the end of our greatest adventure. An adventure that nearly killed us, again and again. But still we sit, still we smile, still we move on for at least another day.

The storm above subsides and the flare goes out. We settle down beside one another and I close my eyes.

"Do you think we'll ever go back? To the city?"

I stare up at the tarp, imagining the dark skies beyond, the moon out once again, maybe a little fuller and fatter than before. "I think we will."

"If we ever make it over this desert," Markus adds.

I close my eyes. "We will, big brother."

"I hope you're right."

Hope—Markus holds it again. I go over our entire journey in my head as we fall asleep, from the moment the black panther first came to us. It feels a lifetime ago. I think about all the people we've met, those poor souls at the train yard, Farkas, Garth, the drunk soldier at the zoo—how he let us go and helped us when our journey could have ended before it even began. I'm surprised to find myself thinking about him, hoping he's alright. Maybe it's because he gave us kindness from where we least expected it to come. I wonder about what awaits us and who lies before us. I hope to see my father and my mother again. I picture their warm faces, knowing they are proud, wherever they may be. But something tells me neither of them are dead, but out there somewhere, in this dry and dusty world, waiting to be saved—waiting for their sons to return.

I think about the men inside the church, trapped by the mad priest and unable to escape. They were from somewhere else, I know it. Maybe soldiers, but good. I hope that we find them, I hope that we can return home one day and destroy the masked soldiers once and for all. Then maybe the world won't end, maybe it can live on. I wish Farkas would be here to see that, but he died fighting, fighting for another day that will come, again and again, as long as we move on and as long as we hope, stick together and watch over each other. The panther showed us the way, brought us this far. Now it's up to us to finish it, to make it to where we need to be. I picture the waves in my mind, wonder how big they'll be, whether the water will taste salty like Markus says.

I fall asleep, remembering and wondering. I fall asleep even more at ease than the night before. I feel strong, my body cleansed of aches and shakes, pure water flowing through me again. My stomach rumbles still and I know the water's strength won't carry us for long, but on we will march in darkness, till we either live or die.

I wake to the sound of Markus pulling down the tarp, revealing a high, midday sun. The day seems to drag on forever as we slowly prepare. Eventually the sky turns pink above, slathered in a wispy haze, and we ready ourselves to head out. We rebuild the harness and fill the canteen with water, even removing the batteries from the torch and filling that up too. We need all the water we can take, but don't have enough ways to carry it.

I climb first, with the satchel and rifle over my shoulder, stabbing the clay walls with our daggers, moving up one thrust at a time until the well narrows at the top and I can use my knees and feet to climb as well. The harness rope is tied around my waist and when I reach the top I lower the harness down as far as I can.

I call to Markus. "Dropping it now."

Even in the late coolness my sweat pours. My chest is heaving from the climb and I rest for just a second. Holding the daggers over the edge of the well, I wait a few moments for Markus to move out of the way. I drop the daggers, hearing them land on the well's bed. Below me, Markus struggles to crawl into view, then staggers to his feet with the daggers in hand. He begins to climb up using the blades as I did, with Farkas' machete on his back. He reaches the harness and I begin to pull. My arms grow weak, but thankfully Markus is stronger now, able to plant his knees and crawl up the final few metres. We both lie panting on the surface but know we must move on. We take a tiny sip of water, just to wet our dry mouths and off we go, the sun nipping at our backs till it slinks away.

We trudge on in the dark, the moon curling joyously across the sky between metallic shields of cloud. Before long, Markus has to use the rifle and machete as crutches. His ankle is completely swollen again. Our pace slows and we drink, moving on, growing weary quickly, our muscles still starved of energy.

The aches set in soon, and Markus and I groan as we stumble towards morning. We rest often, taking small sips, first from the torch that leaks as we walk. After a while the wind picks up, blasting us in the dawn. We quickly cover our faces, tearing our hoodies from our bodies. I unwrap the tarp and pull it over us, and there we lie, battered by walls of needles, the sand charging over us relentlessly. I close my eyes and think of the panther, feeling its eyes running through my veins, lit up like fire and refusing to fizzle out.

After hours the winds finally die and we can move on. The sun emerges and starts to fry us, a little at a time. We try not to stop, to keep moving at all times, as the sand turns white beneath our feet. Markus drags his leg and before long is on his knees, holding his body up by leaning on the rifle butt. I pick him up and walk with his arm over my shoulder, bearing both of us on my tired legs.

We both tumble and fall, kicking up a puff of dust. I land sprawled, my mouth open. The sand touches my tongue and I taste the grit. I lift up my head quickly and look straight ahead because the sand—it tastes salty.

Markus coughs beside me, his chest heaving, but the rest of the desert is dead of sound. Then a squawk sounds high in the sky. A sound I've only heard from Markus, from my father and my mother.

I look straight up and the sun blinds me for a moment. I shield my face and peer out between my fingers at the smooth blue above. There I see it, circling up high, a flash of white in the sky.

36

"Markus, look!"

I point up at the seagull, watching it glide in the currents, not needing to flap its wings, perched on the wind.

I can't believe my eyes and the gull squawks again. Markus sits up to my left and I hear him laugh. I hug him, watching the seagull glide away beneath the sun, swerving off to the south-east.

"The sand is salty."

Markus puts his finger to his lips and his eyes go wide. "Maybe we're almost there."

I jump to my feet and pull Markus to his.

"A seagull! I don't believe it!"

I can't stop smiling and stare out to the east across the horizon. Dim in the distance, I can make out a rise in the land. Low peaks—hills. I search for a shiny glare beyond, the glimmer of waves, but the sun is too bright and the horizon too far away.

I face Markus. "We have to keep going. We must be so close now."

He nods vigorously. "I know... it's just so hard."

I take out the flask and shake it. A final few sips left. "We should have this now," I say.

Markus takes the flask and pours a final few drops on to his tongue, passes it to me. I take the last drops, close my eyes, and we face the east ready for one final trek.

I quickly grow delirious again, drifting in the waves of heat as we walk, longing for waves of cool. But the sand goes on, even as hills rise beside us. We start to pass small shrubs, only skeletons, but still signs of life. The sand before us begins to rise upwards in a gentle slant, and I realise we've been moving gently uphill for quite some time.

Markus crashes to the ground beside me, the burning sun at our backs giving him a final swipe. He tumbles and smacks his head, jerking his neck. He groans and I kneel beside him, helping him to sit up. He doesn't say a word; I just listen to his hoarse breathing, his raspy throat rattling my ears. I listen as the rasp grows deeper, another sound joining in, a quiet rush. I look up and turn around, expecting to see vehicles rolling across the ground.

But there's nothing there, nothing on the desert's fringe, so I step away from Markus and strain my ears again. I close my eyes, trying to block everything out, except the quiet sound of that gentle charge. And I hear it, a roll and crash, a roll and a crash.

"Waves," I whisper. "Waves!"

I heave Markus to his feet, putting his arm over my shoulder. We move forwards like that, stepping slowly towards the sound. The peak of the rise is just up ahead, a long straight band of sand ending in blue sky. I step quicker. Markus' eyes are fierce as he fights the pain. We take the final few steps and are hit with a million tiny sparkles.

The sea stretches out before us.

Blue and deep, it lies glimmering as far as I can see, more beautiful than anything I've ever witnessed. It looks gentle, but also strong, shining brighter than any light, purer, more vivid and real than anything else in this grey world.

I fall to my knees and laugh towards the sky, where a family of seagulls circles over the water. One of them swoops down, slips along the surface of the waves and flies up again, holding something in its talons—a fish.

Markus drops beside me and we hug, laughing and smiling, everything else suddenly gone, wiped clean from our minds.

I stare at my big brother, see the tears in his eyes, but finally they're good tears—because we've made it.

We stand up and charge down the bank of sand, arms spread wide like the gulls above us. The waves sparkle like treasure, the sand begins to grow hard and moist beneath our feet. I turn to Markus and there's a smile on his face so wide, tears rolling down his cheeks. I laugh aloud and run forwards, pulling him with me. His laughter rolls in my ear, along with the sound of the waves, the splash, the rise and fall.

We collapse into the cool water and it burns at first—the salt. But then the burning stops, as if all the bad we've seen, all the misery and pain is cleansed off. Underneath, we're us, we're free. We hug each other on our knees, as another wave crashes down over our heads. We splash and jump and dive until we can no longer move from exhaustion.

I crawl onto the beach and lie in the red sunset. The sea looks pink, a crumpled sheet of metal that glimmers on forever. Markus lies beside me and we watch the mountains in the distance. I think I can see figures moving in the trees, but it could just be the wind moving branches and shadows. I can't tell what they are and right now, I don't care.

I turn back to the water, breathing in the sea air. It's salty, sharp and clean.

"We made it, Markus."

My brother sits up, looking at me and a slight smile pushes out his cheeks.

His hair flops and clumps in the wind. "We did, little brother."

I continue to watch the water, our mission complete. We set out to find the sea and here we are, bathed in its water and now bathing in its glow.

I don't know what lies in the mountains, or beyond. I don't know what we're going to do next or even where we'll sleep tonight.

What I do know is that we made it, against all odds. The panther guided us; came when we needed him most—but it was us who made it, Markus and I.

That's the most important thing. We were never alone, and we'll never be alone as long as we have each other.

As I said, I don't remember much of before, but it was meant to be better—easier. There were things in the world then that won't ever be seen again, and that might be sad for those who remember, but not for me. This is the world I know, this is the world I live in. And after what Markus and I have fought through, I'm not afraid of anything.

The life we had in the city wasn't always easy, but I still miss it. I guess if you live any way for long enough you'll miss it when it's over. We made the best of it, and Markus and I will keep on making the best of it.

We'll find food and we'll keep going, following the line of the waves until we find a stream and water we can drink. The waves will roll over our feet, constantly reminding us of where we are—the sea. I still can't believe it.

We'll walk till we find somewhere safe; maybe we can build a shelter, like the one we had in the metro station.

And then...I can't say. I don't know, I don't care. We'll be Ok. Like my father said, together we'll always be Ok. Markus is of the sea, and here he is, where he was always meant to be. I'm a warrior, and maybe now I'm on my way too. But it's just the beginning of that journey.

Markus sits over my left shoulder, only Markus, and for now, that's all I need to know.

Two thorns beside the sea, growing strong.

About the Author

Maté Jarai was born in Budapest, Hungary, on February 16th 1988. His family moved around a few times, spending time in Ohio, Switzerland and Budapest, before settling in Horsham, Sussex in 1995. Maté studied Film and English at Southampton University, where he then went on to take a Masters in Creative Writing. He lives in Southampton, where he is working towards a PHD in Creative Writing whilst working as a Teaching Assistant. He writes articles for *Screen Robot* and also runs a blog, *IamWendle.com*. His short story, *Bill Jaffa,* appeared in the Southampton University's Creative Writing Anthology, *Prose & Cons*, and his short story, *Incubus,* appeared in Gumbo Press's December 2011 issue, *Silence. In the Panther's Wake* is his first novel.

Acknowledgements

My greatest thanks go to Alison Fell, Rebecca Smith and Will May for all your guidance, and to the Southampton University Creative Writers who encouraged me to turn a small idea into a novel. To Maria at The Booksmith for taking a chance on that novel and making my dream a reality.

To my parents for their endless support. To my grandmothers; Nagyi for telling me the stories that inspired this novel and Grensó for your love of the written word and constant belief in me. To my brother. To all my other brothers around the world. To my family in Hungary. To Emily.

16601244R00139

Printed in Great Britain
by Amazon